Miosotis Flores Never Forgets

Miosotis Flores Never Forgets

Hilda Eunice Burgos

Tu Books

an imprint of Lee & Low Books Inc.

New York

TU BOOKS,
an imprint of LEE & LOW BOOKS Inc.,
95 Madison Avenue, New York, NY 10016
leeandlow.com

MIX
From responsible sources
FSC
www.fsc.org   FSC® C103098

Edited by Cheryl Klein
Book design by Neil Swaab
Typesetting by ElfElm Publishing
Book production by The Kids at Our House
The text is set in Dante MT Pro, with display type in Holla and
handwriting in Bradley Hand and CalliopeMVB
Manufactured in the United States of America by Lake Book

10 9 8 7 6 5 4 3 2 1
First Edition

Library of Congress Cataloging-in-Publication Data
Names: Burgos, Hilda Eunice, author.
Title: Miosotis Flores never forgets / Hilda Eunice Burgos.
Description: First edition. | New York : Tu Books, an imprint of Lee & Low Books Inc.,
[2021] | Audience: Ages 9–13. | Audience: Grades 4–6. |
Summary: "When Miosotis Flores discovers that her sister Amarilis's fiancé is physically
abusive to her, she must decide how to help, while also caring for a rescue dog and pursuing
better grades in school"—Provided by publisher.
Identifiers: LCCN 2021010395 | ISBN 9781643790657 (hardcover) |
ISBN 9781643790664 (epub) | ISBN 9781643790671 (mobi)
Subjects: CYAC: Family life—Fiction. | Dating violence—Fiction. |
Dominican Americans—Fiction.
Classification: LCC PZ7.1.B875 Mi 2021 | DDC [Fic]—dc23
LC record available at https://lccn.loc.gov/2021010395

For Claudia and Ruben

Chapter 1

THE MELTING MARCH SNOW CRUNCHES UNDER my boots as I step off the school bus. "Have a great weekend!" the driver calls. I wave before she closes the door. My weekend *is* going to be great. Amarilis is coming home from college for her spring break.

I picked out the perfect movie for us to watch tonight, with good scary parts but also the lovey-dovey stuff she likes. Tomorrow we'll hang out at the Skatium, and on Sunday we'll go to the mall. She always finds the best outfits for me. I want to spend the whole week with my sister, but Papi won't let me take off school, as if anything I'm learning in sixth grade is important.

"Miosotis, mi amor, is that you?" Abuela pops her head through the kitchen door when I walk in. As usual, the phone is to her ear, and I know she's talking to her sister.

"Say hi to Tía Felicia for me," I call out as I take off my boots.

"No, no, no, that's not how you handle this situation," Abuela says into the phone. "Listen, Felicia, this is what you need to do . . ."

I grab my backpack and head upstairs while Abuela disappears into the kitchen. The toilet flushes as I walk past the bathroom. Huh, did Jacinto skip track practice to welcome Amarilis home too? Before I get to my room, the bathroom door opens, but it isn't my brother who walks out.

"Papi!"

"You certainly seem happy to see me." Papi raises an eyebrow.

"Is Amarilis here?" I rush into my room and look around. No Amarilis.

"Ah, it's not *me* you're happy to see." Papi chuckles.

"Is she here?" I say again.

"No, she's getting a ride with Richard this evening."

"Oh." I plop my backpack on the floor. Can I wait that long?

"But while I have you alone"—Papi steps over the backpack and sits on the edge of my bed—"let's talk about this dog business."

My heart jumps. I have wanted a dog since *forever*. I started reading about them in kindergarten. Ask me any dog question and I can answer it. I even volunteer with foster dogs practically every day. Still, Papi doesn't like the idea of me getting a dog, and he gets annoyed when I remind him—about once a week—that I'm ready for one. But now he's the one bringing it up! Could he have changed his mind?

I sit next to Papi and bounce on the bed a little, holding my breath and trying not to seem excited. "So, can I get one?" I blurt out.

Papi smiles. "Not yet, but perhaps this summer."

I jump up and throw my arms around him. "Thank you! Thank you!"

"Calm down! You haven't heard the conditions yet."

I sit again, my hands underneath me, and bite back a smile.

"First, the dog has to be hypoallergenic. We can't have your abuela sneezing and sniffling and feeling miserable all the time."

"That's no problem." I bob my head up and down. "There are lots of low-shedding breeds that would work, like a poodle, a wheaten terrier, a shih tzu—"

"Okay, but that's not all." Papi looks me in the eye. "This house isn't very big, so the dog must be small or medium-size."

Hmm, I guess I can live with that. My first friend was a small dog. He was my mother's white shih tzu, and he looked like a little teddy bear, so she named him Osito. When I was a month old, he would curl up next to me and we'd nap together. I even have a photo to prove it. I was still a baby when he died, but I know I connected with him. Maybe I can get a dog that's exactly like him. I nod.

"And finally, you need to show that you're responsible and this dog won't be a negative distraction."

I frown. "What does that mean?"

"It means that school comes first, as always."

Of course. I turn away so Papi won't see my eyes roll.

"If you get straight As on your report card for the last quarter of the school year, then you can have a dog in the summer."

"What?! I can't do that." I have never gotten straight As my whole life. "I'm not Amarilis or Jacinto," I say. "It's not my fault I'm not smart."

"You're very smart, but you don't apply yourself." Papi stands. "Perhaps now that you have an incentive, you'll finally work to your full potential."

3

"But that's not fair. You know I can't do this."

"On the contrary, I know you can."

Papi doesn't understand how annoying it is to work hard and still not be perfect like he wants me to be. Why can't he accept that I'm an average student? What do straight As have to do with giving a sweet dog a loving home? This is so unfair. He came up with these conditions just so I can't meet them.

I'll never get my dog.

I stay in my room until I hear Papi leave to pick up Jacinto from track practice. When I look in the bathroom mirror and see my puffy eyes, I decide to wait a little longer before going downstairs. If Abuela sees me now, she'll ask a bunch of questions, and I don't feel like talking about how unfair Papi is being. I open the bottom desk drawer, take out a chocolate bar, and think about my problem while I munch.

My phone pings. It's a text from my sister. *Rich and I are on our way. Tell the fam we'll be there in a half hour.*

I answer with a *k*. Amarilis will help me. She always does. She'll convince Papi that straight As are not realistic for me, even though she and Jacinto always manage them. Papi will listen to her, right? He should, since she's basically perfect and all. By the time I swallow my last bite, I feel better.

When I walk into the kitchen, I close my eyes for a second and take in the delicious smells. "Do you need any help, Abuela?"

"Oh, gracias, mi amor." Abuela plops a handful of green plantains onto the counter. "Why don't you scramble a few eggs for the eggplant?"

I open the refrigerator and take out two eggs. "Are you making meat too?"

Abuela glances at me without turning her head away from the plantain she's peeling. "There's a chicken in the oven, but your sister hasn't been home in two months, and she loves my eggplant."

"I know, I was just wondering."

"Your mother loved my eggplant too."

I was less than a day old when my mother died. Papi, Abuela, and even Amarilis and Jacinto—who were seven and five then—all like to tell stories about her. I never have anything to add, so I usually change the subject. Abuela gets annoyed when I do that. She wants us to always remember our mother, but it's easy to forget someone you never knew.

"Amarilis texted to say she'll be here in a half hour," I say.

"Oh!" Abuela looks at the clock on the microwave oven. "That's soon." She drops a few plantain wedges into the hot frying pan and leaves them sizzling as she peers into my bowl of eggs. "Add another two," she says. "I made three eggplants, and they're pretty big."

Papi and Jacinto walk in the door as I pull two more eggs out of the refrigerator. "Mm, it smells delicious in here, Abuela." Jacinto gives Abuela a kiss on the cheek, then opens his arms wide and comes at me. "Hey, squirt!"

"Ugh, get away!" I hold up my hands, but he hugs me anyway and now I'm covered with his stinky sweat. "Eww, stop!"

"What? I'm saying hello to my baby sister." Jacinto smiles sweetly, as if that will fool anybody.

"Oh, be nice to your brother," Abuela says. "But you are hediondito, papito. Go shower before Amarilis gets home."

"I'll set the table," Papi says after Jacinto and his stench go

5

upstairs. He gets a stack of plates from the cabinet and takes them to the dining room. When he comes back in for the utensils, he stops and looks into the eggplant pot. "That looks good," he says as I stir in the eggs.

I keep my eyes on the sizzling yellowish mixture covering the eggplant. Maybe if I give him the silent treatment, he'll change his mind about those As.

I'm smashing the plantains in the tostonera when I hear a car door slam outside. "She's here!" I leave a half-squashed piece and run to the door. Amarilis and her boyfriend, Rich, are taking her bags out of the trunk. I bolt down the front steps and lunge at my sister. "I missed you!" I breathe in the familiar scent of her citrus-and-mint shampoo.

Amarilis laughs and holds me tightly. Then she pulls away and looks at me, her hands on my shoulders. "Have you grown?"

I shrug. I was the tallest kid in my class back in fourth and fifth grades, but now everyone has caught up to me, and some are taller. It sure would be nice to grow a little more.

"You feel taller." She holds me close again and kisses my forehead, then turns to Rich. "Doesn't she look taller?"

"You bet, and prettier too." Rich smiles as he places my sister's bags next to the car. He closes the trunk and puts an arm around Amarilis. "Just like you."

According to Abuela, Amarilis got all the best stuff in the looks department: our mother's golden eyes and wavy light brown hair (which Abuela calls blond), and skin almost as white as Abuelo's. Abuela feels sorry for me because I got stuck with her dark skin and eyes. Even worse, I have Papi's "bad" hair. I kind of like my thick, fluffy hair, but it's literally a pain to comb out all the knots, so sometimes I do wish I looked more like my sister. Still, Amarilis doesn't think she's pretty. If she had blue eyes like her friend Callie and super straight hair like her friend Emily, she says, she would have had dates in high school. As if Papi would have allowed it.

Rich tilts his head and squints at me. "You look sad," he says.

I'm still thinking about that dog I'll probably never get. Is it that obvious? Maybe not. Amarilis says Rich is really sweet and good at paying attention to other people.

I cross my arms in front of me. "Guess what Papi told me today!"

"What?" Amarilis asks.

"He said I have to get straight As this last quarter if I want a dog in the summer."

"That's great! He's letting you get a dog! See, I told you he'd come around eventually."

She is totally missing the point. "But I *can't* get straight As. He might as well have said I can never have a dog."

"My dad always tries stuff like that too," Rich says. "I don't blame you for being annoyed."

"Well, change his mind." Amarilis gives me a poke on the arm. "How?"

My sister bites her bottom lip. "Did you get any As last quarter?"

"I got one."

"Okay, then negotiate. Tell him you'll get two As this time."

"We'll help you," Rich says. "Come on, let's talk to him now." He picks up my sister's bags and heads for the front steps.

"Thanks!" I follow him, hand in hand with Amarilis.

"Actually, you should do this alone," Amarilis says to me. "If Papi feels like we're ganging up on him, he'll dig in his heels."

"But you'll help me, won't you?" I ask my sister.

"Help you what?" I should have known Papi would be lurking at the door waiting for us.

"Hi, Papi!" Amarilis throws her arms around him, then laughs as Abuela shrieks and hugs her super tight.

Papi shakes Rich's hand and they complain about the awful traffic on the Schuylkill Expressway. I relax because he doesn't ask me any more questions. Actually, I'm always relaxed when my sister is home. She makes everything better.

Chapter 2

ABUELA INSISTS THAT RICH STAY FOR dinner, and no one complains. Usually, Abuela is kind of nervous about sitting at the table with our friends. That's because we always speak in Spanish when it's just the family, but now Abuela will have to work hard to understand the conversation, and she probably won't say much. But Rich is worth it. We all liked him right away when we met him last August, the day Amarilis moved into her dorm at the University of Pennsylvania. He's a junior, so he already knew where everything was, and he helped us carry her stuff in, then showed her the laundry room and told her the best times to avoid the crowds. He didn't ignore me or treat me like a stupid kid when we met; he looked me in the eye and asked about my favorite books and movies, and he listened to my answers. Plus, he's really cute.

When Amarilis came home for fall break, she told us Rich had asked her out on a date. Abuela was thrilled that a handsome americano would be interested in my sister, but Papi didn't think Amarilis should get involved with someone older. Amarilis reminded him that he had been two years older than our mother. And when Rich came over all dressed up to ask Papi for permission to date Amarilis, my father had to agree with Abuela that Rich was very proper and respectful.

"How are your grades this semester?" Papi asks Amarilis.

She swallows a bite of eggplant. "Good."

"Did you tell your family about the calc exam?" Rich says to her.

Amarilis shakes her head and smiles.

"Dr. Flores, your daughter is brilliant." Rich leans forward, looking excited. "Well, I'm sure you already know *that*, but she had a test in calculus and the class average was a *twenty-nine*! Guess what she got? An eighty-eight! The highest score in the class."

"Congratulations, Amarilis." Papi lifts his water glass and holds it toward Amarilis like he's giving a toast.

"Thanks." Amarilis lowers her eyes. "When I went back and looked through the test, I saw I made one careless mistake. I could have gotten a ninety-three easily." My sister never thinks anything she does is good enough.

Rich turns to Jacinto. "And we all know you're a scholar *and* an athlete!"

Jacinto fights back a smile and sprinkles salt on his tostones. "I don't know about that."

"Well, I heard you aced the SAT," Rich says. "And you're the star of the track team."

Jacinto shakes his head. "I did okay on the SAT, but I'm taking it again next week. Hopefully, I'll get a perfect score this time."

Ugh. Just like Amarilis. All Jacinto ever does is compete with her. He'll probably end up with the highest GPA in his class like she did. And he'll also go to Penn, where Papi teaches physics and where our parents first met. Why can't he be his own person, like me? He is so boring.

"Rich ran track in high school too," Amarilis says. "He was really good; he has a ton of medals." She squeezes Rich's arm and looks into his eyes the way people do in those movies she likes.

Rich blushes and takes a sip of water. "I used to run cross country."

"Cross country!" Jacinto's eyebrows jump way up. "You distance guys are tough, running for days and days. I can't handle that."

"Well, sprinters are the tough ones, the way you zoom by people in seconds!"

Rich and Jacinto go back and forth complimenting each other, and Amarilis watches them with a big smile on her face. They're talking fast and Abuela's having a hard time understanding, so Papi translates the conversation for her, and then she smiles too. In a few minutes someone will probably ask me about school and grades and extracurricular activities, and I do not want to talk about any of that. I put a big piece of chicken in my mouth followed by a forkful of rice and beans. Now I can't answer any questions. At least, that's my brilliant plan, but it doesn't work.

"Miosotis, what is it you want Amarilis to help you with?" Papi asks.

"Um . . ." I chew slowly as I look around the table. Rich raises an eyebrow sympathetically, and Amarilis nods at me. I could lie and say I was talking about bras and periods, and then Papi will cough and change the subject real quick. But Amarilis jumps in.

"Miosotis has something to tell you about her fourth-quarter grades."

Papi puts down his fork and wipes his mouth with the edge of his napkin. "Go ahead. I'm listening."

Why isn't Amarilis doing the talking for me? She is so good at explaining things, while I never know what to say. I blow out through my mouth and try to concentrate. I can do this. If I want a dog, I have to do this. "Amarilis agrees it's unfair of you to make me get all As to get a dog."

"What Miosotis means," Amarilis says right away, "is that she would like to negotiate a compromise with you to prove she's mature and responsible enough to have a dog. Right, Miosotis?"

I nod. That sounds way better than what I said. "How about if I get two As? In Spanish, like I did last time, and one more." Papi starts to frown, so I quickly add one more thing. "And no Cs this time. I'll get the two As, and Bs in everything else."

"You got a C in something?" Amarilis looks at me, shocked. Then she turns to Papi. "I mean, that's a great proposal, don't you agree?"

Papi's eyes shift from Amarilis to me, then back and forth one more time. "One extra A is not much of an improvement."

"What if she gets the extra A in the class she got the C in last time?" Why is Jacinto butting in now?

"What?! No, science is too hard," I say. "But I promise to bring that up to a B. Please, Papi."

Papi rubs his chin and stares at his water glass as if the answer were inside. Finally, he looks back at me. "Okay, an A in science, an A in Spanish, and nothing less than a B in anything else." Papi holds his hand out to me. "Do we have a deal?"

12

I glance at Amarilis. She nods and smiles at me. This is better than Papi's original demand, way better. But still, what if I can't do it? Actually, I'm sure I can't.

"She'll take the deal!" Amarilis pulls my hand toward Papi's, and we shake on it.

When it's time for dessert, I help Abuela clear the table and bring out the tres leches cake she made from scratch. "Mmm, this is delicious." Rich closes his eyes and licks his lips. "Delicioso," he says to Abuela. She waves away the compliment. Then Rich turns to Papi and sucks in a deep breath. "Um, Dr. Flores, I'd like to ask you something."

"Certainly. What is it, Richard?" Papi stirs his coffee and looks at Rich.

"Well, um . . . This question is for you too—actually, mostly for you," he tells my sister. He reaches into his pocket and pulls out a tiny box. Amarilis gasps. "Um, I love you so much, I want to spend the rest of my life with you, and I know we were meant to be together forever, so I'd like to ask—with your father's permission"—he gets on one knee, opens the box, and holds it out to my sister—"if you would marry me."

This is so romantic! My sister and Rich stare at each other with sparkly eyes, and Amarilis trembles with happiness. She throws her arms around Rich, saying, "Yes! Yes! Yes!"

Abuela, Jacinto, and I clap when Rich puts the giant diamond ring on my sister's finger. Then we all look at Papi.

"You two are very young," Papi says. "And you haven't known each other for that long. Are you certain you're ready for marriage?"

"Yes, Papi, absolutely." Amarilis gives Papi the look she

uses when she wants something from him. That look always works.

Papi sighs. "I know you have a good head on your shoulders, Amarilis, and your mother and I were about your age when we first met, although we waited until after grad school to get married. When do you plan to do this?"

"Oh, whatever date you pick is fine by me," Rich says to Amarilis.

She looks at Papi. "Don't worry, we won't rush into anything."

Papi looks at the two of them with soft and happy eyes. "All right. You have my blessing."

Amarilis and Rich clasp hands and grin so big it makes me smile too. I love seeing my sister happy.

Chapter 3

Ａfter Rich leaves, Amarilis and I go to our room. I don't mention the movie I had picked out for tonight because there are more important things to discuss. We have a wedding to plan!

"You'll be my maid of honor, right?"

"Are you serious?!" I throw myself at Amarilis and hug her. I mean, I know my sister loves me and all, and she's always super nice to me, but it's big-sister nice, not you're-my-equal-and-I-want-you-to-be-my-maid-of-honor nice. So this is huge.

"You're squeezing me to death!" She laughs and laughs. I've never been a maid of honor before. I've never even been to a wedding before!

"When will the wedding be?" I ask. "Please don't make me wait years and years for this!"

Amarilis chuckles. "I'm not sure. Maybe after I graduate, or after Rich graduates, but no sooner."

"Oh, that's a long time."

"It'll be here before you know it. Besides, weddings take

forever to plan, so we'll be busy until then." She turns on her laptop and searches for bridesmaid dresses.

"Find some maid of honor dresses." I sit beside her on the bed. We look at the different colors I might wear. Amarilis has been shopping for me since I was in kindergarten, so I trust her to pick something nice.

"Yellow will look good," she says. "Mami adored yellow."

"And it'll match your favorite flowers, right?"

"Yep. I love daffodils," she says. "A bouquet of yellow daffodils with white roses would be perfect."

I know that bouquet. I've seen my parents' wedding photo a million times, hanging above the fireplace. In it, the yellow daffodils with white roses hang loosely from Mami's hands, arranged perfectly with sprigs of green in between and tied with a yellow satin ribbon. Our mother designed it herself, Papi says. She was obsessed with flowers and gardening. Papi jokes that he only married him because his last name means *flowers*. And she named all of us after flowers.

I'd be happy with a flower name if Mami had picked a normal one for me, like Rose or Lily, but people screw up their faces and say, "Huh?" when I introduce myself. Jacinto teases me by calling me Forget-You-Yes, and I can't get back at him because his name in English—Hyacinth—doesn't even annoy him. Amarilis is the only one with a normal-sounding name in English. I wish my father weren't the only Dominican in the world who hates nicknames. "Your mother picked out your names so lovingly," he says. "It would be disrespectful to alter them." So I can't even shorten my name to Mia or Missy—or anything else—to help my friends out.

16

"Will you wear Mami's wedding dress?" I ask my sister.

"Yes, absolutely," Amarilis says. "That way I'll feel like she's there, you know?"

I don't know. What would it be like, to have our mother here? How would it feel to be hugged by her, to tell her about my day and hear her laugh when I tell a joke? I shake my head and tell myself to forget it.

"Will you have bridesmaids too?"

"I'm asking Callie and Emily." Amarilis rests her left hand on one of her many embroidered pillows and snaps a photo. "I'll send them this picture without a caption or anything. They'll know!"

After she sends the message, my sister smiles at me. "My life with Rich will be perfect. He'll go to medical school and I'll get a job at a big accounting firm. Then after he graduates, we can have our first baby. I want at least two kids, and they'll be so cute! Won't it be great if they're blond and blue-eyed like Rich?"

"I . . . guess," I say. "But what if they're not?" My sister sounds like Abuela now.

"Well, they don't *have* to be blond and blue-eyed," Amarilis says. "It's just that I love him so much that a mini-Rich would be wonderful!"

Her phone rings and it's a video conference call with Callie and Emily. They both shriek and yell congratulations. "What a beautiful ring!" Emily says. "Are you excited?"

"Yes!!"

"When's the wedding?" Callie asks. "After he finishes med school?"

"No," Amarilis says. "Sooner than that."

"Where is he applying?" Emily asks. "Will you have to move far away?"

Amarilis shrugs. "We don't know yet." Then they talk about nice places to get married and themes and colors.

As I pick up each of the fifteen stuffed dogs from my bed and place them on top of the dresser, I think about Amarilis moving far away. She's only been engaged for two hours, and I was so happy and excited about it at first, but now I don't know. It's hard enough having her a half hour away at college. At least she texts me every day now. What will it be like when she's married? Will she live hundreds of miles away? Will she spend long hours at work and then go home to her kids and never have time to even send a text?

"Hey, mamita, what are you thinking about over there?" Amarilis says.

"Oh, are you finished with your call?"

"Um-hm. Come on, let's keep looking at dresses."

I plop down next to Amarilis. "I don't want you to move far away."

Amarilis looks at me with knitted eyebrows. "I'm not going anywhere. Remember, I still have three more years of college in Philly."

"I know, but after."

"Ay, mamita." Amarilis pulls me toward her and I rest my head on her shoulder. "We don't know where our lives will take us, but that doesn't matter, because we're sisters, and we'll always be close. Besides, Rich and I want to stay in the Philly area. Both of our families are here, and I absolutely want free babysitting from you!" Amarilis laughs and tugs at my ponytail. She looks me in the eye. "Are you okay?"

I nod. She's right. Look at Abuela and Tía Felicia. They hardly ever see each other since my great-aunt is in New York. But they talk every day. And so will we. Always.

Chapter 4

I PRESS THE SNOOZE BUTTON THREE TIMES before I get up Saturday morning. My sister is snoring away on the other side of the nightstand. She was texting with Rich when I went to bed last night, so I don't know what time she finally went to sleep. That's okay. We're not doing anything until the afternoon. Wedding stuff. Skating can wait.

I dress quickly and run downstairs. Papi is on the couch, reading the *Philadelphia Inquirer* as always. "Where are you going so early?" he asks.

"Next door, remember? You ask me this every Saturday." My neighbor Gina works for a dog rescue group. She and her wife, Miss Mabel, foster up to four dogs at a time until they find forever homes. Papi knows I help Gina most days, but he doesn't want me to get attached to the dogs, so he keeps "forgetting" about it.

"Oh, yes." He goes back to his paper.

"You're eating first, right, mi amor?" Abuela walks out of the kitchen wiping her soapy hands on a towel. "And should I fix your hair?"

"Her hair is fine, Doña Marta," Papi says without looking up. The status of my hair is a daily conversation topic between Papi and Abuela.

"Well, as long as you wear a hat," Abuela says. "But listen, it's cold out there. You have to bundle up to go into those woods." Abuela moved to the United States from the Dominican Republic over fifty years ago, but she still isn't used to the cool weather. When I was little she made me wear a snowsuit if the temperature dropped below sixty degrees.

"The Haverford College nature trail is not exactly the woods," I say. Still, I put on my coat and shove a hat on my head, because there's no point in arguing. "I'm not hungry, so I'll just have a banana. I can eat a big lunch when I get back." I finish my banana, then grab my gloves and run out the door before Abuela can chase after me with some scarves and a three-course meal.

Miss Mabel still has her coat on when she opens the door.

"Hello, sweetheart! How are you this morning?" Miss Mabel always calls me sweetheart or honey or sweetie—basically anything except my name. The first time we met, Papi sounded it out for her really slowly—MEE-OH-SO-TEES—and she said it was "beautiful." Yeah, right. She has never said my name again since then.

"Come in, come in." Miss Mabel steps aside and waves me in. "Miss Gina's around here somewhere." Miss Mabel thinks kids shouldn't call adults by their plain first names, even though Gina insists all that "Miss" stuff makes her feel old.

I step inside and enjoy a deep whiff of wet dog and burnt popcorn. When Abuela cooks, our house smells pretty great, but after each meal the heavy-duty cleaners and disinfectants come out, and it's like we never even lived in the place. Gina and Miss Mabel's house always smells like it's full of life. I follow Miss Mabel into the living room and immediately step on a squeaky toy. It happens every time.

Miss Mabel takes off her coat and hangs it on the rack by the stairs. Her pink scrubs seem shiny in the darkened room beneath her salt-and-pepper locs. "You just got home from work?" I ask.

"Yes. I love the night shift. A lot of the other nurses hate it, but not me! I am not a morning person." She tilts her head toward the stairs. "Gina must be upstairs. I'll let her know you're here. Good night!" A shaggy little dog with a curled-up tail bolts down the steps and jumps up to her, bouncing and barking over and over again. "Rory! Why are you down here, boy?" She bends forward and scratches his neck. He closes his eyes and leans his head into her hand.

"He's so cute!" I hold my knuckles out to his nose.

"He joined us last night," Miss Mabel says, "and he's very loving. This little guy needs a lot of attention." Rory lies on the floor and rolls onto his back, showing off a matted belly. "You do the honors, honey. I'm going to get some sleep."

I squat and rub Rory's belly. He holds his front paws by his side, giving me extra room to rub away, but as soon as Miss Mabel starts up the steps, he stands and watches her. "Gina! Your helper's here!" Miss Mabel calls as she walks upstairs. "Get these mutts out of here so I can rest." She chuckles.

When Miss Mabel is out of sight, Rory climbs onto my lap and noses his head under my hand. "You want a neck rub?" I scratch his neck as he rests against my chest and licks his lips. "You're a sweet baby," I say softly. "Yes, you are."

A few seconds later, three other dogs race down the steps ahead of Gina. The biggest one—a three-legged lab mix named Max—pounces on me and licks my face over and over. "I'm happy to see you too, Max!"

Gina limps to the threadbare brown sofa speckled with dog hair, and Max bolts over and gets comfy on her lap. Little Prissy, a tiny Yorkie, gives me a sniff and a short hand lick before heading to the couch, and Pugsley drops his favorite toy on my lap, then jumps up to join Gina.

"Good morning, Miosotis," Gina says, a little out of breath. Her cheeks are pink and her damp hair clings to her neck. "We should get going before someone has an accident. Have you met our new addition?" She nods at Rory, who is now cuddled next to Max. "He's a shih tzu mix and very sweet. You can take him and Pugsley, and I'll follow behind with Max and Prissy." She reaches for Prissy and cups the dog's face in her hands. "Who's the prettiest girl?" she says as Prissy licks her nose. "Yes, of course it's you." She looks at me. "Prissy's the only girl with us right now."

Gina and I know it would hurt another girl dog's feelings to hear her call Prissy the prettiest.

"How many leashes do we need?" I go to the hooks of leashes by the door.

"Your two and one for Max," Gina says. "I'll carry Prissy across Ardmore Avenue and then she'll follow me when we're on the trail."

I grab a handful of plastic bags from the dispenser in the kitchen, fasten leashes on Rory and Pugsley, then open the door to wait for Gina and the other two dogs. There isn't a light at the corner, so we have to wait a while for a break in the traffic.

Then we cross the avenue and walk into the campus. Gina puts Prissy down and unhooks Max's leash. Both dogs stay close to her heels. "How do you keep them from wandering off?" I ask.

"You can tell by the way a dog looks at you whether or not he's a runner. Also, these two have been with me for a while, so they know I'm the one who gives them food and fun toys. They don't want to get too far from all that!" Gina laughs. She keeps her eyes on the dogs and gets a sad look on her face. "I never thought they would still be here after all this time."

Neither did I. People keep passing on Max just because he's missing a leg. And poor Prissy's had a rough life, being forced to breed year after year at a farm in Lancaster. Now that she's old, no one wants her. Except Gina, who obviously loves her. "Won't you miss them if they get adopted?"

"I sure will," Gina says. "Truth be told, sometimes I hope they'll stay with me forever, but I know that's selfish. Max would be happier in an active family with young kids, and Prissy would love to be an only child getting pampered day after day."

We step onto the nature trail, and Rory and Pugsley take off in opposite directions, sniffing all over the place and stretching my arms out to their limits. "I'll take Pugsley," Gina says, "so they can both do their own things."

As soon as I move toward Rory, he bolts forward and I run to keep up with him. "I'll meet you back at the house!" Gina calls to me. It doesn't seem right to ditch her with three dogs, but I know she can handle it.

Rory puts his nose to the ground and zigzags his way along the trail, looking up every now and then to bark at a squirrel scampering up a tree.

"What a cute dog!" An old woman and man walk toward me holding hands. "Look, honey," the lady says, "isn't this the cutest dog ever?" She reaches over and Rory licks her hand.

The man nods in agreement and reaches out for some hand slobbers too. "You're very lucky to have such a sweet dog," he tells me.

"Thank you." I don't explain that I'm not lucky yet.

Rory and I keep going until we reach the duck pond, and he heads straight toward the water. I hold him back. He sniffs his way near a gaggle of geese. They look a little vicious when they stand and waddle toward us, and some are even bigger than Rory, so I pick him up and run back to the trail. This dog definitely needs me to protect him.

He knows it too. When I put him down, he balances on his hind legs and licks my face all over, which tickles and makes me laugh. At the end of the trail, I check for traffic, then cross the street and head home. I stop in front of Gina's house and look over at mine. Rory sits and looks at me, and I'm pretty sure he's ready to follow me anywhere, like Gina said about Prissy and Max. I stand under the pine tree my parents planted in front of our house after their first Christmas together. Rory trots over and sits next to me again.

What would happen if I took off Rory's leash? Would he stick beside me? I know we just met, but dogs always like me, and Rory seems to have gotten attached already. Even though Papi said I have to wait until the summer—and the two As—to get a dog, I wonder what he'd do if he saw Rory. Would he notice that Rory looks like a fluffy teddy bear, like my mother's dog Osito? Maybe Papi would get all sentimental and let me keep him. After all, he gets teary every time he talks about Osito and my mother. "That dog followed her everywhere," he says. "He stopped eating when she was gone."

I get a great idea. I'll take off Rory's leash, he'll follow me home, and Papi will look up from his newspaper. He'll remember my mother's dog, see how much Rory loves me, and say, *Yes, you may certainly keep him right now*. And then I won't have to worry about an A in science, or about any of my other grades.

Just as I unclip the leash, a squirrel scampers down our pine tree and zooms toward the busy avenue. Rory bursts down the sidewalk and chases after the squirrel. I gasp and stare at his blur of a tail, unable to move. He's heading straight into traffic.

I drop the leash and run after Rory.

Chapter 5

T HE QUICK THUMPS OF MY HEART almost drown out the
Saturday traffic whirring past me on the busy street. I look
up and down, but I don't see Rory anywhere. Then I hear a per-
sistent car horn, and then another, and another. In the middle of
the next block, cars are swerving around a white-and-tan mound
of trembling fur.

I run toward him, calling out, "Rory! Rory! Come here, boy!"
I'm out of breath by the time I get close enough to make eye
contact. I squat on the sidewalk and spread my arms open. Rory
turns and darts to the other side of the street, causing more honk-
ing and swerving. What am I going to do? What if Rory gets hit
by a car? What if the geese at the pond attack him? Or a bigger
dog? I will never forgive myself. And Gina will kill me. How could
I have been so stupid? Poor Rory might die because of me.

I keep my eyes on Rory as I wait for the traffic to ease up. He
watches me too, his tail wagging and his tongue dangling. When
I finally run across the street and almost reach him, he turns and
bolts into the condo complex next to the college. "Rory, come

back, please!" He stops once but takes off again as soon as I get close. He looks back a few times as he runs, never slowing down. I'm getting tired, but I refuse to take my eyes off of him.

Then my toe catches on a stone, and I trip and crash onto the ground, landing on a sharp rock that slices into my right sleeve. The white filling oozes out from the blue shell, which is kind of dark and muddy now. How will I explain this to Papi and Abuela? While I examine my torn coat, I hear a heavy breathing sound next to my ear. It's Rory, sniffing me up and down! I quickly wrap my arm around him and scoop him up. Then I cry all over the poor little guy.

Rory licks my tears and watches me. "You're not getting away again." I grip him firmly as I stand. But he doesn't even try to get away now. By the time we get to Gina's house, Rory is snoring with his little head on my shoulder.

Papi, Gina, and Miss Mabel are outside. "Where were you?" Gina cries. "I saw the leash out here and I got worried! I thought you went to your house, but you weren't there. Are you okay?"

I look at my father's frowning face, and I wonder how I can make this sound not so bad. If I tell them what happened, Gina will never trust me again, and no way will Papi let me get a dog, even if I get straight As for the rest of my life. "I—I—well, somehow Rory got away. I think there's something wrong with the leash. Um, it came loose, so I ran after him. But he's fine, I got him."

"Oh, thank you, Miosotis!" Gina lifts Rory out of my arms and covers him in kisses.

"Now that everyone's safe, I'm going back to bed." Miss Mabel yawns and stretches her arms over her head as she walks back to her house.

"Let's head home." Papi puts a hand on my shoulder. When we're inside, he says, "Perhaps working with the dogs is too dangerous. You should tell Gina to find someone else to help her."

"What?! It's not dangerous! I'm fine, and most importantly, the dog is fine and I saved his life."

"Look at your coat." Papi points at the rip. "What if this had been the summer? You'd probably be in the emergency room now."

I roll my eyes. "Why is everything always a big deal with you?" I storm upstairs.

"Whoa, mamita, what's all this stomping about?" Amarilis is still lying in bed in the dark.

"Papi's making a fuss about one of Gina's dogs getting away. He says it's too dangerous for me to keep helping her."

"Too dangerous? How?" Amarilis gets up and lifts the shades. When she turns and sees me, her eyes pop wide open. "What happened to you?"

"Nothing, I . . ." I look down. I'm covered in mud and grass stains, and the arm isn't the only place where my coat ripped. It looks like it went through a garbage disposal. "Well, I fell when I was chasing after the dog, but so what? These things happen, right?"

Amarilis lifts her eyebrows and mumbles, "I guess." She walks out of our room and into the bathroom.

I take off my coat and look in the mirror. There's dirt on my face, and my ponytail is undone. My rubber hair tie is gone, and curls and frizz are flying all over the place. Okay, I get why Papi's worried, sort of, but still, I'm fine, even if I do look kind of a mess. And the fact that I would go through all this to save a dog is proof that I'm cut out to be a dog owner. Right now. Why can't he see that?

I get out some clean clothes and sit on my bed to wait for the bathroom. I pick up my cell phone when I hear it ping. It's my friend Olivia.

Help! I have a zit emergency! Olivia sends me photos of a barely noticeable pimple on her forehead and I suggest parting her hair on the left to cover it up. She tries that and it works. *You're a lifesaver, as always!* she texts.

The whole time I'm texting with Olivia, Amarilis's phone buzzes again and again from her bed. I send a group text to Olivia and our other friend Zoe and get them all caught up on my sister's engagement, how I'm going to be her maid of honor, and the dog deal.

I can help you with your science grade, Zoe says. Which is true.

I'll dog sit for you anytime! is what Olivia has to offer, and I know she's excited about playing with a puppy.

When Amarilis comes back from the bathroom, she grabs her phone and gasps. "Wow, that's a lot of texts."

"All your high school friends probably want to see you," I say. "But we're going to the bridal store today, right?" My sister would never ditch me for her friends.

"Absolutely, mamita. And tomorrow we can go skating or to the mall. Whatever you want." Amarilis scrolls through her phone and giggles. "Oh, all these texts are from Rich."

"I guess he's really in loooove." I make some kissing noises.

She giggles again and sits on the bed, curled over her phone with her legs folded underneath her. I walk into the bathroom and turn on the shower.

When I get downstairs, Amarilis is looking through bridal websites with Callie. Callie jumps up from her seat and gives me a big hug. She and Amarilis have been best friends since kindergarten, and I've known her my whole life. "Are you going to the bridal store with us?" I ask.

"Yep."

"Hurry up and eat, mamita," Amarilis says. "Then we'll leave."

"Is Emily coming too?" I take the bowl of picadillo and rice Abuela hands to me.

"No, her spring break isn't until next week," Callie says. Callie is living at home and commuting to Drexel, which is right next to Penn. She and Amarilis get to see a lot of each other. But Emily is all the way in Boston.

"We'll send her pics of the dresses, though," Amarilis says. "She has great taste in clothes."

I rush and shovel spoonfuls of beef and rice into my mouth. As soon as I swallow my last bite, Amarilis hands me a jacket and we head to Callie's car.

"Will you be home in time for dinner?" Abuela asks from the door.

"Yes," Amarilis says.

"And what about your novio, is he joining us too?"

"No, he went to Vermont this morning to ski with his family." Amarilis puffs out her lower lip and makes a sad face. "I'm going to miss him."

Callie chuckles. "I'm sure you can live without him for a few days."

—≪≪◆≫≫—

We don't have an appointment at the bridal store, so we can't try anything on, but they let us wander around, looking at the dresses on our own. "What about these white ones with yellow polka dots?" Callie runs her hand over a shiny long dress.

"That's pretty!" Amarilis snaps a photo and sends it to Emily.

"Ooh, this one's nice!" Amarilis takes another photo. And another. And a bunch more. Then her phone buzzes. She looks at it. "Emily likes the third one best, but Rich isn't thrilled about any of them."

"You sent the pics to Rich?" Callie's eyebrows crinkle close together.

"Well, yeah. I mean, it's his wedding too." My sister has always said she wants a marriage where she and her husband are fifty-fifty partners.

Callie says, "I guess, but which dress is *your* favorite?"

"Um . . ." Amarilis looks at her phone again. "Actually, Rich has an interesting suggestion. He says the main flower in my bouquet should be the amaryllis. That's a cute idea, right?"

"I thought you wanted daffodils and white roses," I say.

"I thought so too, but I don't know, it might be nice to showcase the flower Mami named me after." Amarilis taps her chin. "Let's look at some red dresses too, since amaryllises are red and white."

I shrug. Callie slips her arm through my sister's as we walk around in search of red. "You know your mom would love anything you pick as long as you're happy," she says.

"I know." Amarilis reaches for me with her other arm. "Do you have any favorites, mamita?"

"Well, I don't want to wear anything poofy." I point to a dress that looks like a balloon made of lace.

Callie and Amarilis laugh. "I concur," Callie says.

"Emily asked what season we're planning for, which is a good question." Amarilis stuffs her phone into her back pocket. "Let's go home and look up wedding venues. We'll have to book a place far in advance, and that will help with all the other decisions."

Callie and I agree. As we leave the store, Callie points to the lacy balloon dress. "But remember," she says, "under no circumstances whatsoever will we wear that."

We laugh all the way to the car.

Chapter 6

PAPI GRILLS ME ABOUT SCHOOL DURING dinner and finds out I have a math test on Monday. "Perhaps you should focus on studying tomorrow instead of ice skating with your sister."

"I can do both."

"Remember our deal." He wags a finger at me.

"That's okay, mamita," Amarilis says. "Go study. We'll skate one day after school this week."

"Are you sure?"

"Absolutely. Your grades—and your dog—are important."

I'm not happy about this, but I know Papi won't change his mind about the deal. "Can I at least study at Zoe's?"

Papi loves Zoe, which is helpful but kind of annoying. Of course, I love Zoe too. But Papi doesn't see that she's funny and generous and loves those killer animal mash-up movies on the Syfy channel. No, all he sees in Zoe are straight As and leadership positions in a bunch of school clubs. So he goes giddy whenever I spend time with her. He thinks she's a "good influence" on me. Olivia, not so much. Her grades are mediocre, like mine.

"Perhaps she'll get a good job with a degree from a substandard college—or with no college at all," Papi says about Olivia, "but no one's going to give you the benefit of the doubt. You have to be twice as good as a white American to be given even half the credit."

Blah, blah, blah. My father and his old-people melodrama.

Anyway, he's happy to give me a ride to Zoe's the next day, especially when he sees my backpack over my shoulder. "You're studying for your math test, right?"

"Uh-huh."

"Good, good." Papi smiles.

Olivia and I get to Zoe's house at the same time. "I made us some flash cards last night." Zoe fans out a stack of cards.

"Oh, please," Olivia says. "We're watching the movie first, right?"

Zoe nods. She wants to see the movie about killer flying squirrels with powerful snapping-turtle jaws just as much as we do. So she gets some snacks and turns on the TV.

We squish together on the loveseat and laugh at the characters' silly conversations. When they stumble into the squirrels' territory, we lean forward and hold our breaths.

"Oh no, get away from them! Get away!" Olivia yells at the television as a teenage girl wearing shorts and a bikini top wanders away from her friends to coo at some cute squirrels in the park.

"I can't watch." Zoe puts her fingers over her eyes but spreads them apart and never looks away from the screen.

Popcorn flies, and the three of us shriek when blood squirts everywhere—even though we knew it was coming.

We sit back in relief when the blood-splattered screen cuts to a commercial. "Who do you think the next victim will be?" Zoe says.

"The guy with the glasses!" Olivia gulps her juice. "And then the super tall girl."

"For sure." Zoe looks at me. "What's your guess?"

"I don't know."

"What's with you?" Olivia asks. "You're being kind of quiet."

I shrug. "I'm worried about this deal I made with my dad. I've never gotten an A in science before. Does this mean I'll never get a dog?"

"Don't worry," Zoe says. "I'll help you."

The commercials end and we turn to the snapping squirrels again, but in the back of my mind, I keep thinking about yesterday with Rory. I almost got the little guy killed, so why am I worrying about my science grade? I probably don't deserve a dog. Plus, was I wrong to lie to Gina about the leash? What if she throws it out and buys another one? She and Miss Mabel aren't rich or anything. Even if they were, that would be a waste. Am I silly to worry about this? I mean, it isn't a big deal, right?

Zoe clicks off the TV when the movie is over. "Okay, time for math."

Olivia and I groan, even though we both like studying with Zoe. She's the best teacher ever. So we study—in between interruptions from Zoe's mom.

"Here's some hot chocolate for you ladies," Zoe's mom says the first time she comes into the room. She places the tray on a bookcase and puts her hands on her hips, looking at us one by one. "Don't you want to do something fun?"

"We already watched a movie," Zoe says. "We need to study now." She turns her back to her mother and proceeds to quiz Olivia and me on long division.

"You're not being a very gracious host," Zoe's mom says when she comes in again, this time with a plate of cookies. "Your guests must be tired of all this studying."

Zoe rolls her eyes. "Will you please stop interrupting us?" After her mom leaves, she leans forward and lowers her voice. "My mom keeps hoping the two of you will be a good influence on me."

"Good influence?" I say. "How?"

"She thinks I need to mellow out about school."

Olivia and me a good influence on Zoe?! What would Papi say to that? This seems so funny to me that I laugh and laugh, and Olivia joins in. Even Zoe stops frowning and lets out a giggle. By the time her mom pokes her head in the door again, the three of us are rolling on the floor, clutching our stomachs and trying to breathe. Zoe's mom smiles and backs out of the room, closing the door behind her.

Chapter 7

ON MONDAY MORNING I TIPTOE PAST my snoring sister as I get ready for school. Abuela is waiting for me when I go down for breakfast. "Ven, ven, siéntate," she says.

I sigh, sit, and pick up my spoon. I want to eat as much as possible before Abuela comes at me with the brush and comb. Every morning I pull my hair back in a ponytail without untangling it. Some strands stick out around my ears and neck, but so what? As long as it's not in my eyes, I'm fine. Abuela disagrees. She's always shocked at the mess on my head, and then she unties my hair and brushes and brushes it until my eyes water.

Today is no different. I can't enjoy my breakfast with all this head jostling. And it is totally gross when a piece of hair falls into my oatmeal. Finally, she ties it in a perfect ponytail and curls the bottom with a wide-tooth comb. It's so tight I can't turn my head as I walk to the bus stop. I sit in my seat on the bus and massage my neck to release some of the hair until I can move my head again. Just like every day.

School is pretty much business as usual too. At the beginning of the year, my teachers expected me to be brilliant because they remembered Amarilis and Jacinto. The only thing worse would have been if my brainy parents had gone to my school too, like Zoe's mom and dad and Olivia's whole family. Luckily, my mother grew up in New York City and my dad in the Dominican Republic. Still, my brother and sister are tough acts to follow.

In first period, Mr. Nesbitt hands back our science reports. "Why didn't you get help from your brother?" He taps my B– paper after putting it on my desk.

"Wouldn't that be cheating?" I shove the stapled papers into my bag.

"No, I wasn't suggesting you have him write the report for you. You're allowed to ask him for ideas or have him review it and give you pointers."

"I did ask him." This is sort of true. I mean, I told Jacinto I had to write a science report and might need help, and he grunted, "Okay, squirt." Then I never mentioned it again. The thing is that when he "helps" me, he takes over and doesn't even explain what he's doing. I'm always more confused after I've gotten Jacinto's help than I was before.

"Hmm, okay." Mr. Nesbitt doesn't look convinced. "As long you did your best."

Yeah, right. Adults always say that, but they never mean it. I used to work hard in school, but every time I brought home an imperfect report card, Papi reminded me how Amarilis and Jacinto always got better grades than me, and I could never match them. So now I don't try hard. I mean, if Papi's going to complain equally about a B+ and a B-, then why bother working for the plus sign?

It's a good thing the science report was the last assignment of the third quarter. Maybe I should be nicer to Mr. Nesbitt now that I want an A for next quarter. Or maybe I should go ahead and let Jacinto do my work for me.

Math class isn't any better. When I hand in my test—which I think I aced, by the way—Mrs. O'Grady clasps her hands together like an excited kid about to open birthday presents. "Did my star pupil come home for spring break?"

I nod.

"Tell her I said hello, and that we'd love it if she came by to visit!"

I nod again and walk out of the room.

Thank goodness it's finally lunch period, even though it is cardboard-tasting pizza day. My friends and I talk about the wedding. "Amarilis says my dress will be a little fancier than the other bridesmaids' dresses," I say, "since I'm the maid of honor."

"You're so lucky!" Olivia squeals. "Did I tell you about my cousin Myrna's wedding?"

She did, but we want to hear about it again. Maybe I can pick up some pointers for Amarilis, so I pay close attention when Olivia describes the dresses, the flowers, the decorations, and the food.

"Abuela wants Papi to ask his cousin in New York to make a Dominican wedding cake," I say. "She owns a bakery."

"Myrna had a chocolate chip cake for her wedding," Olivia says.

"That's what Amarilis wants! She thinks it's silly to bring a cake all the way from New York."

"I can ask Myrna where she got her cake, if you want."

"Won't your grandma be upset?" Zoe says.

I shrug. "Maybe. She did say Amarilis was acting like she was ashamed of her heritage."

Zoe slurps up the rest of her strawberry milk. "Well, *I'm* for sure glad you're Dominican. Thanks to you, I'm not failing Spanish!"

I laugh. "Maybe you'd be getting a B, but you couldn't fail anything if you tried."

"I don't know. This *ser* and *estar* stuff is really stumping me."

"Me too!" Olivia and Zoe pull out their Spanish worksheets, and we go over the sentences one at a time. It's hard to explain the rules on when to use *ser* and when to use *estar*, but I know what sounds right, and that seems to help.

Back at home, Abuela is on the phone having her daily conversation with Tía Felicia. My great-aunt always has drama going on in her life, so I eavesdrop as I pull off my coat and shoes.

"Listen, if you keep bailing him out, he'll never learn! Do you want him to be a criminal the rest of his life?" Tía Felicia's son, Ernesto, probably got arrested again. "Well, go ahead and waste your life savings on that good-for-nothing son of yours! Don't count on me for help. Never again!" Abuela hangs up the phone after shouting, "¡Jamás!" a few times. Then she closes her eyes and takes some deep breaths before looking at me. "Hola, Miosotis, mi amor. When did you get home?"

"Right now. Is Amarilis here?"

"Yes, she spent the day looking for wedding places on the computer. Now she's upstairs working on some secret."

41

I go up and knock on my bedroom door, just in case the surprise Amarilis is working on is for me. It probably is since my birthday will be here soon. When Amarilis calls, "Come in," I turn the doorknob.

"Oh, good, it's only you." She pulls a square piece of fabric out from underneath one of her pillows. "I'm making this for Abuela for Mother's Day. I know it's two months away, but I never have time at school, so I want to get it done here."

"That's pretty." Amarilis is cross-stitching the word ABUELA and a bunch of colorful hearts all around it. It's supposed to be cheerful, but I feel kind of sad looking at it. The frame above my sister's bed has a cross-stitched picture of a red-and-white flower with the word AMARYLLIS stitched underneath. Our mother made it, and she made one for Jacinto too, with three hyacinths, one pink, one purple, one blue. Then there's mine, which is shoved under my stash of candy in the top drawer of the nightstand between our beds. The words FORGET-ME-NOT are neatly stitched across the bottom, but that's it. My mother never finished it. Amarilis has asked if I want her to put the flowers in for me, but I always say no. I don't need some silly flowers above my bed. "It looks like you're almost done," I say.

"Yes, but I still have to make the pillow."

"Did you find any good wedding places?"

"Yeah, I made appointments to see two of them on Friday when Rich is back in town." Amarilis puts the fabric aside and grabs her computer. "Isn't this place gorgeous? It's a little pricey, but maybe worth it."

I sit next to my sister as she scrolls through photos of a giant room with fancy chandeliers and a bunch of smiling people in

42

shiny clothes holding glasses of champagne. "It's beautiful," I say.

"I know, right? And here's the other place. It's a converted barn, so a different feel, but nice too." These pictures show a packed room with wood-paneled walls and a matching dance floor. The women have flowy dresses and the men aren't wearing any ties. Everyone is smiling like in the other place.

"Yeah, that's cute."

"Anyway, once we choose the venue and the date, we can start on the other details." Amarilis picks up Abuela's present and gets back to cross-stitching. "So, how was school today?"

"It was okay. The usual."

"Do you want help with your homework tonight?"

I don't really want to spend my time with her doing homework, but I know it will be good for my dog goal. "Sure, thanks, but I have to go next door first."

"Okay, mamita, see you in a little bit."

As soon as I open Gina's storm door, I hear a chorus of barks and dog nails skidding across the floor. "Come on in!" Gina calls before I even knock. Inside, the dogs are out of control. Gina is on the floor tossing toys around while they chase after them. "Help me up, Miosotis, and we'll take these wild kids to the dog park."

When I give Gina my arm, Rory jumps up and licks my face. "Aww, you're so sweet," I say. "Do you remember me, little guy?" I try to pick Rory up, but he's too wriggly. "I'll get the leashes."

"Don't use the messed-up one from the other day," Gina says.

I pull on my fingers as I face the hooks of leashes. "Actually, it was my fault Rory got away. The leash is fine."

"Really? What happened? Did you forget to clip it all the way?"

"Um-hmm." I grab the leashes and reach for Rory without looking at Gina. At least she won't waste her money replacing the leash. But I still haven't told the truth, and my heart is thumping super fast in my chest.

"Don't worry about it," Gina says. "But be careful from now on."

I nod. I still don't look at her.

We herd the dogs into the car, and Rory curls up on my lap. When we get to the dog park, Gina sits on a bench. "I think rain is coming, because my knee is killing me today." Gina was hurt years ago in Iraq when she was with the army, and some days her knee bothers her more than others.

"You rest," I say. "I'll play with them." I grab an armful of tennis balls and hurl them across the park one after another. Max, Pugsley, and Rory chase the balls and bring them back to me to throw again and again. Prissy sits on Gina's lap. When more people come with their dogs, Pugsley hides under the bench behind Gina's feet. I'm sweating, so I take off my coat—which Amarilis repaired with thick thread weaving through it like an ugly scar—and keep tossing the balls across the field. Soon Rory joins Pugsley under the bench, but Max is still going strong.

I turn to Gina. "I should probably get back to do homework and eat dinner." I love playing with Max, but I know from experience that he never ever gets tired, and I can't stay out here all night.

"Of course, dear." Gina stands and cradles Prissy like a baby. "Thank you for doing this. The boys will sleep well tonight."

In the car on the way home, Rory snuggles next to me and puts his warm head on my lap. I snap a picture with my phone.

I'll show it to Papi tonight when I ask if we can adopt Rory. There is no way he'll resist this adorable face!

—«««•»»»—

"Did you finish your project?" Abuela asks Amarilis during dinner.

"Not yet, but almost. I'll work on it some more tomorrow. Tonight I'm helping Miosotis with her schoolwork."

"Oh, nice." Papi hums as he spoons some beans over his rice.

Now that Papi is in a good mood, I make my move. "Look at this picture. Isn't Rory adorable?"

Papi lifts his glasses onto his forehead and holds my phone close. "Yes, he certainly is a cute little guy."

"OMG. This dog is sooo precious!" Amarilis takes the phone and hands it to Abuela. "Doesn't he remind you of Mami's dog?"

"¡Ay, sí, que lindo!"

"Can we adopt him, please?" I use my sweetest voice as I look into Papi's eyes and blink a few times quickly.

"You mean now?"

"I'll still get those As and definitely no C ever again in my life, honest," I say. "But the thing is, he's available now and he's perfect! Not too big, hypoallergenic. I mean, we don't know if there'll be another dog like this in the summer."

"No. You and I made a deal, and we're sticking to it." Papi turns to Jacinto. "How was your first day of spring track?"

So I guess we're done talking about my thing.

"Pretty good," Jacinto says. "I was voted one of the team captains."

I know I shouldn't complain. Papi is right. We have a deal. We shook on it and everything. But I'm tired of waiting, and good grades have nothing to do with taking care of a dog. Why can't Papi see that?

Chapter 8

Papi and Abuela shoo us upstairs and say they'll clean the kitchen without our help. "You only have a few more days to study for the SAT," Papi tells Jacinto. "And you"—he points at Amarilis—"help your sister with her homework. She certainly needs it."

I breathe in hard through my nose. What does he mean by that? Papi tells me I'm smart, that he believes I can do anything if I try, but then he says stuff like this, so I know what he really thinks. I turn and head upstairs.

"Okay, what are we working on tonight?" Amarilis follows me into our room.

"My geography project is due tomorrow." I pull a large folded sheet of paper from my backpack and place it on the desk. "We have to pick twenty countries and identify them in some way, like flags or coins or foods." I unfold the map of the world and smooth it out. "I'm doing flags." I turn on the computer.

"Flags?" Amarilis crinkles her nose as if I'd put smelly socks in front of her. "That's kind of boring. Don't you want to do something more challenging?"

"What's wrong with flags?"

"Well, nothing, but I'll bet a lot of kids will choose flags," Amarilis says. "It's not hard to look up a flag on the internet."

"I know, that's why I picked flags." I sit and search for a photo of the flag of the Dominican Republic.

"Knock, knock," Jacinto says from outside the open door. "Guess who called me?" He lopes into our room and plops himself on Amarilis's bed.

"Rich?" Amarilis smiles.

"Okay, I guess I should have figured you would know."

I swivel in my chair and face them. "Why did Rich call you?"

"He asked me to be a groomsman at the wedding."

"I hope you said yes?" Amarilis sits next to Jacinto and pokes his arm.

"Um, let me think." Jacinto strokes his chin. "Oh, yeah, now I remember! I did say yes!"

Amarilis swats Jacinto on the back with a pillow. "I'm glad family is important to Rich." She holds the pillow close and hugs it. "We're so much alike. I'm marrying my best friend."

Jacinto gives Amarilis a little squeeze on the shoulder. "That's pretty cool." He glances at the computer screen. "What are you doing over there, squirt?"

I explain about my geography assignment.

"Don't you think flags are boring?" Amarilis asks him.

"Yeah, everybody'll pick flags. You want to stand out."

"What about famous landmarks?" Amarilis says.

"Or local foods?"

"Oooh, maybe animals. You like animals, right?"

"I just want to do flags," I say.

As usual, they ignore me. Next thing I know, "we're" research-ing national flowers. Amarilis and Jacinto agree on a few things: I have to include the DR, and the other countries should be spread out on the map and all have different flowers. But then they start to argue. "Picking Holland for the tulip is too predict-able," Jacinto says. "What about Hungary or Turkey? Which one would you prefer, squirt?" he calls to me from the computer.

I'm on my bed now, scrolling through puppy Instagrams on my phone. "Whatever, I don't care."

"I wouldn't rule out the Netherlands," Amarilis says. "Just because it's obvious to you doesn't mean everybody thinks of Holland when they see tulips."

"They most positively do!"

My brother and sister go on and on for a while until they agree on something, and then they move on to the next argument: is Ethiopia's lily—calla—different enough from Italy's to include both? I doze off, and when I wake up they're discussing whether they've chosen too many red flowers and should make some changes. I remember I'm supposed to read two chapters of *Catherine, Called Birdy* for English, so I get the book and cover my ears while I read. By the time I finish, Amarilis and Jacinto are stepping back from my map and admiring their work. "Doesn't this look great?" Amarilis says.

It does look great. And why wouldn't it? A high schooler and a college student should do a fabulous job on a sixth-grade project. I can't believe they're actually proud of this accomplishment. I'm not, since I had nothing to do with it.

Chapter 9

THE NEXT DAY MR. NESBITT EXPLAINS how he will grade us for the fourth quarter. Weekly homework assignments will be worth a total of thirty percent of our grade. Two tests will be worth fifteen percent each, and a final project will make up forty percent. Then he gives us some details about the final project: We have to find a recent news article about something scientific and present a slideshow on it in front of the class. The presentations will be during the last two weeks of May, and he'll hand out a schedule by the end of the week.

I take notes as he gives us pointers on getting started. This business of taking notes is new for me, but if I'm going to get an A, I figure I should change things up a bit.

"Isn't this exciting?" Zoe says as we sit in the cafeteria. "The science in the news project sounds like fun. And an A in that will guarantee you an A in the class."

I squint at Zoe. "You're the math whiz, but I don't think that's right."

"She's got you there." Olivia laughs.

Zoe sighs. "You for sure can't fail everything else and still get an A, but it shouldn't be hard to get As on your homework. Just show it to your dad or your brother before you turn it in."

"And the tests?"

"Those you study for." Zoe reaches over and grabs my hands. "I'll help you, and you'll do great, for sure!"

"I don't like science either," Olivia says, "but the news project does sound cool. Since we can pick any topic we want, I already know what I'm going to look for: makeup."

"Makeup?" Zoe lets go of my hands and gives Olivia an exasperated look.

"Yeah, it's chemistry, right?" Olivia pops a baby carrot into her mouth and crunches. "Plus, the slideshow will be fun to do. We can make ours all artsy and stuff. If you want, I can help you with that part, Miosotis."

"Thanks." I twirl my plastic fork around and around in my spaghetti. When it snaps in two, I feel like I might snap also. "I don't want to learn about science in the news. I don't want to make a fancy slideshow. And I don't want to give a speech in front of the whole class. All I want is a dog. Is that too much to ask?"

------≪≪◆≫≫------

Abuela is sitting on the couch when I get home from school. She has the phone to her ear and she's scolding Tía Felicia, but I don't stick around to find out why. I head straight upstairs where Amarilis is leaning against her pillows, typing away on her laptop. "Hey, mamita, look what I made." She swirls the laptop around to face me.

51

I drop my backpack and bend over for a closer look. "What's the spreadsheet for?"

"For planning my wedding. I read a bunch of wedding planning articles and guides today. They were so helpful." She points at her screen. "These are the tasks we should complete at least a year before the wedding, and then, as we get closer to the date, we have to do all these other things. I've planned everything out month by month over a fifteen-month period."

"So . . . your wedding's in fifteen months?"

"We don't have the date yet; figuring that out is one of the first tasks. But, for the purposes of this spreadsheet, I had to pick something."

My sister is so organized. "Your wedding will be perfect." Just like her.

"Oh, gracias, mamita." Amarilis stands and lifts her arms over her head. "I've been hunched over this computer for hours. I need a break. What are you up to now? Do you want to go skating?"

"I can't. I have to go to Gina's. Do you want to come?"

"Nah, I'll see if Abuela needs help with dinner. Those dogs are too slobbery for me."

I smile. I love my sister, but I don't understand her sometimes. I mean, there's no such thing as too slobbery when it comes to dogs. "I won't stay long today. Maybe we can watch a movie tonight?"

"Or do your homework," Amarilis says.

"Ugh."

"Or both. What's due tomorrow?"

"Just a science worksheet." I reach into my backpack and

find the worksheet. "It's only one page, so it shouldn't take long."

"Great! Popcorn and a movie when we're done with this!"

—⋘◆⋙—

"Guess what!" Gina says as soon as I arrive. "Rory and Pugsley both found forever homes today! Pugsley's new dad will be here in about an hour, and Rory will be picked up later tonight. Isn't this great?"

I stare at Gina. "Yeah, I guess."

"Aren't you happy for them?"

"I am, but I'm going to miss Rory, and this seems quick." I kneel and rub Rory's neck. He rolls onto his back and licks his lips while I massage his belly. "I thought I might be able to adopt him myself."

"Oh, I'm sorry, sweetie." Gina pats my back. "I didn't know your family was interested in adopting. Your dad should fill out an application."

"The thing is, he says I can't get a dog until the summer."

"But you should get your application in now anyway." Gina opens the top drawer of her filing cabinet and pulls out a sheet of paper. "In fact, Rory's new family filled out an application a while ago; they were waiting for the right dog to come along."

"Hmm, that's a good idea." I take the paper from Gina and fold it. "Thanks." I tuck the application into my pocket before we clip the dogs' leashes on and head outside. As I watch Rory bounce through the nature trail, sniffing each twig before peeing on it and growling at the bigger dogs we pass, I feel more hopeful. Maybe I can find a science article about dogs. I could definitely make a good slideshow about them. Yes, I can get an A in science, and I will have my dog the day after school ends.

-◄◄◄◆►►►-

"Um, Papi?" Amarilis says during dinner. "I was reading some wedding planning guides today, and they all say the first thing to do is figure out a budget, so we should talk about that."

"Yes, you're right." Papi takes a sip of water and sighs. "Weddings are expensive these days, aren't they?"

"Yes, but I have money saved up, since I didn't have to use my whole college fund because of your faculty discount. We can use that money."

Papi nods. "I agree. However, I looked into the discount, and it only applies to dependent children. You might not qualify if you're married."

Amarilis frowns. "Oh, I hadn't thought of that. Does this mean we can't get married until after I graduate?"

"Listen, three years will go by fast," Abuela says. "Between your studies and preparing the wedding details, you'll be so busy, you'll be glad you waited."

"Yeah," I say. "There's a lot on your spreadsheet. We can spend the summers getting it all done. I'll learn calligraphy and help you address the invitations." I have to admit I like the idea of taking our sweet time to prepare for the wedding. Even though Amarilis says I won't lose her, things will be at least a little different, and I'll need time to get used to those changes.

My sister pokes her beans with her fork and pushes the rice around on her plate. "I guess you're right," she says softly. "I hope Rich doesn't mind."

Abuela puts her hand over Amarilis's. "He won't mind. He loves you. But tell me, how do his parents feel about your marriage?"

Amarilis perks up now. "They're really excited. His mom offered to lend me her diamond earrings so I can have something borrowed. And she's already talking about the menu for the rehearsal dinner. They live in one of those mansions in Gladwyne, so they have plenty of room."

Abuela smiles real big and looks at Papi. "Ay, Oscar, you must be honored that those people are happy to accept someone like us into their family."

"Honored?" Jacinto almost chokes on his food. "Why? They're not better than we are."

"Oh, you know what I mean."

"Actually, Abuela, I don't."

"Jacinto, don't be rude to your grandmother," Papi says. He turns to Abuela. "Amarilis is a gem, and anyone would be happy to accept her into their family."

"Por supuesto." Abuela's voice is soft and swirly, like a lullaby to calm an unreasonable toddler. She smiles at Amarilis, who smiles back.

Jacinto rolls his eyes, and I shrug at him. I'm surprised Amarilis doesn't even look our way. Usually, it's the three of us shaking our heads at the silly things Abuela says. Today it seems like she agrees with Abuela. Should she? Are Rich and his parents really so great?

—«‹◆›»—

"What's this?" I walk into our room after dinner and pick up the paper on my bed.

"I finished your science worksheet," Amarilis says. "Now we can watch the movie."

"Oh." I'm not sure about this. I mean, I guess I'm glad Amarilis made my life a little easier. But why did she do it? Is she like Papi and she believes I can't do my own homework? And what would Mr. Nesbitt think if he knew? He did say getting help wasn't cheating, so maybe he wouldn't mind at all.

"Do you want me to explain it to you?" she asks. "You should understand this in case it's on a test."

"Okay."

Amarilis goes on and on about weather patterns and atmospheric pressure. I try to understand it all, since I need to for my A, but I have to admit I'm a little confused. Still, I don't say so. I'll figure it all out before my test, right? I put the worksheet away and go downstairs with my sister.

We sit in front of the TV with our microwaved popcorn. We hold hands when the heroine walks through a creepy park by herself and sigh when she runs into her crush. Amarilis dabs her eyes with a tissue when they declare their love for each other and kiss. And I forget all about school and homework.

Chapter 10

AMARILIS IS WHISPERING INTO HER PHONE in the middle of the night. "I'm sorry if I hurt your feelings. I guess I didn't explain it well. Absolutely, I love you. I'll always love you, no matter what." She looks at me when I sit up. "Sorry," she mouths. "I woke up my sister," she says into the phone. "Are we okay?" She sniffles. "Okay, I'll talk to you tomorrow."

"What's going on?" I ask.

"Nothing. Rich saw my text about our wedding date and he got a little upset."

"Why?"

"He said he's afraid I don't actually want to marry him." She chuckles. "Isn't that absurd? Anyway, he understands now. Sorry I woke you. Go back to sleep."

I'm exhausted when my alarm buzzes in the morning. I drag myself out of bed, and I don't try too hard to be quiet as I get ready for school. Still, Amarilis doesn't stir.

Mr. Nesbitt smiles as he looks over my science worksheet, and Ms. Wilson uses my map as an example for social studies class. But I have to sigh when Papi turns to me at the dinner table and asks how I did on my math test.

"B plus."

"Not bad."

"Yeah," Jacinto says. "You're getting better. But if you want, I can help you go over the ones you got wrong."

"And next time," Amarilis chimes in, "you'll absolutely get an A."

"I remember the first time your mother got a bad grade." Abuela looks at me with a sad little smile. "She was so upset. But she turned it around, and so will you."

I palm my forehead and roll my eyes. To most people, a B+ is great. But not to my family. "Whatever." I put a piece of concón in my mouth and chew it slowly, hearing the toasty rice crunch in my ears as I think about my math test. The thing is, I studied a lot this time, and I thought I had an A. This is why it's better if I don't bother studying. No matter how hard I work, I still manage to disappoint my family.

"Is everything okay with Rich?" I ask Amarilis after dinner.

"Yep! I made appointments to look at more wedding places every weekend for the next month. We both agree it's good we'll have time to plan the perfect wedding." Amarilis turns on her computer and pulls up the spreadsheet. "We also have to finalize the guest list. Rich's mom said she'll send me her list, and I need to find out who Papi and Abuela want to invite."

"Do you think our family will come from far away for the wedding?" I ask.

"Nah. Well, Tía Felicia and the other New York people will be there, but the DR folks probably can't afford the trip."

Amarilis shows me photos of the other places she's going to look at with Rich and then asks about my homework.

"I have to read two more chapters for English, plus solve these problems for math."

Amarilis handles the math while I read. She finishes it in a few minutes, then calls Rich and giggles on the phone while she works on Abuela's Mother's Day gift. I stare at the math problems. Most of Amarilis's answers make sense to me, but some don't. Will Mrs. O'Grady know I didn't do this myself? What will my next test be like if I don't understand this? Amarilis chatters away without noticing me. I put the worksheet in my backpack and get ready for bed.

—«‹‹◆›››—

Callie is at our house when I get home from school the next day. She and Amarilis usher me into our room and show off the pillow for Abuela. "I finished it at Callie's house today," Amarilis says.

"I love Thursdays." Callie lies on my sister's bed and spreads her arms wide. "No classes on Thursdays."

I leave them talking about wedding colors and places and flowers, and I head over to Gina's. She has a new dog, Buster, who's as big as a horse. He runs up to me, knocking over a lamp on the way. His tail thumps against the floor and his tongue dangles sideways when I scratch his neck. Max gives me a friendly yip from under the coffee table, then goes back to ripping into a long bully stick.

"Let's grab the leashes so these guys can get some exercise," Gina says.

A low growl followed by a quick bark comes from the dining room. "Who's in there?" I ask.

"That's Freckles, but we'll leave him behind." Gina scoops Prissy up from the couch. "He's been hiding under the table all afternoon."

I go into the dining room and crouch down to get a look. Freckles trembles and growls at me, baring his little teeth. He isn't much bigger than Rory, with little brown spots on his mostly white face. "Hey, little guy." I get a little closer. Freckles snaps at me and I back away. It's kind of amusing how he thinks he's tough, but I don't want those little teeth clamping down on me. "It looks like he's sitting on a puddle of pee," I say to Gina.

"I know. I'll clean it later. The poor thing is terrified. Leave him be for now."

We walk to the college, where I am in charge of holding Buster's leash as he gallops all over the place. I hang on with both hands because no way will I let him get away. By the time we get back to Gina's house, Buster is tuckered out and so am I. He slurps up a bunch of water, spilling half of it all over the kitchen, then, sounding like a pile of firewood clattering to the floor, he plops down in the middle of the living room. Freckles is still under the dining room table. He growls a little when I look at him, but mostly he shivers even though it's warm in here. That is one strange little dog.

-‹‹‹‹◆›››-

There are seven of us at dinner tonight, so we bring down a desk chair and squeeze it in. "How was your ski trip?" Callie asks Rich.

"It was okay, but I'm glad to be back with my sweetie." Rich

60

and Amarilis hold hands and stare at each other with giant smiles on their faces.

Abuela nods at Papi and purses her lips toward Rich.

"Oh, yes," Papi says. "Richard, we'd like to invite you and your family over for Easter dinner if you're available."

"Thank you, Dr. Flores. I'll ask." Rich pulls his phone out of his pocket and sends a text.

"We don't have a lot of room," Amarilis says. "Wouldn't it be better if we got together at a restaurant?"

"¿Un restaurante?" Abuela opens her eyes wide. "Restaurant food isn't as good as anything I can make."

"I agree," Papi says. "Restaurants are stuffy and impersonal. We want to chat and take our time getting to know one another."

Rich's phone beeps, and he looks at it. "They said yes. My mom's super excited to meet all of you!" He puts his phone back in his pocket and turns to my sister. "Do you mind if she comes with us to see that barn tomorrow?"

"Of course not," Amarilis says. "I'd love to get her opinion."

After dinner—and a *very* long discussion of the pros and cons of a bunch of wedding venues—Amarilis goes out on the front porch with Rich and Callie. It's Jacinto's turn to help with the dishes, and I don't have a lot of homework, so I grab a sweater and sneak out to join them.

"I'm glad we're doing Easter together," Rich is saying to Amarilis. The two of them are on the porch swing, and Callie is in the chair near the railing. I sit down on the steps. "With your family around, maybe my dad won't lecture me."

"What does he lecture you about?" Callie asks.

"Oh, everything. Pulling up my grades, applying to med school, that sort of thing."

Callie tilts her head and gives Rich a confused look. "So, you don't want to go to med school?"

"No, I do, just not right away. Plus, I know he has connections, so I'll get in somewhere. He doesn't have to hassle me."

"Hmm." Callie taps her chin.

"Rich is really good with kids," Amarilis says. "He'll make a great pediatrician." She puts her hand over Rich's. "Remember that little girl who was riding her bike on Locust Walk?"

Rich smiles and nods.

"She fell," Amarilis tells Callie, "and she was crying and crying. Rich was the only person who could calm her down!"

"Well, I have class tomorrow." Callie stands and shoves her hands into her pockets. "I'll see you guys later. Have fun at the wedding barn. It looks amazing!"

After she leaves, Rich asks, "Why was Callie being sarcastic?"

"Sarcastic?" Amarilis says. "About what?"

Rich sits up straight and uses a super high, shrieky voice. "Have fun at the wedding barn. It looks amazing!"

"She wasn't being sarcastic," Amarilis says.

"Hmph." Rich crosses his arms and sits back.

I've never seen Rich frown before. Callie sounded cheerful when she said goodbye. Why is he being weird?

"Did you finish your homework, mamita?" Amarilis says.

"No." I get up and open the door. "I have to read a few chapters for English. Um, see you tomorrow, Rich." I hope he doesn't think I sound sarcastic too.

Rich gives me a thumbs-up. "Sure thing, little sis."

Chapter 11

M R. NESBITT HANDS OUT THE SCHEDULE for our final project presentations, and Zoe is thrilled to be presenting on the first day. "I don't want to see what other people are doing, because then I'll for sure compare myself to them."

"I can't wait long either," Olivia says, "but going first would be tough. I'm glad he put me on the second day."

I'm scheduled to present three days after Olivia, on the Friday before Memorial Day. "I guess Mr. Nesbitt knows us all well," I say, "because I want mine over with before the long weekend."

"I already found the perfect article," Olivia says. "It's about the harmful chemicals in lipstick. I'm sure other makeup has a bunch of bad stuff in it too. That's probably why my face breaks out."

I shrug. "I'm not allowed to wear makeup yet, and I get pimples all the time."

"Oh, please!" Olivia says. "Your skin is perfect."

"Are you kidding me?!"

Zoe rolls her eyes. "Can we get back to talking about the science project? I'm trying to pick between two articles: one about how to clean up all the plastic that's found its way into our oceans, and one about the possible extinction of a bunch of tree species in the Amazon forest. They're both so fascinating, it's hard to narrow it down."

Zoe and Olivia are super excited about this project. That's typical for Zoe, but Olivia too? Maybe if I find an interesting dog article, then I can do a good job on my presentation. I might even learn something new, something I'll remember for more than a week. After Amarilis goes back to school, I'll look through Papi's newspaper every day. Better yet, I'll search online.

"You should make a spreadsheet of the articles you find," Amarilis says at home. "Like this, see?" She shows me her laptop, with a table of wedding venues sprawled across the screen. The places she plans to see are listed on the left, and the things they have—both good and bad—are across the top. She's marking the boxes for the place she and Rich saw today.

"But I don't have any articles yet," I say.

"I know, but if you make a list, you won't feel like you have to find the perfect article right away," Amarilis says. "You can read a bunch of articles and then pick the best one, based on what you want. If I expected to find the perfect wedding venue on the first try, I'd be too stressed to look at anything."

"I guess that makes sense." Still, it sounds like a lot of work. I promise to think about it, and then I leave for Gina's.

-‹‹‹◆›››-

Amarilis is going back to school on Sunday, so we go ice skating on Saturday afternoon. When we get back home, Abuela tells us she just finished preparing food for Amarilis to take back to school. "I packed a week's worth of lunch and dinner for you." She opens the freezer and points to the pile of plastic containers inside. "Make sure you put it all in the refrigerator as soon as you get to your room tomorrow."

"Gracias, Abuela." Amarilis gives Abuela a smile that doesn't reach her eyes. She's been quiet all day, even while we were skating. When I asked her what was wrong, she said she was tired. But I don't know. I think she's sad about something.

Abuela notices as well. "Ay, mi amor, we'll miss you too." She strokes my sister's hair. "Also, I washed and folded your clothes and put them on your bed."

"You didn't need to do that," Papi says. "Amarilis can do her own laundry."

"I know, but I like taking care of my babies."

Papi chuckles. "Corazón used to say that too. Jacinto always wanted to be carried, and she would indulge him, the little haragán."

"Hey, I was little! Would a lazy person do this?" Jacinto holds up his trowel and gardening gloves on his way to the backyard. He inherited our mother's green thumb, and he spends hours fiddling with our flowers.

"She was a good mother, my Corazoncito," Abuela says.

"She certainly was." Papi sighs.

I turn away. I have nothing to add.

-‹‹‹◆›››-

Abuela insists we go to church on Sunday before Amarilis goes back to school. After Mass, we stop at the graveyard. Abuela wipes down my mother's and Abuelo's tombstones, and Papi sends Jacinto to the garden store across the street to pick out some perfect flowers for the two of them.

"Are you okay?" I whisper to Amarilis while we're waiting for Jacinto. "You seem sad."

Amarilis tugs at my ponytail and gives me a half smile. "I'll miss you, mamita."

I give my sister a hug. I'm going to miss her too, but she wasn't gloomy like this when she left after winter break. "Are you sure that's all?"

Amarilis nods, then turns to watch Jacinto come back with an armful of flowers. Papi and Abuela arrange the flowers carefully, talking to Abuelo and my mother the whole time.

"Amarilis is marrying a very nice and handsome young man," Abuela tells them. "You would really like him."

"We need to get going," Amarilis says. "Rich is picking me up in a half hour."

-<<<•>>>-

I go next door after my sister leaves. "Thank goodness you're here," Gina says as soon as she opens the door. "Freckles won't let anyone touch him, although he finally came out from under the table to drink some water a few times. As soon as he sees a leash, he bolts back under there."

"Hmm." I bend to look at Freckles. "Why is he like that?"

"The poor thing was likely abused," she says. "I think someone hit him with a leash."

I gasp. How could anyone hurt such an innocent little guy?

"He likes Prissy," Gina says. "Because, really, who wouldn't?" She uses her talking-to-a-baby voice as she nuzzles Prissy. "I'll try to get him to follow her to the backyard. But take Buster and Max out of here first." She gives me a fistful of plastic bags and grabs two leashes.

"Um . . . you want me to walk both of them at the same time?"

"Don't worry, you can handle it. Max is extremely well-behaved and Buster has been imitating his every move." Gina hooks the leashes onto the two dogs and hands them to me.

I'm nervous, but I know I can do this if I try. Plus, if this is how Gina needs me to help her, then this is what I'll do. I take Max and Buster to the college nature trail, where they sniff the ground, pee on twigs, kick up dirt behind them, and make gigantic poops. Which I have to pick up all by myself.

Hmm, maybe it's a good thing Papi insists I get a not-too-big dog.

When some joggers go past us, Buster decides to join them and drags me along. Max wags his tail and trots beside him, so the three of us run for a little while, until Buster sees another dog and loops around to smell her. Max grabs a giant stick and looks at me. When Buster is done sniffing, I try to continue on the trail, but Max won't budge. "Do you want to go home now, Max?" I ask. He takes off running toward home.

I'm exhausted by the time we get back to my street. Four people—a man, a woman, a little girl, and a littler boy—are sitting on Gina's front steps. "Oh, this must be him!" the woman says. Buster yanks away from me and practically knocks the woman down, slobbering all over her face. She laughs and turns to the tiny boy. "Do you want to say hello?"

Before the kid can answer, Buster is all over him. The boy lies on his back and giggles while Buster licks and drools all over him. "It looks like we found our dog." The man chuckles.

"I want this one," the girl says. She's still sitting on the steps, and Max is right next to her with his head leaning on her shoulder. She pets him gently, a big smile on her face.

The parents look at each other. "Do we want two dogs?" the man says.

The woman shrugs. "I hadn't considered it before, but that might be okay."

Gina's door opens and she comes down the steps with Prissy in her arms. "Oh, good, you got to meet Buster. So"—she bends over, puts one hand on her knee, and faces the little boy—"what do you think about taking him home to be a part of your family?"

The boy nods and smiles and smiles, and the parents explain that they want Max too. I go over and give Max a hug. I'm happy he found someone to love him forever. Those two kids sure are lucky. They're too young to worry about school and grades. And still, their parents are letting them have two dogs just like that.

Chapter 12

On Monday Mr. Nesbitt hands back our homework assignments from last week. "Excellent job, Flores." I look at the big red A+ on the top of my paper. A Flores did in fact do an excellent job on this assignment, but it wasn't me.

"You're on your way to that A in science, for sure." Zoe holds out her fist to bump mine when we sit at lunch.

I shrug. "Amarilis went back to school, so my homework won't be perfect anymore."

"Oh, please, you still have your brother to help you," Olivia says as she organizes her food in an artsy pattern on her tray.

"And your dad," Zoe adds.

"I guess, but . . ."

"But what?" Zoe crinkles her eyebrows together and crunches on a crouton.

"But I'm not learning any of this science stuff," I say. "I'm probably going to fail the tests."

"No you won't." Zoe shakes her head. "We'll study together, and you'll get it then."

I hope she's right, but I'm still a little worried.

"Are you excited about your birthday party?" Olivia always knows when to change the subject.

My twelfth birthday is on Thursday, and I'm having a pottery/slumber party on Friday. Papi wants me to invite more kids from school—some A students—but Olivia and Zoe are all I need. Well, also Amarilis. When she texted me this morning, she said she's coming back for my party but can't stay all weekend. Like I told her, that's fine as long as she celebrates with me like always. She's never missed my birthday.

"I am excited," I say. "After pottery, we'll stay up all night watching scary movies."

"Ooh, fun." Zoe shivers. "I'm already getting goose bumps!"

"Let's coordinate our outfits for the pottery place!" Olivia leans forward and claps.

It takes us the rest of our lunch period to agree on what to wear: black jeans, gray sneakers, and the tie-dye shirts we made together at Zoe's party last summer. We'll wear our matching charm bracelets, but Zoe and I will take off our earrings since Olivia doesn't have pierced ears. We pour out of the lunchroom when the bell rings, still arguing about our hairstyle.

"Miosotis should decide," Zoe says. "It's her birthday."

My party is going to be perfect.

-«««•»»»-

When I knock on Gina's door in the afternoon, a soft yip comes from inside, but no barking or running around. "Where are the dogs?" I ask as I step into the house.

"Poor little Freckles needs a lot of attention, so I'm going to devote myself to rehabilitating him," Gina says. "I told the rescue group no new dogs for now."

"Is he still under the table?" I walk into the dining room and squat. Sure enough, Freckles is there, and he gives me a short growl.

"He comes out when it's only Prissy and me here," Gina says. "Hopefully, he'll trust you and Mabel soon." Gina picks Prissy up from the couch and kisses the top of her head over and over again. "You can take the week off, Miosotis. I want Freckles to relax and feel like this is his home. By next week I expect that he'll be ready to do more, and then you can come help me with him."

"Oh, okay." I can't imagine a whole week without dogs. Prissy gives me her paw to say goodbye, and I go back to my house.

"That was quick," Abuela says when I walk in.

"Gina doesn't need help this week," I say. "I'll get a head start on my schoolwork." I go upstairs and turn on the computer. I should look for a science article, but I keep thinking about Freckles and wondering how Gina's going to help him.

I search for the term *abused dogs*, and I'm a little surprised by what I learn. There are so many ways abuse can mess up a poor dog. One website says to be a detective and learn about the dog: pay close attention and figure out what scares him and which things he likes. Another one says to hand-feed your dog to build trust. All of them say the most important thing is to be patient and show him unconditional love. Don't make him work for treats or pets—just give, give, give. I can do these things. I will be ready to help Gina with Freckles when I go back to her house next week.

On Tuesday and Wednesday after school, the house is quiet since Jacinto has track practice and Papi is still at work. Abuela paces the living room listening to Tía Felicia on the phone, and I go upstairs to do my homework. I study each science question and look up the answers in my textbook. I even read a little extra to make sure I understand it. Then I move on to social studies, and then math. I think I get what we're working on now, but the math test I had last week keeps popping into my mind. I pull out my math book and review the tricky problems I got wrong. I'm pretty sure I can get a B in math this quarter, but I don't want to take any chances. And I'm nervous about my science grade.

As soon as Jacinto gets home, I run everything by him. He looks over my work and makes a few changes. "There, I'm positive you'll get As on all of this now," he says as he hands it back.

I feel happy when I turn in my homework assignments. With each good grade, I'm closer to getting my dog.

―⟪⟪◆⟫⟫―

Zoe and Olivia make a big deal about my birthday on Thursday. They decorate my locker with streamers and signs and photos of dogs. Lots and lots of dogs. "This is so cute!" I say when I see them. "Thanks, guys."

We spend our whole lunchtime talking about my party. "I'm a little sad Amarilis isn't home," I say. "I mean, I know I'll see her tomorrow, and I never celebrate on my actual birthday anyway." It's the day my mother died, so everyone is always sad. "But still, Amarilis used to surprise me with a little special something on my actual day. She'd give me a cupcake or a candy bar, or she'd watch a Syfy show with me even though she hates those things. You know, something we can only do if we're together."

"How do you know she won't do that this year?" Olivia says.

"She already sent me a birthday text this morning, and she can't come over on a school night."

Zoe gives my hand a squeeze. "It's rough when our kids grow up and move out."

Olivia laughs, and so do I. "You're so silly." I squeeze Zoe back.

When I get home from school, Abuela gives me a tiny flan. "I know your party is tomorrow," she says, "but I made this for a little birthday celebration today. Plus . . ." She holds up a bag of candy bars.

This reminds me of Amarilis, which makes me sad again. I know Zoe is right, that people grow up and get on with their lives, and I guess I will too someday. But it seems so much is changing now that Amarilis is away at college. We went from seeing each other every day to texting daily when she went away to school. This week she skipped two days, saying she was so busy she didn't see my messages. Will she be even busier after she's married? "Gracias, Abuela," I whisper before I sniffle and wipe my eyes.

"Ay, ay, ay." Abuela holds me and rocks us back and forth. "I know this is an emotional day. I'm sad too." She pulls away and rubs the tears from my cheeks with her thumbs. "But listen, I'm so happy to have you in my life. You bring a lot of joy to this family, mi amor."

I force myself to smile. I can't tell Abuela I'm not crying about my mother. If I do, she'll think I'm an awful person. But I never even knew my mother. How can I miss her?

The house phone rings over and over all evening. My father's cousin from New York says she wants to wish me a happy birthday. Then she speaks with Abuela, who cries on the phone and says, "Thank you for thinking of me," and "I miss her all the time, especially on this day." When an uncle from Florida and my other grandparents in the DR call, it's the same thing. Even Papi tears up when he gets on the phone with them. Of course, Tía Felicia calls, and this time speaks with me after talking to Abuela. "Estas son las mañanitas . . ." she sings in her gravelly voice as soon as I get on the phone. "Your cousin Ernesto wishes you a happy birthday too," she says when she finishes singing.

"Gracias, Tía." I give the phone back to Abuela, who doesn't scold her sister about anything today.

—«‹‹•›››—

Zoe and Olivia take the bus home with me on Friday. We drop off our book bags, then Papi drives us to Pots 'n' Things. "Is Amarilis meeting us there?" I ask him.

"I believe so," Papi says. "But text her and tell her to call if she wants me to pick her up at the train station."

I'm sorry, mamita, Amarilis replies to my text. *Something came up and I can't come. Will call tomorrow to explain, and I'll absolutely make it up to you. Love you!*

I stare at my phone. I can't believe it. Amarilis won't be at my birthday party? She's not married yet, but she's already too busy for me. I blink and blink as her text gets blurry.

"She's not coming," I say after a minute.

"Why not?"

I shrug. Is this how it's going to be with Amarilis from now on?

"She's probably busy with her schoolwork," Papi says. "That's okay, you three girls will have a great time together, right?"

"Yeah." My friends are here for me and they deserve to have fun. I put my phone away and wipe my eyes with a tissue. "It's going to be wonderful." I turn and smile at them.

Zoe, Olivia, and I create some cool stuff at my party. Zoe makes a fancy vase with a pattern of neat, identical daisies along the top edge, and Olivia, who is definitely going to be a famous artist one day, paints a perfect self-portrait in the middle of a shiny blue plate. I try to make a dog sculpture, but it looks like a rabbit. "At least bunnies are cute," Olivia says.

Even though Amarilis said she couldn't come, I keep glancing at the door in case she was joking and planning to surprise me. But she doesn't show up.

Abuela makes arroz con pollo for dinner, and it is delicious, as always. The chicken is juicy and the rice is the perfect blend of soft and chewy. And she only added a few peas since she knows too many vegetables ruin any dish for me.

But then Papi decides to be embarrassing. "Are the three of you in all the same classes this year?" He points his fork at Zoe, Olivia, and me, one at a time.

"The two of them are," Olivia says. "But I'm in a different English and social studies class."

"We all have math, science, and Spanish together," Zoe says.

I roll my eyes. "Could we talk about something other than school?"

"Certainly!" Papi smiles. "Tell me about your hobbies, girls."

I groan and bite into a piece of chicken. Clearly, there is no way to avoid this parental humiliation.

Zoe sits up tall and folds her hands on the edge of the table. "I'm in the speech and debate club, which will be a big help when I become a lawyer."

"Excellent!" Papi says. "Public speaking skills are useful for any profession. Why don't you join the club, Miosotis?"

"For sure!" Zoe shrieks. "We could work together!"

"No, thanks. Is it time for cake?" I stand and pick up my plate.

"What about you, Jacinto?" Olivia bats her eyes at my brother and fluffs out her hair. "Are you in speech and debate?"

"Nope. No time with sports." Jacinto shovels a forkful of food into his mouth without looking up.

I help Abuela clear the table and I stay in the kitchen to put the candles on my cake. "Go sit with your friends." Abuela tries to shoo me away. "I'll do this."

"But I want to help." Zoe is now talking about math club and tutoring, and I'd like to stay away from that conversation.

"It must be hard to be an athlete," Olivia is saying to Jacinto when Abuela and I come in with the cake.

My brother shrugs and grunts.

They all sing "Happy Birthday" to me. It doesn't sound the same without Amarilis's off-key voice drowning out everyone else's, but it's better than nothing. And getting presents is always fun. Olivia gives me an adorable pink T-shirt with a rhinestone *M* in the middle, and Zoe's gift is a book of dog breeds. The nightgown from Abuela is so cute with paw prints all over it, and I'm glad Papi gives me cash again. I'm a little surprised when

Jacinto hands me a box that's neatly wrapped in shiny paper with a matching bow on top.

"It's from Amarilis and me." It's a leather leash! "We know you'll make the grades for your dog."

I throw my arms around him.

There's a light knock on the door, and I gasp. *Amarilis!* I run to the door and fling it open.

"Happy birthday!" Gina has Prissy in one arm and a bouquet of flowers in the other. "I don't want to interrupt anything. Just dropping these off."

"Ohh . . . thanks!" I take the flowers and give Gina a hug. I hope she can't tell I'm a little disappointed. Because I *am* happy to see her, honest.

"Come in, come in," Papi says. "Have some cake."

"I'd love to, but Mabel's home watching the other dog, and he's a bit unpredictable, so I need to get right back."

Abuela takes Gina's arm and leads her to the kitchen, where she wraps up two giant slices of cake and hands them to her.

"Thank you. This looks delicious!"

"Thanks for the beautiful flowers, Gina," I say as she walks out. "I'll see you Monday?"

"Sure thing! Looking forward to it!"

"Your brother is sooo cute," Olivia says when we settle into our sleeping bags in front of the TV in the living room.

"Eww, that flying rhino is cuter than my brother." I point to the television.

Zoe chuckles.

"Oh, please! You're such a mean sister!" Olivia throws her pillow at me and giggles.

We miss half the movie with our pillow fight, and one pillow bursts open. It is definitely a fun birthday party, even though Amarilis isn't here.

Chapter 13

I'M NOT SURE WHAT TO DO after Olivia and Zoe go home Saturday afternoon. Gina probably thought she was being nice by giving me my birthday weekend off, but I've been thinking about that cute little Freckles and I want to get to know him. I should do more research about abused dogs so I can be ready when I get back to Gina's. Maybe I'll find an article for my science project.

A few minutes after I turn on the computer, my phone vibrates. It's Amarilis.

"Hey, mamita, how was your party?"

"Good, but it would have been better with you there."

"I'm so sorry I missed it." My sister really does sound sorry.

"What happened? Why couldn't you come?"

"It was poor Rich. He needed me."

"Why? Is he sick? Did you have to take him to the hospital?" Papi always talks about college kids not taking good care of themselves.

"No, it's nothing like that," Amarilis says. "He was depressed because his biochemistry professor gave him another failing grade, so he's probably not going to graduate on time, and maybe he'll never get into med school."

"Wow, that is depressing." I'm sure Rich worked hard. And now he might not get to be a doctor like he wants. If I try and try to get good grades and still end up without a dog, I'll be so upset. Poor Rich.

"I know, and I swear that professor is out to get him; it's not fair. Rich is brilliant; it doesn't make sense that he would fail anything!"

"What's he going to do?"

"I don't know. His dad said that as long as Rich graduates, he might be able to pull some strings and get him into a med school somewhere," Amarilis says. "But let's talk about something happier. Do you want to visit me for a few days during your spring break?"

"Really?!"

"Yes! I know how pathetic it is to watch your friends go away for spring break every year while our family stays behind," Amarilis says. "University City isn't exactly a beach resort, but at least it's a change of scenery."

When she was in high school, Amarilis begged Papi to take us on a trip for spring break. We went to the Dominican Republic once to visit family, which my sister complained about because they don't live anywhere near the beach. But at least we got away and we met all these people we'd been hearing about our whole lives. I'd like to go back, but Papi says we can't afford it for a while. I see the big checks he mails to our relatives in the DR every month, and I know we could take lots of trips if he didn't do that. Amarilis knows it too.

"You should come on Sunday," she says, "and go to class with me Monday. We'll hang out so you can see what college life is like."

"Awesome! But . . . won't it be better if I come for the weekend? That way I don't have to sit through a bunch of boring classes."

Amarilis laughs. "I only have two classes on Mondays, and they're my favorites: marketing and accounting. You'll love them!"

"Okay." It's hard to say no when she's excited, but I'm pretty sure I won't actually love these classes.

※

When I get to Gina's house on Monday after school, she's cradling Prissy like a newborn baby. "She hasn't eaten in two days," she says. "I'm getting worried. She's been lethargic lately, and now . . ." Her voice trails off and she closes her eyes and sniffles.

"Did you call the vet?"

Gina's eyes pop open. "What time is it? We have a three thirty appointment." She rummages through cushions and dog toys and mutters about her car keys.

I look under the dining room table. Surely Freckles won't still be there. But he is, shivering and looking at me with big eyes. "Hi there, little guy," I say. He doesn't growl, but he whimpers a little. Is this a good sign? Maybe.

"You'll stay here and keep an eye on Freckles?" Gina's keys jingle in her hand. "Mabel's asleep upstairs."

"Sure. Should I take him out?"

"Only if he wants to go. I was trying to feed him. His food is over there." Gina points to a bowl in the corner of the dining room. "Truth be told, he's probably too shy to eat in front of you, but stay close in case he needs anything. Don't touch him, though; he gets frightened easily."

"Okay." I shut the door behind Gina and Prissy, then go into the dining room and lie on the floor facing Freckles. One website I read said you should always speak quietly to a dog who has been abused and let him know he's loved. "Hello, Freckles," I whisper. "Come hang out with me?"

Freckles shivers and pees on the floor.

Oh no. Poor Gina is already stressed about Prissy being sick. And Miss Mabel probably worked all night. They don't need to deal with a pee puddle. I get up, go into the kitchen, and pull at the roll of paper towels until I have a nice big wad around my hand. Then I kneel and reach under the table.

Freckles watches my arm, then jumps up and backs away when it gets close to him.

"It's okay," I say in a soft, high-pitched voice. "I'm going to clean this up so you don't have to sit in your own filth." His front paw is right in the pee, so I wipe that off first.

As soon as I touch him, Freckles yelps and nips at my hand.

"Ouch!" I leap back into the kitchen. There are faint teeth marks on the paper towels. This is irritating. Doesn't Freckles see I'm trying to help him? Why would he attack me?

"Gina? Are you in here?" Miss Mabel comes into the kitchen, squinting and yawning. "Oh, hi there, sweetie. What's going on?"

"Gina took Prissy to the vet and asked me to keep an eye on Freckles. He just tried to bite me." I stretch my hand toward her.

82

"Oh, are you okay?" Miss Mabel puts the wad of paper towels on the counter and turns my hand back and forth as she examines it. My hand is fine. "It's a good thing you had all those paper towels. We used welding gloves when we first handled him."

"Really? Even Gina?"

"Especially Gina. You have to be very careful with a skittish dog. He's not aggressive; he just snaps a little when he feels cornered and scared." Miss Mabel bends over and looks at Freckles. "But you're coming along, aren't you, baby?"

"He peed under there and I was trying to clean it up."

"I'll get it. He's not afraid of me anymore." Miss Mabel wipes up the pee and puts the stinky paper towels in a plastic bag.

"I'll put that in the trash." I take the bag and walk outside, feeling a little jealous that Freckles let Miss Mabel near him, but not me. "Dogs usually love me," I say when I come back inside. "But Freckles doesn't seem to want me here." My brain is telling me to be patient, but I can't help how I feel.

Miss Mabel puts her hands on her hips and cocks her head to one side. "You can't take this personally. He acts this way with everyone at first. He'll come around."

I glance under the table, and Freckles is peering at me. He whimpers when we make eye contact.

"I know," I say. "But the one thing I've always been good at is getting along with dogs, so I don't want to mess this up."

Miss Mabel chuckles. "I'm sure you're good at other things too. Do you want to be a vet?"

I shrug. "My dad says it's harder to get into vet school than medical school, and my grades aren't great, so . . ."

"You're only in middle school, right?" When I nod, Miss

83

Mabel waves her hand like she's smacking something away. "You have plenty of time to pull up your grades."

"I guess, but . . ."

She looks at me and crinkles her eyebrows together. "But what?"

"But . . ." I look at my hands and shift my weight from one foot to the other. "School isn't my thing. I'm not that smart, and it's kind of boring."

Miss Mabel leans against the counter and folds her arms across her chest. "When I was in eighth grade, my grades were terrible. Always had been. Never anything better than Cs."

"Cs!"

"Yep. It drove my parents crazy. But I figured they didn't know what they were talking about. I didn't need to know world history or algebra or any other stuff they were teaching in school. So why bother studying?"

Now she's making sense. And she got into nursing school!

"Then you know what happened?" Miss Mabel stands up straight and points at me. "My grandmother had a stroke."

Huh?

"I loved my grandmother. She lived next door and babysat me after school when I was little." Miss Mabel shakes her head and her eyes get watery. "I visited her in the hospital and at the rehab facility, and I met all these wonderful nurses, and I thought 'This is what I want to do when I grow up!' And when I started high school, I *wanted* to learn, not only biology but my other subjects too, because the fact is they're all related somehow. I wasn't the valedictorian or anything, but my grades were pretty good when I graduated. Because I was motivated."

"So, you're saying I can get good grades if I decide I want to be a vet?" I say.

"No, I'm saying that if you want to learn, you will put the work into it, and the good grades will follow."

"Hmm." I'm not convinced.

"And by good grades, I don't mean you'll get straight A-pluses—even though you might. But if you focus on really learning the material, you'll benefit from that knowledge."

I sigh. "The thing is, my dad doesn't care if I learn anything. He just wants me to get As."

"I find that hard to believe."

"But it's true!" I say. "He even said so. He won't let me get a dog unless I get two As this quarter."

"He's probably trying to motivate you," Miss Mabel says. "But if grades don't motivate you, maybe there's something else that makes you excited about learning? Talk to him about your concerns."

She doesn't know Papi.

"Well, I need to shower and get ready for work," Miss Mabel says. "Think about what I said, okay?" She pats my shoulder, then heads upstairs.

I sit on the floor but not too close to Freckles. He scoots back to the other side of the table, as far away from me as he can get without coming out. I reach into his bowl and take out a handful of food pellets. "Are you hungry?" I say in a soft voice. Then I roll one piece of kibble across the floor to him. It lands right in front of him.

Freckles sniffs the pellet, then looks at me. He sniffs again. And again. Then he rolls it around with his nose and bats at it with his paws. He sits up and barks at it. Finally, he swoops down and gobbles it up. When he's done, he looks at me, waiting. I roll another food pellet toward him, and he goes through the same routine. By the time Miss Mabel comes back downstairs after her shower, Freckles has finished all his food. But he's still under the table.

"You got him to eat?" Miss Mabel sounds impressed. "That's progress."

I smile. Before I can say anything, Gina bursts in the door.

"There's nothing they can do!" she cries as she reaches for Miss Mabel with one arm.

"Oh, honey, what happened?"

Gina sobs and hiccups and sobs some more. "They—want—to—put—her—down. Kidneys—shot—and—lungs—and—"

She looks at Prissy, who is sleeping peacefully in her other arm, and the tears stream down her face.

"Honey, you gave her a good life these past two years." Miss Mabel strokes Gina's hair and kisses her cheek. "You can feel good about that."

Gina takes some deep breaths and closes her eyes. She leans her head on Miss Mabel's shoulder and cries quietly.

Freckles has fallen asleep under the table, so I stand and slip out while Miss Mabel holds Gina and rocks her back and forth.

Chapter 14

"LOOK AT THE PAINTINGS I MADE." Olivia takes out her phone at lunch the next day. She shows us some beautiful pictures of people wearing lipstick in different colors and some without any makeup at all.

"Wow, these are great!" Zoe and I say at the same time.

"They're for my science project." She puts the phone down and leans forward with her elbows on the table. "You see, some colors are more toxic than others, so I'm going to talk about that. Plus, no lipstick is the best option, and these people look great without makeup, right?"

"Wow, you've really thought this through." I'm pretty impressed.

"For sure," Zoe says. "Your project is very informative."

Olivia smiles. "Did you pick an article yet?"

Zoe nods. "My article is about the plastic in the oceans. It's a pressing problem, and I've researched the different contributing factors and the things we, as individual consumers, can do to help." She looks at Olivia. "Although I'm going to use photos for my slide show, since I don't have your artistic abilities."

"Oh, please!" Olivia fluffs her hair. "I can make some drawings for you if you want?"

"Nah, I'm okay. I've found a lot of pictures that'll work well with my theme. But thanks."

"No problem. What about you, Miosotis? Did you find a good article?"

"No, but I know what I want to look for," I say. "Gina has this little dog in her house who was obviously abused, and she's working on teaching him to trust and be happy again, so I want an article about helping abused animals."

"That's fascinating!" Zoe says. "Like a psychology theme. I'll help you look for an article!"

"And I'll draw the pictures for your slide show," Olivia says. "Like maybe some sad dog pictures in charcoal for the beginning, and then some bright watercolors for the end!"

"You'll for sure get an A," Zoe says.

"Thanks." Between the two of them, my friends can help me make an A+ presentation. I think about what Miss Mabel said, though. This is a topic I'm really interested in. Maybe I should concentrate on learning about it and not worry about the grade. But my grade is important if I want my dog. And I really do. I shouldn't take any chances.

That afternoon Gina and Prissy are glued to each other. Gina holds Prissy on her lap, brushing her and cooing and telling her she's beautiful.

"Um, should I take Freckles out or something?" I say.

Gina looks at me like she's surprised I'm there. "Sure. Mabel told me you got him to eat his food. He might follow you to the backyard too."

I walk through the dining room and into the kitchen. "Do you want to go out, Freckles?" I call as I open the back door. I step outside in case he decides to follow me. He doesn't. I come back inside and look under the table. "Come on, Freckles, let's get some fresh air," I say in a soft voice.

Freckles won't move. At least he doesn't growl.

I grab some kibble out of his bowl and put one piece on the ground at the edge of the dining table. Then I step back and put down a trail of kibble all the way to the back door. I sit on the deck steps and wait. I figure if I stay inside and watch, Freckles won't come out. But maybe this way . . .

Right when I'm about to give up and go back inside, I see a pink nose sticking through the doorway. I want to jump and cheer Freckles on, like I do at track meets when Jacinto is almost at the finish line. But I know it would freak the little dog out if I yell. So I sit there and watch, my fists pumping as I root for him in my head. Finally, finally, he steps outside, looks at me with squinted eyes, walks around and around in a tight circle with his nose to the ground, and poops.

I can't hold it in any longer. "Yes!" I shout. "You go, Freckles!"

He runs back inside. Darn. But still, I'm smiling. As I stuff my hand into a plastic bag to pick up Freckles's waste, I think I must be really weird. How can I be so happy about poop?

－≪≪◆≫≫－

On Wednesday, Gina comes to the door with a smile on her face. "She's getting better." She strokes and kisses Prissy. "I'm taking her to the vet today to confirm."

Prissy lets out a soft, short bark, and Freckles runs out from

89

under the table. My heart skips when I see him. "Hey, Freckles. Are you saying hello to me?"

He goes straight to Gina, jumping and scratching her knees.

"Oh, my, what's going on here?" Gina sits on the couch, and Freckles jumps up next to her and licks Prissy all over. She puts her head on the cushion and closes her eyes. "Aw, they're buddies," Gina says.

Prissy's little chest heaves, and I don't understand why Gina thinks she's getting better. Freckles nuzzles against Prissy when he finishes licking her. She stretches out her little paw and caresses his face. Then they look into each other's eyes. Are Freckles and Prissy saying goodbye?

"Okay, time for our appointment," Gina says. "You'll stay here with Freckles?"

I nod.

As soon as Gina leaves, Freckles goes back to his spot under the table. No amount of coaxing or bits of kibble will get him out. I sit on the floor and take out my phone. Olivia sent me a photo of a charcoal drawing of a sad-faced puppy. *Maybe you can use this for your project*, she says. Zoe texts that she hasn't found any articles about depressed dogs yet. *But I'll keep looking.* Freckles inches his way out from under the table and sits next to me.

OMG, I say in a group text to Olivia and Zoe. *Freckles just sat next to me. He is so adorable.* I stand slowly and, without looking at him, go out the back door. I make sure to hold back my squeals when he follows me out, lifts his leg over a fallen twig, and squirts it with pee.

I think I want to adopt him.

Miss Mabel is home when I come by the next day. "I took the day off," she says. "We lost Prissy last night."

Gina is sitting on the couch petting Freckles absentmindedly He lifts his head and licks her tears.

"I'm so sorry, Gina." I sit on her other side and take her hand.

"Thank you, Miosotis. You're a good friend."

Freckles jumps off the couch and goes to the back door.

"I'll let him out." I'm sad for Gina, but I don't know what to say or do to make her feel better. I'm glad when Miss Mabel takes my place on the sofa, and I stay outside with Freckles for a while. I smile as he sniffs all over the place like a happy dog.

Gina is super mopey on Friday and Saturday, so I make sure to be there for Freckles as much as possible. "Remember I won't be here tomorrow or Monday or Tuesday," I tell her before I leave on Saturday. "I'm visiting my sister. But will you be okay? Because I can go see her later in the week if you need me here."

"No, you go ahead," Gina says. "I must get back into the swing of things anyway. You've been a great help, but Prissy would want me to take care of her little buddy."

"All right, if you say so." I worry about both Gina and Freckles as I walk out the door.

Chapter 15

JACINTO GOT HIS DRIVER'S LICENSE LAST month, and he begs Papi to let him drive me to see Amarilis. My brother is the most cautious driver in the world, and I'm worried it will take him two days to get me there. Papi knows about Jacinto's slowpoke ways too, but he thinks it's a good thing. So he says okay.

"Hey, squirt," Jacinto says when we're in the car. "Can you help me with something?"

"Me? With what?" My brother has never asked for my advice before.

"I want to invite Miranda to junior prom, and I need a good idea for a promposal."

"A what?"

"A promposal. You know, a creative way to ask a girl to prom."

"Hmm," I say. "Is Miranda the girl from track?"

"Yeah . . ." Jacinto stares at the red light in front of us and smiles. "And calc, and AP English, and AP US History."

"So . . . you basically see her all day. Why don't you just go up and ask her?"

"Never mind. I'll see if Amarilis has any ideas. You don't understand." Jacinto rolls through the green light, very slowly, and looks straight ahead while three cars pass us on the left.

"I'll help with your prom thing." I pull out a notebook (which Papi insisted I bring to take notes in Amarilis's classes) and ask him a million questions about Miranda. It's a little weird that he knows the answers to all of them—her favorite color, food, subject in school, track event—but also kind of cute. He *really* likes this girl.

"And she loves marigolds," Jacinto says, even though I didn't ask about flowers.

I pull out my phone and look up promposals, then I check my notes and I get an idea. "I got it! I got it!"

"Calm down!" Jacinto sounds like Papi. "You'll make me have an accident."

I shake my head. My brother is such a nerd. "Since Miranda runs the four by one hundred and the four by two hundred relays, you should buy four aluminum batons, all in orange, which you said is her favorite color, right?"

"Um-hm."

"Okay, then you write in permanent marker on each of them, *Will you* on the first one, *go to* on the second one, *prom with* on the third one, and *me?* on the last one. You get three friends to give her the first three, and then you give her the last one. So, what do you think?"

Jacinto nods, but he doesn't look at me because he won't take his eyes off the road. "I like it. I'll give her some marigolds with the last baton too. But this is good. Thanks, squirt! I'm positive she'll say yes!"

When we get to Amarilis's dorm, Jacinto drives around the block a few times looking for a parking spot. "Drop me off here." I point to a no-stopping zone in front of the dorm.

"Hmm." Jacinto drives past it and around the block one more time. Finally, he turns on his blinkers and pulls in. "Okay, see you on Tuesday."

I hop out and grab my stuff. I step into the lobby, then turn and wave at my brother through the glass doors. He waves back and inches out of sight. I text Amarilis. *I'm downstairs.* Then I sit and wait. Kids walk in and show their IDs to the front-desk people, who buzz them in through the turnstile into the building. I look at my phone. *Are you coming to get me?* I text.

About five more minutes go by before my phone pings. *I'm sorry, mamita. Something came up so now isn't a good time. Maybe another weekend.*

I stare at the phone. What the heck? *Can you at least come and say hi? And wait with me for Jacinto to come back?*

Sorry, no. At the library.

What? Doesn't Amarilis remember our conversation? Did she even mean it when she invited me over, or did she say that so I wouldn't complain about her missing my birthday party? And now that I'm here, doesn't she want to see me? How hard would it be for her to walk over from the library for a few minutes? Or I could go to her. *Where is the library? I can come see you.*

Then I wait. And wait. For about ten more minutes. With each second I get madder and madder. I know Jacinto won't answer his phone while he's driving, so I can't get ahold of him until he gets home, then I'll have to wait for him to come all the way back, which will take forever. But still, I don't want to sit in here anymore. I pick up my stuff and walk outside.

Amarilis's room is on the second floor at the front of the building. I remember looking out her window the day she moved in. "You're across the street from Wawa!" Jacinto said. He *loves* Wawa. Now, as I stand outside and watch people swarm in and out of the convenience store like ants, I look up to Amarilis's room. There she is, her back to the window, talking to someone I can't see.

My mouth drops open. She lied to me. She so didn't want to see me that she flat-out lied. After I trekked all the way out here to spend time with her. Why does my sister hate me?

I wipe the tears from my face as I run across the street and call my brother.

-⟨⟨⟨◆⟩⟩⟩-

"You're sure it was Amarilis you saw?" Jacinto asks while he drives me home.

I nod and cry some more. "Why would she do this?"

Jacinto shakes his head and inches through West Philadelphia without another word. I rest my head on the window and wonder what I did to make Amarilis mad at me. Because she has to be mad to do this. Am I too whiny? Is she tired of helping me with my homework? Is she ashamed to have a sister who would get a C in science?

Bright red-and-blue lights and a wailing siren jolt me out of my thoughts. Jacinto pulls over and gives me a confused look. He rolls his window down when the police officer stands beside it. His chest is heaving, and I'm scared too.

95

"License and registration, please," the policeman says. "And keep your hands where I can see them."

Jacinto keeps his hands on the steering wheel. "Um, I have to get the registration out of the glove compartment."

The police officer nods. I open the glove compartment, and Jacinto takes out the registration and hands it over. "My license is in my wallet in my back pocket."

Why is my brother giving the cop a play-by-play of everything he's doing? I mean, where else would his license be?

The policeman nods again, and Jacinto pulls out his license.

"So, you're a new driver." The officer examines the license and the registration paper. "This is a nice car. Who's Oscar Flores?"

"My dad."

"Really! What kind of job does *he* have?" The officer laughs.

Why is he asking that? Papi's job has nothing to do with anything.

"He's a college professor." Jacinto's hands are back on the steering wheel, and he's staring at the windshield. He takes in a deep breath and blows it out before adding, "Sir."

"Does your dad know you're driving his fancy SUV?"

"Yes, sir. Would you like to call him, sir?"

The police officer rests his arm on the edge of Jacinto's open window and looks at him and then at me. My brother is still facing front, but I look right at the cop's face and watch his shifty eyes and yellow teeth. "No, that's okay, but you be careful and stay out of trouble." He hands the documents back to Jacinto and walks away, saying something garbled into his walkie-talkie.

After the police car zooms away, Jacinto stays with his hands on the steering wheel, staring ahead and not moving. His breathing slows little by little. I put my hand on his shoulder. "Are you okay?"

Jacinto looks at me. "I wasn't even doing anything wrong. He just didn't think a brown kid should be driving a Lexus. Cops always assume we're criminals for no reason." He clenches his jaw, and he doesn't look scared anymore. He's angry. He puts the car in drive and takes off. When a bunch of pedestrians jaywalk in front of us, he slams on the brakes. He honks and yells out some curse words I have never heard him say before.

We continue in silence all the way home.

Chapter 16

ABUELA IS YELLING INTO THE PHONE when we walk through the door. "How could you do something so stupid? Now those kids will starve! And you can forget about getting any help from me!" She slams the phone down and turns to Papi, Jacinto, and me. "Can you believe what Felicia did this time? Ernesto asked her for money to buy food for his kids, and she gave it to him! Instead of getting the food herself. Surprise, surprise, he spent it on drugs, and now the mother—who's also a good-for-nothing— is crying that her babies are hungry! That's it, I'm done with her."

"Cálmese, Doña Marta. You'll make yourself sick." Papi pats Abuela's shoulder, then looks at me. "What happened with Amarilis?"

"I'm going to my room." Jacinto keeps his head down and runs upstairs, taking two steps at a time.

"What's bothering him?"

So many questions. I'm still mad at Amarilis, but the thing in the car was more upsetting. Too upsetting to talk about. "Amarilis said she was busy with something and this wasn't a good time for a visit."

"She could have told you before you went all the way down there."

I shrug. "Things happen, I guess." I glance at the steps and wonder if I should tell Papi about the police officer.

"Is Jacinto angry she made him drive out there twice?" Papi says. "He seemed happy when you called. He said he'd get more driving time in."

"He's not mad at her. But . . . we got stopped by the police."

Papi and Abuela gasp. "Are you okay? Did they hurt you?"

"We're fine."

Papi rushes up the stairs and knocks on Jacinto's door.

"Poor Jacinto." Abuela closes her eyes and does the sign of the cross. "It's a good thing your father had that talk with him last year about his scar."

I remember that talk. Papi never mentions the scar on his forehead, but last year he finally told Jacinto how he got it, and Jacinto told Amarilis and me. "Late one night his junior year in college, Papi was walking back to his dorm from the library when three Philly police officers grabbed him from behind and slammed him onto the pavement," he said.

I was shocked. Papi never even walks across the street if there's a red light, so I could not imagine him breaking any law. "Why?" I yelled.

"They said they had a description of a Black or Hispanic male wearing a denim jacket who had taken a lady's purse. Papi was wearing a gray sweater and he didn't have any purse on him, but that didn't stop them from gashing his face open." Jacinto looked like he might vomit.

"A Black or Hispanic male?" Amarilis said. "What kind of description is that? It includes at least half the men in the city."

Jacinto shrugged. "And there's more. They wouldn't let him go until the lady saw him and said it wasn't him. Even after he showed them his student ID and said he had been in the library for hours. *And* they told him to be careful because he might be picked up again. As if they hadn't done anything wrong. As if it made sense for them to grab him in the first place!"

"I don't understand," I said. "How come he never told Amarilis this, even though she's older?"

My brother dropped his head into his hands. "Amarilis is super pale, and she's a girl, so she doesn't need to know about these things. I'm the one people are afraid of, the one the cops might attack." He looked at us with tears in his eyes. "He said I need to learn to be careful, but I kind of wish he hadn't. What good does it do to know about this? How do you avoid something like that? What could Papi have done differently?"

I'm relieved Papi had that talk with Jacinto. That's how my brother knew to tell the cop he was going to reach into the glove compartment and into his back pocket. That's how he knew to stay calm even though he was scared to death. But none of this makes it any less unfair.

"Are you okay, mi amor?" Abuela pats my arms as if she's looking for broken bones. "When your father was attacked by those crooked policemen all those years ago, your mother was so upset. She wasn't there, but it affected her anyway." Abuela holds my face in her hands and gives me a concerned look. "Listen, you and Jacinto will be fine."

I give her a hug. I hope she's right that this was a one-time thing and Jacinto and I will eventually forget about it. But I keep thinking about what my brother said. Is that policeman really

100

"crooked"? Is he the exception to the rule? Or is Philly full of cops who assume all brown boys are criminals? If Jacinto is right, how can he be safe? He can't whiten his skin and uncurl his hair every time he leaves the house.

When Amarilis calls to apologize for blowing me off, I don't pay much attention. She talks about Rich and some professor who hates him because he's jealous or something, which doesn't make any sense, but I'm still thinking about my brother and wondering if he should stop driving around Philadelphia, so I just say, "Uh-huh, uh-huh," a bunch of times.

"You're still mad at me," Amarilis says.

I sigh. "I saw you."

"Huh?"

"You weren't in the library," I say. "I saw you in your room. Through the window of your dorm. You were talking to someone."

There is silence for what feels like forever.

"Amarilis? Are you still there?"

"Yeah, but you probably saw my roommate's friend. Everybody says we look a lot alike."

I've never seen this other girl, but I'm pretty sure I'd recognize my own sister. I do want to believe her, though. "Okay."

"I have to go now," she says. "We're good, right?"

She hangs up without waiting for me to answer.

Amarilis might say we're good, but we're not. Things are changing between us, and I don't like it.

Chapter 17

GINA IS SURPRISED WHEN I SHOW up at her house on Monday. "My sister was too busy for a visit," I say before she can ask anything.

"Truth be told, I'm glad to see you," she says. "I have some errands to run, but I didn't want to leave Freckles alone. Now you can hang out with him."

"Sure!" I gather up a few squeaky toys and sit on the floor in the dining room after Gina leaves. Freckles watches from underneath the table as I play like a little kid putting on a puppet show. "Hello, Mr. Mouse, you look tasty," I have the lion say. "What?! You're going to eat me?" I jiggle the mouse and use a trembly voice.

Freckles sits up and his ears get pointy. His eyes shift from me to the two stuffed animals, back and forth. "Please don't eat me!" I press on the mouse to make him squeak. Freckles runs over, grabs the mouse, and dives back to his spot under the table. I laugh. "Are you saving the mouse, Freckles?"

He lies with his head on the mouse—looking adorable—and

keeps an eye on me. At least he's not growling or peeing under there. I get up and go to the backyard, leaving the door ajar just in case. I take a seat on the deck steps and pull out my phone. There's a message from Olivia with a photo from the beach in Florida, and a bunch of questions about how to talk to some cute guy at her hotel. Zoe sent us a long text about the Louvre. I giggle at the photo of her mother modeling a new outfit from a shopping trip at a fancy boutique in Paris. Zoe's caption has no words, only an eye-roll emoji.

Freckles slips through the door, the toy mouse in his mouth, and trots over to me. He drops the mouse in my lap and runs to the edge of the yard to pee. Then he comes back, takes the mouse, and plops down beside me. I send Olivia and Zoe a photo of Freckles with his toy. *I am so in love with this dog.* I pet him gently on the head with two fingers. He closes his eyes and dozes off.

When I get back home, Abuela tells me to gather up my jeans for the laundry. "Remember to take everything out of the pockets." We have had unfortunate incidents with tissues and candy bars.

I reach into one of my pockets and pull out a folded piece of paper. It's the dog adoption application Gina gave me a few weeks ago. I look at it and think about Freckles. I never thought I would want a little dog who's afraid of everything, but I love being with him, and it will be hard for him to get used to someone new. He's been through so much already.

After I put my pants in the washing machine, I go to the kitchen. Papi got home from work early, and he's making his famous spaghetti and meat sauce. "Dinner's almost ready," he says as soon as I walk in.

"May I ask you something?" I unfold the adoption form and smooth it out on the counter. "This is the application to adopt a dog from Gina's rescue group."

Papi shakes his head as he places the colander in the sink. "Miosotis, we've already discussed this. You keep your end of the deal, and then we'll get the dog."

"I know, but the thing is, Gina says people fill out the applications first, and then they don't get their dogs for months. Won't it be better if we're ready to pick up a dog at the beginning of the summer? Then I can train it before I go back to school."

Papi has his I'm-thinking look as he pours the water and spaghetti into the colander. The steam rises and fogs up his glasses. He puts the pot back on the stove. "Leave the application on my desk and I'll take a look at it."

I run out of the kitchen before he changes his mind.

-«‹‹◆›››-

I bring my backpack to Gina's house the next day.

"Your teachers gave you homework over break?" Gina asks.

"Sort of," I say. "I have a big project due in May."

"Well, good for you!"

"Should we try to take Freckles to the nature trail today?"

"I don't think so," she says. "He still freaks out whenever he sees a leash. I spoke with the Happy Puppy team, and we agreed I should go ahead and bring in another dog or two. It might be good for him."

I look under the dining room table. "Do you think he'll be ready to be adopted by the summer?"

"I certainly hope so."

"Because . . . I was wondering, if maybe I could adopt him?" I reach into my bag. "My dad filled out the application." I don't tell her Papi said I should make it clear to Gina that this is not a definite thing. He wrote in the day after the last day of school as the date when we will be ready to adopt, but if I don't get those As, the deal is off. Gina doesn't need to know all that, though, because I *will* get those As.

I also don't tell her the application is missing something. After Papi signed it, he told me to check off the necessary boxes, like the one asking if anyone in the family is allergic to dogs. The thing is, since we don't know what breeds Freckles has in him, I don't know if he's hypoallergenic. I'm sure Abuela will be fine, but what if the rescue group decides to give him to someone else to be safe? It's better if they don't know about Abuela's allergies.

"That's wonderful, Miosotis! He's already warmed up to you, so this would be perfect!" Gina takes the application and stuffs it in a yellow folder. "Well, since you're here now, I'll go clean the bathroom while the two of you spend quality time together."

I sit on the floor where Freckles can see me, and I take my science textbook out of my bag. Maybe Miss Mabel is right and learning about conserving energy is actually related to working with animals. I don't really see how, but it is kind of interesting, so I try to understand the information in the textbook. I'm getting engrossed in energy-efficient home designs when I feel warm air on my ankle. I look up and there's Freckles, lying near my feet and sniffing my leg. "Hey, cutie." I want to scoop him up and give him a hug, but he might get freaked out. I go back to my book and act calm and nonchalant.

A few minutes later, I put the book down and stand. Freckles follows me to the back door. Outside he sniffs all along the edge of the yard, lifting his leg and squirting pee every now and then. When a dog barks in the distance, Freckles stands still as a statue, with one front paw hovering over the ground. Then he plants all four feet down and barks back.

My mouth drops open. This is my first time hearing Freckles bark. "You must feel at home now." I reach over to scratch his neck, and he gives my hand a quick lick.

Chapter 18

JACINTO IS KNEELING BY THE SIDEWALK, yanking at something in the front yard when I go back home. "What are you doing?" I say.

"Pulling weeds." He spears a trowel into the ground with one hand and grabs a lump of green with the other.

"Um, are you okay?"

"Yeah, why?" He doesn't look at me while he works.

"Because that was pretty upsetting, what happened on the way back from Penn."

Jacinto puts the trowel down and sighs. "Yeah, but it wasn't the first time and it won't be the last. I can't let other people's ignorance ruin my life; I just have to keep going."

"What do you mean?" I ask. "Has this happened before?"

Jacinto stands and stretches his arms over his head. "One time at a track meet, a girl from another school accused Devante and me of stealing her cell phone, even though we were nowhere near her and her stuff. Coach made us empty our bags and pockets to prove she was wrong. He didn't tell any of the white kids

107

to show their stuff." He shakes his head and squats back down, trowel in hand.

I watch him work, wondering what it's like to be him. I wish everyone knew how super smart, hardworking, kind, and loving he is. But when strangers look at my brother, what do they see? Are they afraid of him? Do they assume he's up to no good? Still, other people's wrong assumptions about him don't stop Jacinto from being a great guy. That police officer made him angry for a day, but he didn't change my brother. No one can turn him into the person they think he is. Would I be strong enough to stay so true? I honestly don't know. "You're kind of awesome," I say.

My brother flashes me a big smile. "Yeah, I know."

I roll my eyes and laugh.

"And Miranda agrees."

"Ooh, did you do the promposal thing?"

"Yep, at track practice today." Jacinto grins and grins. The more intense members of the team stayed in town for spring break, so they're still having daily practices. My brother loves to run, plus he gets to see Miranda every day, so he says this is the best spring break ever.

I sort of want to hug him, but he's all sweaty. I give him a thumbs-up. "That's cool. Congrats."

Jacinto goes back to weeding, humming while he works, and I walk into the house.

Abuela is on the phone. "Stop crying, of course I'll help you," she says. "You're my baby sister. I would never abandon you."

I smile. It's been only two days since Abuela swore she was done with helping Tía Felicia. I knew she didn't mean it. She never does.

108

I tiptoe upstairs and walk into my room. Someone is sitting at the desk, bent over and writing. "Amarilis?" I squint and walk toward her.

"Hey, kiddo." Callie turns around.

"Callie!" I give her a hug. "Why are you here? Are you with Amarilis?" I peek out the door to see if my sister is in the bathroom.

Callie has a sad look on her face. "No, I came by to leave this for her." She folds a piece of paper and puts it in an envelope. She licks the envelope's seal, then presses it shut. "Could you give it to her when she comes home for Easter?"

"Um, okay." I take the envelope and look at it. "But why don't you text her or send an email?"

Her shoulders slump. "She's mad at me. She's not answering my texts or anything."

"What happened?"

Callie shrugs and waves her hand in front of her face. "You know how it is with us—we fight one minute and we make up the next." She takes in a deep breath and stands. "I'll give you my number so you can get ahold of me." We put each other's numbers in our phones. "See you later, kiddo." She squeezes my hand, then walks through the door and down the stairs without looking back.

I put Callie's envelope on one of Amarilis's pillows, then I turn on the computer to look for a science article. I find a bunch of stories about people doing awful things to dogs, and I mean *really* awful. I need to get those pictures out of my mind, so I pull a chocolate bar out of the desk drawer and unwrap it while I wait for the video of the day I was born to boot up. I like to watch it every now and then, just because.

I take a big bite of chocolate. My mother is lying in the hospital bed, her amber eyes looking exactly like my siblings'. She reaches for the bundle someone puts in her arms. I'm wrapped in a striped blanket, my face is pale and puffy, and I resemble a Q-tip with that cap on my head. My mother smiles and blinks back tears. "Hola, Miosotis," she says softly into my face. "I love you, my beautiful baby." My eyes are wide open, and I don't take them off her for one second. Like I know this is the last time I'll ever see her. Like I know she won't live long enough to see me again.

Watching this video wasn't such a good idea. It definitely didn't cheer me up. Now I have to find something else to help me forget about my mother. Some TikToks with dogs doing cute stuff should do the trick.

Chapter 19

WHEN I COME HOME FROM GINA'S on Thursday afternoon, Abuela puts me to work. Easter is three days away, and Abuela wants to get started on the meal she'll serve Rich and his parents. She prepares her secret concoction for seasoning the pernil, while I pick stones out of a pound of beans and wash them again and again. "Is this enough beans?" I ask as I fill the pot with water for the beans to soak. Abuela makes sweet beans only once a year, so I don't want them to run out fast.

"Oh yes, that's plenty," Abuela says. And then, as if reading my mind, she adds, "I'm making a carrot cake too. Ricardo and his family have probably never heard of habichuelas con dulce. They might not like it."

"As long as there's enough for me," Jacinto says from the doorway.

"When did you get home, papito?"

"Right now. Last day of practice. Coach told us to finish by running a mile, so I ran home." Jacinto is sweaty and out of breath but smiling.

"You'll be home tomorrow?" Abuela says. "Good, you can help get things ready."

For the next two days, Abuela keeps us busy vacuuming, dusting, and cooking. Jacinto grates a million carrots for the cake. I'm on habichuelas con dulce duty, so I mash and strain the beans, then stir in the milk, sugar, nutmeg, and cinnamon sticks. Abuela doesn't trust me to peel and cut the sweet potatoes, but I get to taste them when it's all done. The house phone rings as Jacinto and I are putting the beans into two big containers.

"Hola, Amarilis." Abuela listens for a little while, her smile turning into a frown. "That's not necessary. We have plenty of food."

I glance at Abuela as I put the containers into the refrigerator. She has that look she gets when Tía Felicia is annoying her. Is Amarilis backing out of this dinner?

Abuela throws her hands up in the air after she hangs up the phone. "Your sister wants us to order food from a restaurant, in case we don't have enough. When have I ever not cooked enough food?"

Jacinto laughs and gives Abuela a hug. "Don't be insulted. She's just nervous."

Abuela sighs. "I suppose you're right."

After we get home from church on Easter Sunday, Abuela tells me to keep on my fancy little-girl dress with the giant bow at the waist. And she insists I already messed up my hair, so she glops more gel in it before she brushes it straight and pulls it up in a too-tight bun. Amarilis gets home about an hour before Rich and his family are supposed to arrive.

"Hola, mija." Papi kisses Amarilis on the forehead. "Why

112

didn't you call? I would have picked you up from the train station."

Amarilis shrugs. "It's a nice day for a walk."

"You look beautiful, Amarilis!" Abuela throws herself at my sister, who winces and pulls away from her hug.

"You're crushing me, Abuela!"

Amarilis looks weird to me. "Are you wearing makeup?" I ask.

"Absolutely! What do you think?" She turns her head back and forth, modeling her face. I guess she's happy with that stuff that looks like paint. It's the same color as her skin, so what's the point?

"Um . . ."

"You look very grown-up and sophisticated." Abuela pats my sister's shoulder.

I nod. I don't want to hurt Amarilis's feelings.

"Can we open a window?" Jacinto says. "I'm sweating in here!" He frowns at Amarilis. "Aren't you dying of heat in that turtleneck?"

My sister shakes her head. "You know I'm always cold."

I never knew that. From the way Jacinto is squinting at Amarilis, I can tell he never knew it either.

Rich and his parents arrive right on time. He and his dad are wearing matching pastel-colored polo shirts, and his mom is in a black-and-white outfit that looks perfect with her white pearls and black-and-gold bracelet. We all hug awkwardly when Rich introduces us, and his dad hands Papi a bottle of wine. "This pairs perfectly with pork," he says.

"It looks lovely." Papi holds the bottle in both hands and takes his time reading the label. "Thank you."

Rich's mom puts an arm around Amarilis. "We love Amy so much. I'm thrilled to finally get a daughter."

Jacinto raises an eyebrow at me. How long has Amarilis been Amy? I look at Papi, who is biting his lower lip.

When we sit at the table, Rich's parents rave that Abuela made so many beautiful dishes, and we all fill our plates.

"Thank you so much for inviting us," Rich's mom says. "We've heard wonderful things about all of you."

Papi thanks them for coming and compliments them for raising such a nice young man. The parents go back and forth fawning over their kids, and they make sure to include Abuela and speak slowly so she can understand. Then Rich looks at Jacinto. "I heard you got busted by the cops."

Jacinto blinks a few times. "Well, I got pulled over, yes."

"Were you speeding?"

"No!" I say. "He wasn't doing anything wrong."

"Well, that doesn't make any sense." Rich's dad sits back and shakes his head. "No one gets stopped for no reason. What did the officer write on the ticket?"

"He didn't give me a ticket."

"Huh?" Rich says. "Then why did he stop you?"

"You'd have to ask the police officer." Papi shrugs. "Only he knows what was going on in his mind."

"Yes." Rich's dad takes a sip of wine. "He probably had a good reason. Just trying to keep us all safe. Amy, did Rich ever tell you about the time he got arrested in high school?" Amarilis shakes her head, and he goes into a whole long story about Rich and his friends getting drunk at a party and being picked up by the police after driving into some neighbors' mailboxes.

"We had to go get him in the middle of the night." Rich's mom laughs and musses his hair. "The little rascal."

"Did you go to jail?" I ask.

"Oh, no, not at all." Rich's dad shakes his head. "We simply paid a fine and bought some new mailboxes. It wasn't a big deal. After all, boys will be boys."

Abuela once told me about the first time Tía Felicia's son, Ernesto, went to jail. He was a teenager and jumped a subway turnstile in New York City. He hadn't destroyed anything or put people in danger, but he still spent a few nights in a prison cell. What Rich did sounds way worse than what Ernesto did, but nobody laughed and said Ernesto was just being a boy. It seems unfair that Rich and Ernesto would be treated so differently.

After dinner, Papi, Jacinto, and Rich's dad go to the living room and talk about sports. Rich's mom wants Abuela's carrot cake recipe, so I get a piece of paper and write a translation of what Abuela dictates. Mostly Abuela pulls ingredients out of the cupboard and says, "A little of this," and "A pinch of that," so I don't know how much help this recipe will be to Rich's mom.

Amarilis and Rich are still at the table, holding hands and talking with their heads close together. Rich's mom goes to them when we finish with the recipe. "I'm sorry I wasn't able to see the arboretum with you," she says. "Was it nice?"

"It was," Amarilis says. "But we won't make any decisions until we've visited all the places on our list."

"We have four more to go," Rich says. "And all the information is going into the handy spreadsheet."

"It's great that you're so organized." Rich's mom smiles at my sister.

"It really helps," Amarilis says. "I know we have a lot of time, but I don't want anything to slip through the cracks."

"That's an excellent plan, Amy. Have you decided how many bridesmaids you're having?"

Amarilis and Rich look at each other. "We're still trying to figure that out," my sister says.

"Oh, what factors are you considering?"

"Well, Mom, Amarilis has this friend she asked to be in the wedding, but now we're thinking she might not be a good choice."

"Which friend?" I ask.

Amarilis lowers her voice. "Callie." She doesn't look at me.

"Callie! Your best friend since kindergarten?"

Amarilis closes her eyes for a second and takes in a deep breath. "It's complicated. Let's talk about something else now."

So we do. We talk about wedding venues, school, and dogs. Before she leaves, I give my sister Callie's note.

"What's this?" She squints at the envelope.

"A letter from Callie."

Amarilis glances at Rich, folds the envelope in half, and puts it in her pocket. "I'll look at it later."

She could have looked at it now. It's not like she rushes out or anything. She packs up leftovers to take back to her dorm, plus some for Rich's parents and some for me to take to Gina and Miss Mabel. I follow her upstairs, hoping to talk about Callie a little, but she hurries into the bathroom, saying there's no time. I hope she makes up with Callie soon, because not having her best friend at her wedding would be ridiculous.

Chapter 20

OLIVIA IS EXCITED TO SHOW OFF her tan on our first day back to school, so she wears a cute white tank top. As soon as we walk into Mr. Nesbitt's classroom, she shivers. "Ugh, I forgot about the AC in this room," she says. "It's freezing in here!"

I raise my hand. "Can I go to my locker and get a sweater for Olivia?"

Mr. Nesbitt tells me to be quick.

When I open the locker, my phone is pinging. I look around to make sure no teachers are in the hallway, then I reach inside. Callie has sent me a text. *Did you give Amarilis my note?*

Should I tell Callie that my sister is thinking of kicking her out of the wedding? Maybe Amarilis will change her mind. Then Callie doesn't need to know. Ever. *Yes,* I reply.

And? What did she say?

That she'd read it later.

Oh. Thanks.

I put the phone back, grab the sweater, and run to class.

"Guess what?" Zoe smiles when we sit down to lunch.

"I found the perfect article for your science project."

"Really? What is it?"

She pulls three sheets of paper out of her bag and hands them to me. "The link is on there so you can look it up, but I printed it out anyway. See, isn't it perfect?"

Pioneering Vet Helps Canine Bones Heal in Record Time

"Hmm," I say.

Zoe looks at me like I said something mean. "What's wrong with this article?"

"Nothing! It's just that I've been looking for an article about an abused dog like Freckles. I haven't found one yet."

"The article has to have been written within the last six months," Zoe says. "You might not find what you're looking for."

I nod. "This *does* look interesting. Thanks for finding it."

Olivia looks over my shoulder as I read it. "Ooh, I can paint dogs with broken legs, and dogs wearing cones, and then healthy ones at the end. That's actually much easier than showing depressed and happy dogs."

"Believe me," Zoe says, "with this article, you'll for sure get an A."

I flip through the pages again and study some of the words. *Humerus*, *femur*, *vertebrae*. They definitely sound scientific. I look at my friends. "You're right."

It is a good, interesting article. But it makes me think I don't actually want to be a vet. I mean, broken bones are creepy. And when I hang out with dogs, I don't want to fix what's wrong with them physically. That's what the vet is for. But I want to get inside Freckles's head and figure out how to make him happy and comfortable. At home, I keep looking for articles on dog behavior and psychology. Still, it's good to know I have Zoe's article in case I don't find anything else.

⫷⟡⫸

On the day of Jacinto's first big track meet of the season, I step outside after school and walk around the corner to the high school field. Papi and Abuela are already on the bleachers.

"Over here!" Papi waves his arms over his head. As if I could miss them. Abuela is small, but she sure stands out, wrapped in a red blanket over her green coat with matching hat, scarf, and gloves. Everybody else is wearing sweatshirts or light jackets. Papi jumps up as soon as I reach them. "It's about to begin." He lumbers down the steps and stands by the fence at the edge of the track, next to the intense parents who take notes and yell out suggestions for improvement every time their kids cross the finish line.

I sit next to Abuela. "Who's that girl with Jacinto?" she asks.

I follow her gaze and see Jacinto looking all shiny-eyed with a goofy smile on his face. He's talking to a girl with dark braids pulled back in a neat bun. "That's Miranda, the girl he's taking to junior prom."

"Oh, he's taking her?" Abuela looks around. "Why doesn't he go with a pretty girl like that one?" She purses her lips toward a pale girl with a blonde ponytail.

"He might not even know that girl," I say. "And Miranda is pretty!"

"Eh, she's okay, for her type."

Miranda is looking starry-eyed right back at Jacinto, and I can see her long eyelashes from all the way up here. The dimples on her cheeks stand out as she laughs at something he says. How could Abuela not think Miranda is pretty?

Of course, I know the answer. When Abuela looks at Miranda, all she sees is one thing: her brown skin.

"You know," I say, "she's the same color as us."

"Is she?" Abuela peeks at the skin under her glove as if she's never seen it before.

"Yes, she is!"

"Hmm. Well, your brother should be trying to improve the family, make it whiter, like I did and like Amarilis is doing." Abuela points at me. "Listen, you might be dark like me, but you have Abuelo's thin lips and nose. If you stay out of the sun and fix your hair, you could be pretty."

I roll my eyes and blow out hard through my mouth. Does Abuela think it's a compliment to tell me I *could* be pretty *if* I change the real me? Abuela has been saying stuff like this my whole life, and I've never questioned it. To be honest, I even believed it. After my mother died, Abuelo retired from his job, and he and Abuela moved here from New York to help Papi take care of us kids. When I was little, I hung out with Abuelo while Amarilis and Jacinto were at school. He taught me to ride a bike and play catch, and we watched baseball games on the couch while he explained the rules and called me his princesa linda. I was eight when he died of cancer, and Abuela and I cried and cried.

I always thought it was sweet that Abuela raved about how

handsome he was. And he *was* handsome. But wouldn't he still have been good-looking and wonderful if his hair hadn't been straight and his eyes hadn't been green? Not according to Abuela. And, to be honest, I sometimes wish I looked more like him and less like her. But now, as I watch Miranda, I know I've been wrong to listen to Abuela. Miranda is pretty, smart, and athletic. She's always nice and she makes Jacinto happy. Why would she want to be different? Why should I?

After the girls' one hundred-meter race starts, I get up and go stand next to Papi.

"Jacinto's friend won!" Papi puts two fingers in his mouth and whistles. "Good job, Miranda!" He claps and claps.

Miranda smiles and waves at us, then walks onto the grass to cool down.

"The boys' one hundred is next," Papi says.

Jacinto jogs to his lane and adjusts his feet on the starting block. He stares ahead as we wait for the starting gun. Then he takes off.

"Go, Jacinto, go!" Miranda jumps up and down for the whole race.

Papi whoops and high-fives me when my brother crosses the finish line in first place. One of the intense moms comes over with a stopwatch in her hand. "Eleven seconds even," she says. "Not bad."

Papi nods and smiles at her, then looks up at the bleachers and gives Abuela a thumbs-up. "Why aren't you sitting with Abuela?"

I sigh and watch the mile runners set up. "She was kind of annoying me."

"Really? Why?"

I look at my father. "Do you think Abuela's racist?"

"Uh-oh." Papi tilts his head. "What did she say now?"

"She said Miranda's not pretty. That Jacinto should take some random blonde girl to prom."

"You know how your abuela is. She'll change her tune when she gets to know Miranda."

"She thinks I'm ugly, and she's known me my whole life," I say.

Papi puts an arm around my shoulders. "First of all, you're beautiful. Don't ever forget that. However . . . as your mother used to say, colonialism and slavery messed with a lot of our heads." He lets go of me and shoves his hands into his jacket pockets. "Your grandmother grew up hearing that people with lighter skin and straighter hair were to be envied." He shrugs. "Unfortunately, so did I."

"Yeah, me too," I say.

Papi looks at me with sorry eyes.

"But you always stick up for me when Abuela complains about my pelo malo and tells me to stay out of the sun," I say. "I like when you do that."

Papi gives me a little smile. "Your hair is beautiful, just like you. I know for a fact that Abuela loves you very much, and she certainly doesn't believe you're ugly. But she can't shake her ingrained ideas of colorism, especially not at her age." Papi looks at Abuela on the bleachers with sad eyes. "Like all of us, Abuela has flaws. But she did a fabulous job raising the wonderful woman I married, and you're turning out pretty great too."

I wrap my arms around Papi, put my head on his chest, and hold on tight.

Chapter 21

AMARILIS TEXTS ME THE AFTERNOON OF Jacinto's prom. *Tell Papi to take lots of pictures of my handsome baby bro and his gorgeous date!*

Papi is driving Jacinto to pick up Miranda and then to a friend's house, where a group of kids are gathering to hang out and snap photos before taking a party bus to prom.

Okay, I text back. *Did you call Callie?* I ask every time we text, and her answer is always the same.

Not yet. Then she changes the subject, like always. I answer her questions about school and Freckles, and I read her list of pros and cons for a bunch of wedding places. But we don't talk about Callie, which is annoying. Callie keeps texting me and I don't know what to tell her.

When Jacinto comes downstairs in his fancy tuxedo, Papi, Abuela, and I clap and hoot at him. I snap a photo and send it to Amarilis. *What a good-looking guy!* she replies.

Abuela opens the refrigerator and gets the corsage Jacinto picked out for Miranda. "Listen, remember to be a gentleman."

She presses the flowers into his hands. "And have a nice time, mi papito lindo." She kisses his forehead, pats his arm, and walks the three of us to the door.

I wave to Papi and Jacinto, then head to Gina and Miss Mabel's house. "Hello, sweetie!" Miss Mabel is all smiles when she answers the door. "It's great to have a relaxing evening off!" Her fluffy slippers slap the floor all the way to the kitchen.

Gina is sitting on the couch with a tiny black dog in her arms and Freckles by her side.

"He's not under the table!" I clap my hands.

Gina puts a finger over her lips. I know she wants me to play it cool, so I sit on the edge of the couch and pet the new dog.

"Who is this?" I ask.

"This is Teacup," Gina says. "She's a toy poodle, and a nasty breeder in Chester County abandoned her because she gets seizures."

"Aw, poor thing."

"Yes, but she already has a bunch of people asking about her cute self," Gina says. "We're going to be losing this baby soon, but I'm sure she'll be very happy in her new home, wherever it is."

I don't know how Gina opens her heart to these dogs time after time, and then she has to hand them over and never see their sweet faces again. She does it with a smile even though I'm sure it hurts. I wish I could be like her, but when I look at Freckles, I feel like there is no way I can watch him go to another home. I sure hope I get that A in science. And that Abuela isn't allergic.

Miss Mabel comes back with a cup of tea. She sits on the armchair and lets out a satisfied sigh. "Hey, sweetie, are you going to your dad's job next week?"

"My dad's job? Why?"

"It's Take Your Children to Work Day on Thursday. They're making a big deal about it at the hospital."

"Oh." I forgot about that. "I went with him last year, and it was kind of boring, but . . ." A day off from school would be sweet.

"Well, you don't have to go with a parent," Miss Mabel says. "I could take you to the hospital. It's a very well-organized program and you could learn a lot about the medical profession. You might even learn something that excites you. We have therapy dogs you could meet."

"Really? That would be okay with you?"

"Certainly! Just ask your dad. And tell him to give me a call if he has any questions."

"Thanks!"

I spend a whole hour with Freckles. He eats his dinner, then chases me while I run around the yard. When I throw a ball across the grass, he stares at it, then looks at me with his head cocked to the side, like I'm acting weird, and I have to laugh. He is so cute! Maybe one day he'll learn to fetch a ball, but, as Gina says, we have to take baby steps. And Freckles is taking those baby steps in the right direction.

Chapter 22

AFTER HE SPEAKS WITH MISS MABEL, Papi is thrilled about me going to the hospital with her. "She says there'll be about twenty kids," he says, "and many wonderful planned activities. Who knows? Perhaps you'll decide a career in medicine is perfect for you!"

"Um-hmm." I'm glad I don't need to sell this idea to Papi, but I just want a day off from school. Hopefully, I won't have to spend the next five years listening to him report on all his research about the best premed programs.

When Miss Mabel and I get to the hospital, she signs me in and introduces me to the people in charge. "This is my dearest friend, Mr. Matt." She hugs a tall man with bulgy muscles.

"Welcome, Miosotis," Mr. Matt says. "Don't you worry about a thing, Mabel. I'll take good care of her."

"We sure will," says a lady who tells me to call her Nurse Jane. "You can come back for her at five."

"See you later, sweetie." Miss Mabel puts her hand over her mouth to cover up a yawn. I feel a little guilty about her changing her schedule for me, and I told her she could drop me off and then go back home to sleep, but she said no, that she would go ahead and work a few extra hours while I was at the hospital too.

I join the other kids to wait for the program to start. The little nine- and ten-year-olds are talking loudly and quickly, and some are giggling. A few high school kids stand apart from the rest of us, like they think we have cooties, and stare at their phones. When Nurse Jane announces that all electronic devices have to be put inside a locker, the older teenagers groan. Then she divides us into three groups. "You're all going to see the same areas," she says, "but not at the same time." My group goes with Mr. Matt.

We gather around him and he makes us introduce ourselves. "I'm Matt. I've been working here for ten years and I went back to school this year for a master's degree in nursing." He turns to the smallest person in our group. "Now tell us about you."

Each kid says their name and how old they are. Nine-year-old Greg and fourteen-year-old Ronaldo both plan to be doctors when they grow up, and best friends Amanda and Mitzi want to find the cure for cancer. Some kid whose name I don't hear whispers that he's eleven and would like to see dead people. I step away from him.

These kids are all so sure of their futures in medicine. They're probably super smart. When it's my turn to speak, I keep my eyes on the floor, feeling like I don't belong here. "My name is Miosotis, I'm twelve, and I'm in sixth grade."

"And I understand you're interested in a career in veterinary medicine," Mr. Matt says.

I shrug. "Maybe."

Mr. Matt hands out papery jumpsuits and tells us to put them on over our clothes. He also gives us hair bonnets and rubber gloves. "Cleanliness is very important," he says, "especially at our first stop: the central sterile supply area."

At the central sterile supply area, a woman holds up metal operating tools and shows us how to clean them with a special machine, which is actually kind of neat. But then she grosses me out describing the infections people could get if the tools aren't extra-special clean. After that we go in a room with X-rays on light boards all over the walls, and a man explains how to understand what we're looking at. "Is this bone broken?" the dead-people kid keeps asking with a huge smile on his face.

Our last stop is the room where the therapy dogs hang out. There are three dogs, all looking cute in red bandanas that say *therapy dog* on a patch in the middle. We meet a big brown lab named Sammy, a medium-size orangish dog with floppy ears named Penny, and a little guy that reminds me of Rory. His name is Taco. "All right, children," the lady in charge says. "Break up into groups of two, then pick the dog you want to work with."

I don't move fast enough, so, before I know it, the dead-people kid is standing next to me with a weird grin on his face. "We're partners," he whispers. Great.

I raise my hand. "Can we have Taco?"

"We want Penny!" Mitzi and Amanda say.

"Okay," the lady says. "You two will work with Sammy," she tells Greg and Ronaldo.

The dead-people kid and I walk over to the smiley guy

cuddling Taco. His name tag says ROGER. "Hello there, young people," he says. "Welcome, welcome." He puts Taco on a foam exercise mat. "Come get to know him."

I kneel and hold my hand out for Taco to sniff. He follows his nose all the way up my arm and then sniffs at my paper gown and back to my jeans, taking a long time to examine my knees.

"You must have a pet," Roger says. "He smells something interesting on you."

"Probably my neighbor's dogs," I say.

"Does he have any superpowers?" the dead-people kid whispers from his hiding spot behind me.

I roll my eyes.

"Why, yes, as a matter of fact, he does!" Roger says. "Taco's special talent is that he calms patients and helps them feel relaxed no matter what. People hold him when they're getting a shot or if they're feeling anxious about an upcoming procedure."

Hmm, that does sound like a superpower. I turn to the dead-people kid and nod.

"It's important for Taco to be healthy and calm," Roger says. "Good dental hygiene is paramount to overall health, so we're going to brush his teeth." Roger shows me how to hold Taco's mouth open the right way to run the toothbrush across all his teeth. "You're a natural at this."

If only Papi could hear that.

Then we play ball with Taco. Roger tells Taco to stay, then tosses the ball. "Fetch," he says when the ball is across the room. Taco's little legs are a blur as he runs for the ball. He brings it back to Roger and holds it in his mouth until Roger says, "Leave it." Then he drops it right away.

129

"Do you want to try?" Roger hands the ball to the dead-people kid, who shakes his head and backs away. So I get to play with Taco the whole time, which is cool.

"He's so obedient," I say after we have Taco sit, stay, and roll over a few times.

"That's crucial," Roger says. "We can't have the dogs running amok here. But some dogs forget the commands, so we practice them every day."

I should talk to Gina about working with Freckles. He would probably like having a mini training routine. Maybe I could study to be a therapy dog trainer. If I go home and tell Papi that, he'll get me a dog, As or no As. For my future career and all.

Before I know it, the day is over, and we're back at the check-in desk waiting to be picked up. "Are you Miosotis?" the lady behind the desk asks when I am the last person waiting. I nod. "Mabel called and said she was running a little late in the emergency room."

"Do you want me to take her there?" Mr. Matt asks the desk lady.

"Sure, thanks!"

I follow Mr. Matt through a million corridors to the emergency-room waiting area. He tells the person at the reception desk that I am waiting for Mabel Gordon, pats my shoulder, and says, "It was a pleasure to meet you, and good luck with everything." Then he winks and walks away. I sit and pull out my phone to text Olivia and Zoe about my day.

I've just unlocked my phone when I hear a familiar voice at the check-in desk behind me. "You won't call my family, right?"

I turn around. Amarilis is standing there holding a bloody

paper towel against her cheek. Tears are pouring out of her swollen eyes.

I jump up and run to my sister. "Amarilis! What happened? Are you okay?"

Amarilis looks at me with big eyes. Blood oozes through the paper towel onto her fingers. She grabs my arm with her other hand and looks around the room. "Is Papi here with you?" she whispers.

I shake my head. "What's wrong? Did you get mugged or something?" Now I'm getting scared.

"No, no, no," Amarilis says. "It was just an accident, but I'll be fine."

"What kind of accident?"

Before Amarilis can answer, a woman in scrubs comes out to get her. I ask Amarilis if she wants me to go with her.

"No, I'm fine," Amarilis says. "But promise me something." She looks me in the eye. "Do *not* tell Papi or Abuela or Jacinto you saw me here, okay?"

"Why?" If Amarilis was in an accident, wouldn't they want to know?

"Promise me, please!"

"Okay, I promise." The woman leads Amarilis through a swinging door as I stay behind. This is so weird. Amarilis doesn't have a car, so if someone else was driving and they had an accident, wouldn't the driver be here too? Why didn't Rich come with her? And why doesn't she want the family to know about this? I should have insisted on going back there with her. There's something fishy about this and I want to know what it is. I shove my phone deep into my back pocket.

131

"Excuse me," I say to the lady at the front desk. "I was here for Take Your Children to Work Day, and I left my cell phone in the lobby. Can I go back and get it?"

"Um, I guess," the woman says. "But I'm not supposed to let you in by yourself."

"I'll be right back," I say. "I know exactly where it is."

The woman looks around. "Let me page a volunteer." She picks up the phone receiver, presses a button, and says, "Volunteer to ER reception, volunteer to ER reception."

My heart thumps as I wait. How will I find out about Amarilis with someone following me around?

A white-haired lady comes into the room. "You asked for a volunteer?"

"Yes, this young lady needs to go back to the main lobby. She was here for Take Your Children to Work Day, and she left her phone there."

"My pleasure, follow me." The volunteer swipes her key card and walks through the swinging door. I follow closely behind her, looking for my sister. All around the floor are rooms closed off by curtains, so I edge near them and try to listen to the conversations inside. When the volunteer steps through another doorway and down the maze I walked through with Mr. Matt, I hang back. I hold my head up and walk back toward the curtained rooms, slowing down a little in front of each room. I listen for my sister's voice, but I don't stop. I want to look like I know where I'm going so the medical people around me don't get suspicious.

When I circle around a second time, I hear a woman's voice say, "Amarilis, you don't have to tell me who did this to you, but

132

I promise no one will call your family if you decide to talk about it." I get on one knee and untie my shoe, then tie it again very slowly. I can hear Amarilis sniffling. Someone did this to Amarilis on purpose? Why? And who? Anger bubbles up inside me and I want to go find that person and make them pay for this.

"Was it your boyfriend?" the woman says softly. Her boyfriend?! Why would she ask that? Amarilis doesn't answer, at least not with words. But I know she must have nodded because the woman starts talking again. "Oh, honey, this is nothing to be ashamed of. It's good you came in. There are lots of people you can talk to. They dedicate themselves to helping victims of domestic violence. Here, I'll get you some pamphlets and phone numbers."

My shoelace is tied now, but I don't get up. I can't believe what I just heard. Rich seems so sweet—definitely not the kind of person who would beat anybody up, especially not someone he loves. Maybe it was an accident, like Amarilis said. I really hope so. But I think about Amarilis's bloody cheek and puffed-out eyes, and how scared she was to see me here. She looked so lonely in the waiting room, like she didn't have anyone to take care of her, like she didn't have a fiancé who loved her. I don't want to believe it, but I know this was no accident.

Chapter 23

"WHAT ARE YOU DOING HERE?" THE volunteer has come back, and she glares at me with her hands on her hips.

"I found my phone." I stand and hold it out. "See, I had dropped it here. I tried to tell you but you walked too fast, so I figured I should stay here and wait."

"Hmm." She heads back to the waiting area and holds the door open for me.

"Thanks for your help," I say.

A moment later, Miss Mabel rushes out. "I'm sorry to keep you waiting!"

"No problem," I say. "It wasn't that long."

Miss Mabel is super chatty on the way to the car. I walk behind her, my sister's swollen, teary face on my mind. "Did you enjoy your visit?" Miss Mabel says. "What was your favorite part? Was it the dogs? I figured it would be the dogs, but you never know. You could surprise yourself and find another passion unexpectedly, right?"

"Yeah, I liked the dogs." I step into the car and buckle my seat belt.

"What's wrong?" Miss Mabel squints at me with that grown-up worried look. "Did someone upset you? Are you queasy? I hope you didn't catch anything." She feels my forehead with the back of her hand, even though she's told me a hundred times that that's no way to tell if someone has a fever.

"No, I'm fine," I say. "But . . . I—I saw a girl, a teenager, in the waiting room, who looked kind of beaten up."

"Oh my." Miss Mabel clucks her tongue. "Was she in a fight?"

"I heard her say it was her boyfriend."

"Ah, that's sad." She pulls out of the parking lot and drives in silence for a few minutes. "Was she alone?"

"Yeah. Why do you ask?"

"Well, a lot of times people in abusive relationships drift away from their friends and family. I hope that girl has someone in her corner." She checks her side mirror before swerving around a bus. "At least she came in for help. That's a good sign."

I don't say much more the rest of the ride home. A few times I fake chuckle or say "uh-huh" when Miss Mabel talks about her day or tells me a story about something funny Mr. Matt said or did. But I'm not really listening because I can't stop thinking about Amarilis. Is it good that she went to the ER for help? How many other times has this happened? Is this why she didn't go to my birthday party or let me visit her? Did she have black eyes or a split lip those times? And was she covering up bruises under her makeup and long-sleeved turtleneck on Easter?

"Okay, sweetie," Miss Mabel says. "I'll see you later."

I look up and see we're home.

"Thanks, Miss Mabel. I'm glad I went with you today. This was a great experience." I know I sound like a robot, but I feel like one too. The words come out of my mouth because they're what I'm supposed to say. I can't tell Miss Mabel what I really think—that I'm scared for my sister and confused about what's happening to her.

⟨⟨⟨◆⟩⟩⟩

The table is already set when I walk in the house, but I don't have much of an appetite. How can I sit here eating when Amarilis is out there hurt?

"Did you fill up on junk food at the hospital?" Abuela asks.

"No. I'm just tired." I mix my rice and beans together again and again.

"Ha!" Papi says. "Now you see how tough the working life is."

"Did you watch any surgeries?" Jacinto asks.

"No. I saw before and after X-rays, and the tools they use for different kinds of operations." I had wanted to tell my family about the therapy dogs, but I don't feel like talking anymore. I do wonder about Freckles, though. Did he miss me today? Roger said dogs are happiest when they stick to a routine. Is Freckles confused because I didn't come over this afternoon? He's already been through so much pain in his life. I should do all I can to help him. I eat a little more food, then put my fork down. "Can I go next door and see if Gina needs anything?"

Abuela frowns. "But you hardly ate."

"It's okay if she misses one meal." Papi turns to me. "Put your leftovers away; perhaps you'll feel like eating later tonight."

I don't think so, but I nod and carry my plate to the kitchen.

"Hi, Miosotis!" Gina hugs me with her free arm. "I wasn't expecting you tonight. Mabel said you had a busy day."

136

"Yeah, but I wanted to say hi to Freckles." I look at the little dog cuddled against Gina's chest. "And who is this?"

"Her name is Pepper," Gina says. "She's a Pomeranian mix. Isn't she adorable?"

"She is." I rub behind Pepper's ear. "Was Teacup adopted?"

"Yep, and hopefully this little girl will find a forever home soon too. Her owners just up and decided they didn't feel like having a dog after all. Can you believe that?"

I cannot. What is wrong with people? "How can anybody not want to keep you?" I say to Pepper in that Gina baby-talk voice. Pepper licks my nose, then sneezes. "Gee, thanks." I laugh as I wipe my face with the back of my hand.

"You're part of her family now," Gina says.

"So . . . where's Freckles?"

A soft bark comes from underneath the coffee table.

"Oh, you found a new comfortable spot." I kneel and hold out my hand.

Freckles comes out and sniffs me all over. Then he looks me in the eye, crawls onto my lap, and nuzzles against me. I can tell he knows I'm sad and he's trying to help me feel better. And it's working. I told myself I was coming to see Freckles because he needs me, but I'm the one who needs him.

"Should I take him outside?" I ask Gina.

"No, thanks, we came in right before you got here."

"Okay." I close my eyes and put my cheek on Freckles's back as I scratch his neck. Should I tell Gina about my sister? Maybe she and Miss Mabel can help. Amarilis didn't make me promise to keep this from them, just from Papi and Abuela and Jacinto. But still, she might get mad and stop talking to me. Miss Mabel

137

said it's dangerous for someone in an abusive relationship to drift away from family and friends. I'd better not take any chances.

I sit up and Freckles lifts his head and licks my arm. Then he climbs off my lap and goes back under the coffee table. "I'll see you tomorrow," I say as I stand.

"Sure thing!"

When I get back home, I have a bunch of text messages from Olivia and Zoe, talking about their days and asking about mine. Should I tell them about my sister? I don't know. I definitely don't want to say anything in a text. *Day was good. Tell u more tomorrow. Going to bed now.*

Then I text Amarilis. *How do you feel?*

I wait and wait, staring at my phone.

Finally, she replies. *I'm fine now. Don't worry. Good night.*

I stare at the phone some more, wondering if I should ask more questions. She probably won't answer. At least not now. Rich might be sitting next to her this very minute.

I curl up in bed and wonder how I can help my sister. Why does she stay with Rich if he hurts her? Did she call the police when this happened? Maybe they didn't believe her or maybe Rich convinced them this wasn't a big deal. Why did I promise not to tell Papi and Abuela and Jacinto? I shouldn't have, but I did, and I don't want to break a promise. Will Olivia and Zoe have any ideas? Or what about Gina and Miss Mabel? But would it be right to tell someone outside the family? I don't want to embarrass us by airing our dirty laundry, as Papi sometimes says. But if I can't talk to Papi, Abuela, Jacinto, or anyone outside the family, how will I figure this out? I have to do something to help Amarilis.

When Abuela, and then Papi, come in to say goodnight, I pretend to be asleep. Then I open my eyes and worry into the morning.

Chapter 24

"WHAT'S WRONG?" ABUELA ASKS WHEN I come down for breakfast the next day. She tells me to sit and feels my forehead. "Hmm, you don't seem warm . . ."

I know I have dark circles under my eyes, but do I really look terrible?

"Are you hungry?" Abuela puts a plate of scrambled eggs in front of me.

I take one whiff, clutch my belly, and run to the bathroom. Even though I hardly ate anything for dinner, I manage to empty my stomach into the toilet.

"Were you eating chocolate bars all night?" Abuela is outside the bathroom with her hands on her hips. "You promised you wouldn't eat more than one each day if I let you keep them in your room!"

"I didn't have any, honest," I say truthfully.

"Hmm, okay, then back to bed, mi amor. I'll tell your father to call the school before he leaves for work."

I don't argue. Abuela escorts me up the steps, helps me into my pajamas like a little kid, and tucks me in. Once I'm alone in my room, I send Zoe and Olivia a quick text letting them know I won't be in school today, then I curl up and close my eyes. Thoughts of my sister still race through my mind, but I manage to fall asleep. Finally.

When Abuela opens my door a while later to peek inside, I keep my eyes closed and breathe deeply. I'm not ready to go downstairs, and I don't want to talk. I wait until her footsteps are safely back on the first floor, and then I sit up. Amarilis's bed is neat and empty, as it has been ever since she left after her spring break. But there's something sticking out from under one of her pillows. Something I hadn't noticed before. I get up and reach under the ruffled edge of the sham. It's the envelope with Callie's letter. I saw Amarilis put it in her purse, so she must have slipped it under here when she came up to use the bathroom on Easter. Why would she do that? And why didn't she tell me?

I peek inside the now-open envelope, expecting it to be empty, but it isn't. Should I read what's inside, or would I be invading Amarilis's privacy? Maybe she left this here on purpose so I would find it. I pull the letter out.

Dear Amarilis,

I'm sorry I offended you when I asked if Rich has been hurting you. It's just that we've been best friends since we were five, and you seem so different when you're around him, so I was worried. But, of course, if you say he's good to you and you're happy, then I'm happy for *you. Please don't shut me out of your life. You're like family and I really miss you. Call or text me, okay?*

Love, Callie

I fold the letter back slowly. Is it good that Callie already knows about Amarilis? Maybe. I mean, that way she can help me help her. But how did Callie figure this out, and when? Are things worse than what I saw? Is that even possible? When I open the envelope to put the letter back inside, a tiny piece of paper flutters out. This note is in Amarilis's neat handwriting.

Thanks for the note, Callie. I've missed you too! Rich will be thrilled to hear you're not out to get him and trying to break us up. He was worried about that. I'll call you after I talk to him. (I shared my passwords with him, so I don't want him to see I called you again and then get suspicious.) Anyway, I'm excited about chatting again! —A

Why didn't Amarilis give this note to Callie, or at least ask me to get it to her? And why would she give Rich her passwords? Why is she even still planning to marry him? Everything is so weird. I have to talk to Callie. Amarilis wrote her this note, so she must want me to give it to her. But what will I tell Abuela? She won't let me go anywhere if I'm still sick. I have to get well right now.

I wash my face and brush my teeth, then put my clothes back on. I comb the knots out of my hair, slather some gel on it, and tamp down the frizzy curls with a hairbrush. Then I stand back and examine myself in the mirror. Yes, I definitely look like a healthy person. And, now that I can talk to Callie about Amarilis, I feel healthy again. But I am really, really hungry. Abuela will be happy to hear that.

When I get downstairs, Abuela cups my face in her hands. "Ay, mi amorcito! How do you feel?"

"Much better," I say. "It was probably a one-day bug."

"I'm sure you caught something in the hospital. Those places are germ factories."

"Is there anything to eat?"

"Of course, of course!" Abuela smiles like I knew she would. "I'm making sancocho."

"Um, can I have toast?" The thought of a thick stew is making me queasy again. But Abuela has to think I'm well enough to leave the house after school is over. And that is in—I look at the clock—an hour and a half. "I'll save the sancocho for dinner, okay?"

"Yes, yes, you can't have anything heavy on an empty stomach." Abuela makes me a soft-boiled egg and some toast, which are delicious. I feel better now, so I tell her so. "¡Ay, qué bueno!" she says. "But, listen, take it easy. Thank goodness it's only Friday. Now you have all day tomorrow to relax and get better. Remember, Sunday is a big day."

Sunday would have been my mother's fiftieth birthday. We're going to the cemetery to spend the day with her. We go every year on her birthday, but this year Papi and Abuela are making a super big deal out of it. Will Amarilis show up? Or will she make an excuse to stay away so Papi, Abuela, and Jacinto don't see her cuts and bruises?

143

I sit in front of the TV and send Zoe a text. *Can I come by your house and pick up the homework?*

She doesn't answer right away. She wouldn't have her phone during class, so she won't see my text for another forty-five minutes. Zoe lives around the corner from Callie. After Papi picks up Jacinto from track practice, I'll ask him to drop me off at Zoe's so she can fill me in on everything that happened at school today. I don't want to lie to Zoe, but I probably have to. I'll tell her Papi is waiting at the corner, grab the homework, and walk over to Callie's. Then I'll give Callie Amarilis's note and tell her what I saw at the hospital. Callie will know what to do.

My phone pings in the middle of a game show. *Don't worry about coming over. I'll bring the homework to you.*

Aw, man, why does Zoe have to be so nice? *Thanks, but I feel much better and I really want to get out of the house.* That should do it.

K. I'll be home at 4:30, after yearbook meeting.

Whew. Now I have to wait two hours. Or more, if Jacinto's practice runs late. And I don't even know if Callie will be there. What if she has late classes today? I send her a text. *Can I come to your house at 4:30? It's about Amarilis.*

Callie answers right away with a *yes!!!* I sit back and stare at the TV screen, my heart pounding and my mind racing. I hope Callie has some good ideas, because I can't figure out what to do.

Chapter 25

ABUELA IS ADAMANT THAT I SHOULD not go next door today so I call Gina and tell her I can't make it. She's really sweet and tells me to feel better and not to worry about Freckles because he'll be fine. I know she's right, but I can't stop thinking about him and all the ways he reminds me of Amarilis. It feels weird to compare my sister to a dog, since that's supposed to be a not-nice thing to do, but I know it's actually the best compliment ever. I mean, is any human as great as a dog? I think about how I was kind of mad at Freckles when I first met him, just like I was upset when Amarilis started acting weird. Then I found out Freckles had been abused and I was patient with him. I worked hard to help him, and now he is much better and he even seems happy. But the first step with Freckles—the one taken by the rescue group—was getting him away from the people who were mean to him and hit him with leashes.

So I have to get Amarilis away from Rich. Then I'll be able to help her too.

Papi and Jacinto get home as I finish eating a bowl of

sancocho. "You couldn't wait for us, squirt?" Jacinto points to my empty bowl.

Abuela caresses my head and pats my back. "This is a light snack for now. She was sick today and couldn't eat before. Are you hungry, papito?"

"Nah, I need to shower first."

"You sure do." I pinch my nose.

Jacinto takes off his sweaty T-shirt and tosses it on my head.

"Ewww!"

"Okay, you two, that's enough!" Papi laughs. "Get cleaned up, Jacinto." He hands the shirt back to my brother.

After Jacinto goes upstairs, I turn to Papi. "Will you drop me off at Zoe's for a little while? She said she'll give me the home-work and explain what I missed in class today."

"Certainly, what time?"

"Now?"

"Okay, let's go!"

I jump up and head to the door. "Wait, I need my backpack." I run upstairs and grab the envelope with Callie's and Amarilis's notes, stuff it into my bag, and come back down.

"Should she be doing all this running around after being sick today?" Abuela is saying to Papi.

Usually when it comes to health issues, Papi does whatever Abuela says, like slathering Vicks VapoRub all over our chests and noses whenever we get the tiniest cold. I bite my lip and hope he doesn't change his mind now. "It's not running around, Doña Marta. She's going to sit at a friend's house and talk about their classes." Thank goodness Papi is obsessed with school.

Once we're in the car and buckled in, I wonder how I'm going to sneak over to Callie's, what I'll say to Zoe, whether I should tell Papi since it wasn't fair of Amarilis to make me promise not to tell—

"How is science class coming along?"

"Huh?"

"Science? Remember, the class you're getting an A in this quarter?" He chuckles.

I nod and force myself to smile a little.

"Well?"

"I got A pluses on all my homework assignments so far."

"Fabulous! I knew you could do it if you tried!" Papi is smiling so big. I thought he made this deal because he thought I couldn't do it, because he doesn't really want me to ever have a dog. But now I'm not sure. He seems honestly happy about my news. Unfortunately, I don't feel the same way. I mean, Amarilis and Jacinto did my homework for me.

"If you ever have questions, remember you can ask me anything."

"Sure, thanks." So now I guess he'll do my homework if I ask him to. Obviously, he doesn't care if I actually learn anything.

"What about your other classes? Are you keeping your grades up in those too?"

"Yes! I got an A minus on my math worksheet, a B on a social studies quiz, and an A minus on an English paper." These grades I'm super proud of. I got them all by myself.

"Good job," Papi says. "Too bad about that quiz, though. Perhaps you'll do better next time."

I cross my arms and look out the window without saying another word the rest of the way to Zoe's.

"What time should I pick you up?" he asks when we arrive.

"Maybe in . . . an hour?" How long will it take me to talk to Callie and come up with a plan to help Amarilis? Is an hour long enough? "Or two?"

"Call me when you're ready. But don't stay too long."

I step out of the car and walk up Zoe's front steps. "Hello, Miosotis!" Zoe's mom gives me a hug. "I'm sorry you weren't feeling well today. Would you like a cup of hot tea?"

"No, thank you." I don't have a lot of time. "My dad's waiting for me, so could I get the homework from Zoe now?"

"Oh?" Zoe's mom pokes her head out the door and looks left and right. "Where is he?"

"Um, around the corner." I know I'm not making any sense, and Zoe's mom must know it too. I stare at my shoes to avoid seeing the funny look she's giving me.

Luckily, Zoe shows up. "You want to come up to my room?"

"Yeah." I run up after her. "Listen, Zoe, I can't stay long. I'm going to Callie's house about something important, but I don't want my dad to know." So much for lying to Zoe. I knew I couldn't do it, so I don't even try.

Zoe takes my hands in hers and studies my face with a worried look. "What's wrong?"

"I'm sorry, but I can't tell you right now. Amarilis needs help with something serious, so I have to talk to Callie."

"Okay." Zoe fishes some papers out of her backpack. "Here's the homework we got today. Call if you need help. I'll walk you over to Callie's."

"Thanks." I give Zoe a hug.

When we get to Callie's house, I turn to Zoe. "I might have

to come back to your house in about an hour for my dad to pick me up. Is that okay, or will your mom get suspicious?"

Zoe shrugs. "She doesn't worry about anything." Zoe sure is lucky. "See you later," she says before walking away.

Callie opens the door as soon as I knock. "Come on in."

I follow her into the family room and pull the envelope out of my backpack. "I'm sorry I read this, but Amarilis answered your letter and I thought you would want to see it."

Callie's eyes open wide. She smiles, grabs the envelope, and fishes out Amarilis's note. She frowns as she reads it, then tosses it aside, sinks down on the couch, and covers her face with her hands.

"You were right." I sit next to her.

Callie looks at me. "What do you mean?"

"I saw her. Amarilis." I pull at the strings on my bag. My eyes water. "I was at the hospital for Take Your Kids to Work Day, and she was there too. Her face was bleeding and her eyes were puffy and red. I heard her tell the nurse Rich did it to her."

Callie gasps and stands. She paces back and forth a few times. "What did she say to you?"

"That it was an accident. She begged me not to tell the rest of my family. She made me promise!" I cry for real now. "I don't know what to do! Will Amarilis be mad if I tell Papi and Abuela? Will she be mad I told you? We have to get her away from Rich, we have to!"

Callie sits and puts her arms around me. "Shh, shh," she says. "You were right to tell me, but maybe we shouldn't share this with the rest of your family yet."

I sniffle, but I feel better. Callie will take care of everything, and I won't have to worry anymore. "What are you going to do?"

Callie glances at the clock on the wall. "I'll go see her now." She steps out of the room and calls into the kitchen. "Mom, I need to run an errand before dinner, but you guys can start without me if I don't get back in time."

"Okay, sweetie!"

Callie comes back in and puts her hands on her hips like a superhero. "I'll let you know how it goes."

I feel like Callie took a heavy box from me and offered to carry it, and my shoulders relax right away. But not for long. Something doesn't feel right. A box this big shouldn't be carried by one person alone. "Can I come with you?" I ask.

Chapter 26

MY HEART THUMPS AS I DIAL my home number and listen to the phone ring on the other end. I just practiced this with Callie and cleared it with Zoe. "Hello?"

"Papi, hi!"

"Are you ready to be picked up?"

"No, um, Zoe's mom invited me to stay for dinner. Can I?"

"Well, I don't know . . . do you feel well enough?"

"Yes, they're having pasta, which I'll eat plain, so it won't bother my stomach," I say as rehearsed. "And there's new math stuff I don't understand. Zoe said she would explain it to me after dinner." That ought to do it.

"All right, if that's acceptable to Zoe's mom."

"It is! I'll call you later to pick me up. Thanks!" I hang up right away and follow Callie outside.

Callie's hand trembles as she fumbles to put the key in the car's ignition.

"What will we do when we get there?" I ask. I get why Callie is jittery. I'm nervous too. Like how I felt right before going on stage for the school spelling bee. The thought of all those lights and eyes on me, and the fear of making a big mistake . . . but now I can't believe I was worried about that. A spelling mistake is no big deal compared to this.

"I don't know." Callie bites her lip as she pulls out of the driveway. "I guess we tell Amarilis we know and we're here for her, and then see what she says."

"That's it?" Callie's idea seems too simple, and it probably won't work. "How will we get her away from Rich?"

Callie shrugs. "We can't force her to do anything."

"But . . . we'll convince her to break up with him, right?"

"I don't think we should try to do that," Callie says. "She has to decide for herself. We just let her know we're on her side no matter what."

Callie is annoying me now. I would never have been able to help Freckles if he were still with those mean people, and we can't help Amarilis as long as she's hanging around with Rich. I stare at the back of the SEPTA trolley slowing us down. Callie turns up the radio and strums her fingers on the steering wheel. Clearly, she has no more of a plan than I do. Maybe it's unfair of me to be upset with her since I sprang this on her less than a half hour ago. But still, we should both have the same goal—getting my sister away from Rich—and now I wonder if we do.

When we get close to Amarilis's dorm, Callie slows down. "There's a spot." I point to the next block. She speeds through the yellow light, then spends forever parallel parking her tiny car into a huge space. I don't complain because, to be honest, I'm in no hurry. What will Amarilis look like when we see her? What if she's all black-and-blue and swollen?

Callie looks at me after she turns off the engine. "Rich's room is down the hall from hers, so we might see him."

"I hope we do. I'll give him a bloody face like he did to my sister."

Callie grabs my hand and looks me in the eye. "You will do no such thing. I've been reading about abusive relationships, and if we let him know we found out about this, he might get angry and lash out at her."

"But—"

"But nothing. If we see him, we'll be nice to him."

This is ridiculous. I step out of the car, cross the street, and walk in silence into the dorm. Callie follows behind me.

"We're here to see Amarilis Flores," Callie tells the girl at the front desk. "She's on the second floor."

"Your names?" the girl asks.

"I'm Callie and this is her sister, Miosotis."

The girl scrolls through the computer. Then she picks up the phone. "Hi, is this Amarilis? You have two guests here to see you. Callie and, um, your sister." The front desk girl blinks and nods a lot while Amarilis's voice buzzes through the phone. "Okay, I'll let them know," she says before hanging up. "So," she says to Callie. "Your friend isn't ready for visitors right now."

Callie and I look at each other. "Well . . . when will she be ready?" Callie asks. "We can wait."

The girl shakes her head. "She said to come back another day and to call first."

"But it's a family emergency." Callie starts to cry. "Please, you have to let us in!"

Callie's not lying. This is an emergency. If we don't get my sister out of here, horrible things could happen. What if Rich breaks her arm or her leg, or even kills her? Suddenly, I'm crying too, sobbing into Callie's shoulder. The front desk girl stares at us with her mouth hanging open.

"Okay, well, I need to see some ID from you," she says to Callie. "Then I'll buzz you in."

Callie and I sob all the way to the elevator. Once inside, she pulls two tissues out of her purse and hands one to me. "We have to get it together and be calm when we see her."

I nod and blow my nose. Callie dabs her eyes dry. We take deep breaths as the elevator door opens, then step into the hallway hand in hand.

When we knock on Amarilis's door, I panic. My sister will probably tell us to go away, and then what? We have to get in there and drag her home. We just have to. My heart leaps when I hear shuffling and the door opens right away. But it isn't Amarilis.

"Little sis! It's good to see you." Rich pulls me in for a hug, a big smile on his face. "Callie," he says with a nod.

"Hey, Rich." Callie tilts her head. "Always a pleasure to see you. Where's my best friend?"

"She stepped out for a bit. But you two can come back any time." Rich holds my shoulder to keep me in the hallway and starts to close the door.

"We'll wait inside." Callie shoves her foot into the doorway and elbows her way past Rich.

Right away I'm sorry about thinking anything bad about Callie in the car. What would I have done without her? I quickly follow her in before Rich blocks my way.

"I thought you weren't here?" Callie says.

Amarilis is on her bed with an open book on her lap. She looks up and says, "Umm," then shifts her eyes toward Rich.

"What's that?" I say, pointing to a puckered red oval with two black dots on her left cheek.

Amarilis puts her hand over her cheek. "Umm," she says again, this time staring at her book.

"She had a little accident," Rich says. "But I took her to the hospital, they stitched her up, and she's good as new! Right, sweetie?" He looks at Amarilis and smiles like an angel.

I glare at Rich, ready to hurl myself at him and wring his lying neck. Callie hooks her arm through mine and holds me close. "Okay . . . well, that's good." Callie pulls me toward the bed and sits next to Amarilis. She reaches for my sister's hand. "I'm sorry you had an accident. It's a good thing Rich was here to take care of you."

What is Callie doing? Does she actually believe these lies? I told her I saw Amarilis in the hospital yesterday, and Rich was definitely not with her. Not only did he do this to her, he didn't even have the decency to go with her to get help.

Amarilis smiles. "Thanks, Callie. It's good to see you again! We need to catch up on stuff."

"Yeah. Did I tell you I changed my major again?" Callie drones on and on about her classes and professors, and she and Amarilis trade stories about obnoxious know-it-all kids in their schools. When Rich yawns, I figure this is a brilliant plan to bore him to sleep so we can sneak Amarilis out. I keep my mouth shut, even though I really want to grab my sister and go home.

"Why don't I get us dinner?" Rich says. "Hoagies from Wawa?" He stands and pulls out his phone. "I'll order now on the app so they'll be ready when I get there." He doesn't wait for an answer and he doesn't ask what kind of hoagies we want. When he finishes with the order, he sticks the phone back in his pocket and walks to the door. "I'll be right back."

As soon as he steps out, I jump to the door and lock it. "Okay." I turn to my sister. "The real reason we're here is to take you home and get you away from that creep. Let's pack your stuff and leave before he gets back."

"What?"

"Yesterday at the hospital, I heard you tell the nurse Rich did that to you. Now, come on, let's go." I open the closet and rummage around for her suitcase. "We don't have to bring everything now, just what you need right away. Papi and Jacinto can come back this weekend to get the rest."

"Miosotis, what are you talking about? I'm not going anywhere."

"What do you mean you're not going anywhere?"

Amarilis is sitting at the edge of her bed, gripping her knees. "Look, I'll admit Rich and I hit a bit of a rough patch lately, but he was truly sorry when he realized what he did. He apologized and promised never to do it again." She looks at me and then at Callie. "We love each other and we're going to make it work."

Callie puts her arm around Amarilis. "We understand," she says. "Just know we're here for you no matter what. Also, Miosotis said the hospital gave you some numbers to call. Why don't you reach out to one of those places and see if they can help you two sort things out?"

Amarilis looks at Callie like she's thinking that over. "Yeah, you're probably right. I still have those numbers in my desk. I'll call tomorrow."

"WHAT. ARE. YOU. TWO. TALKING. ABOUT!" I yank the suitcase out of the closet and slam it onto the floor. "You can't sort things out with someone who would do that to you! Look at your face! Just look at it!"

Amarilis hunches up her shoulders like she's trying to make herself smaller. Tears roll down her cheeks.

"Come on, let's get your things and go." I open the suitcase. "He'll be back any minute."

Amarilis shakes her head without looking at me.

I put my hands on my hips. "Are you serious? Are you so stupid you'll stay and be somebody's punching bag?"

Callie glares at me. Her face is so red her freckles have nearly disappeared. I don't care. I'm telling the truth. Somebody has to.

"Come on! Let's go!"

"I'm not leaving him!" Amarilis is sobbing now.

Callie holds Amarilis and strokes her cheek. "We're here for you if you need us," she says again. "We're always here for you, whatever you need."

"What you need is to get away from that creep! Honestly, Amarilis, I always thought you were so great and I wanted to be just like you. But you embarrass me. I'm ashamed to be your sister!" I throw the door open and run right into Rich.

Chapter 27

"**W**HOA, WHAT'S GOING ON HERE?" RICH holds up his hands in surrender, and the plastic Wawa bag dangles from his arm.

Right away Callie swoops over and puts her arm around me with her fingers pinching my shoulder. "They found out there's been a death in the family," she says. "Miosotis wanted to tell Amarilis in person. But she's very upset, so I'll take her home now."

"Oh, I'm sorry." He walks into the room and hugs Amarilis, who's still crying. "Who was it?" He looks at me with concerned eyes.

"A relative in the DR," Callie says. "Beloved by the whole family."

"Ohhhh." Rich holds onto Amarilis and rubs her back. "I'm here for you, sweetie."

How dare he call her sweetie. I open my mouth to yell at him—

"Okay, we're leaving now." Callie pushes me out the door.

"Wait!" Rich chases after us in the hallway. "Take these hoagies for the road." He presses the bag into Callie's hand. "Hang in there, little sis," he says. Then he trots back to Amarilis's room.

"How can we leave her there with him?" I say to Callie.

She takes my hand and we walk to the elevator. "It's better than yelling at him and then leaving," she whispers. "If we upset him, he'll take it out on her."

I look down the hall at my sister's door. "But we don't have to go."

"We can't stay all night," Callie says. "She doesn't want us to."

"But . . ."

Maybe Callie's right. She did say she read about this. I researched dogs and learned how to help Freckles, so Callie's research might be right too. But I feel useless. How can I walk away from my sister when she obviously needs help?

"Come on, don't cry." Callie hugs me as we step into the elevator.

Inside the car, she hands me a wrapped hoagie. "Your dad will expect you to have eaten when he picks you up."

I take the hoagie and turn it over but don't unwrap it. I don't want anything from Rich. "I'm not hungry."

Callie keeps an eye on the traffic as she pulls into it. "Look," she says, "Amarilis feels awful enough already. Insulting her and yelling at Rich isn't going to help."

"Well, then, what will help?"

Callie shrugs. "I'm not sure but, to be honest, you probably made things worse."

"Me? What did I do?"

"You called her stupid."

"I was trying to talk her into leaving him," I say. "And staying *is* stupid."

"If you make her feel like she's dumb, then she won't have the confidence to walk away from him."

Callie isn't making sense. "Everyone knows Amarilis is super smart, so obviously she doesn't think of herself as dumb. Right?"

"Amarilis is brilliant," Callie says. "But she's feeling insecure right now, and it's up to us to boost her up."

I turn away from Callie and look out the window. A giant billboard shows a smiling city council candidate, and a man stands in the middle of the street trying to sell something from a box to any car that gets stuck at the light. Everywhere I look, I see the hurt look on my sister's face when I yelled at her. Did I really make things worse?

—«‹‹◆››»—

Olivia is at Zoe's house when I get back. "Is everything okay?" she asks.

I shake my head.

My friends huddle close with their arms around me. "We're here for you," Zoe says.

"Always," Olivia says. "Things seem bad now, but they'll get better, and we'll help if you want."

"Thanks, guys," I say. "But let's talk about something else. I don't want to look sad when my dad gets here."

"Okay, let me see . . ." Olivia rubs her chin and looks at the sky. "Oh, I forgot to show you! Zoe told me your science project should start with a short lesson on dog anatomy, so . . ." She taps her phone a few times, then turns the screen toward me. "Ta-da!"

160

It's a drawing of a see-through dog, and all its bones are labeled.

"Wow, that's cool." I take the phone and examine the drawing. "But I haven't written anything yet."

"Don't worry about that," Zoe says. "I'll write everything out for you on index cards so all you have to do is read it. You've got a lot on your mind right now."

"You shouldn't do my project for me," I say. "You have your own work."

Olivia puts a hand on her hip and tilts her head to the side. "Please, you know you'd do the same for us. You already have."

She's not wrong. Last year when Olivia and I were assigned to work on a Civil War project together, I did the whole thing by myself because her new baby brother wouldn't stop crying all night every night, and poor Olivia was exhausted. Schoolwork is fun for Zoe, so she would never want help with that. But in fourth grade before her parents got divorced, Zoe couldn't stand to listen to them argue all the time. She stayed at my house for a week and I let her have my bed while I slept in a sleeping bag on the floor, because that's what she needed. And now I need an A in science so I can have Freckles. I guess it's my turn to be helped.

"Okay, thanks. You're the best," I say.

-《《《◆》》》-

"How do you feel?" Papi asks when I get in the car.

"Tired. I'm going straight to bed when we get home." I have a lot to think about, and I need time alone.

"Good idea. Get some rest. We have a big day on Sunday."

He drums his fingers on the steering wheel and hums along to the radio.

Should I tell him about Amarilis in the ER? Will he believe me if I do? Will Amarilis never speak to me again? Even if Papi does believe me, what can he do about it? He thinks everyone should always follow the rules, so maybe he would call the police, but maybe not. I mean, why would he trust them? If it's Amarilis's word against Rich's, would the police even listen to her? My sister needs serious help, and I want to scoop her up and make everything better, but I don't know how.

Chapter 28

I GO TO GINA'S HOUSE AT MY usual time on Saturday morning, even though I spent most of the night tossing and turning. My eyes tear up when Freckles runs over and licks my face, his little tail wagging happily. Finally, something is going right. Freckles loves me and trusts me. He will be fine. But what about my sister?

"Isn't he doing great?" Gina says. "Let's take him for a walk today."

"Really, you think he'll come?"

"Truth be told, he'd follow you anywhere!" Gina says with a laugh. She reaches for a leash and hands it to me.

"Come, Freckles." I hold the leash toward him, but before I can clip it onto his collar, he whimpers and runs under the coffee table.

"Hmm," Gina says. "I'll take the leash, and you carry him to the nature trail, okay? Hopefully, when he sees Pepper on a leash, he'll realize no one will hurt him with it."

So that's what we do. I turn to Gina at the start of the trail. "Should we put the leash on him now?"

"Nah, let him walk beside us. I'd hate to traumatize him on his first trip here."

"But . . ." I think of Rory, and I clutch Freckles tightly. "What if he runs away?"

"I don't think that will happen. He's pretty attached to us now."

Maybe she's right, but . . .

"Gina, I have a confession," I say quickly. She squints and gives me a confused look. I have to get this out before I lose the nerve. "Remember when Rory got away? There wasn't anything wrong with the leash and I didn't mess up clipping it on. I took it off. On purpose."

"Why?"

"I wanted him to follow me, the way the dogs always follow you, so I"—I put my forehead on Freckles's back—"I took it off," I say. When I look at Gina, she has a slight smile on her face. "I'm so sorry. And I'm sorry I lied about it."

"Don't worry about it." Gina puts Pepper down and wraps her arms around me. "Rory didn't get hurt, and we all make mistakes, right?"

"I guess. But now I'm worried the same thing could happen with Freckles."

"There aren't any cars here, and we know Freckles and he knows us. Rory was brand-new to my home back then. Believe me, I see how Freckles looks at you. We have nothing to worry about."

I lower Freckles to the ground slowly. He had already started to squirm, and he jumps out of my arms happily. Then he stands by my feet and watches me with his little head craned all the way back.

"See?" Gina says. "He's waiting to see where you go, what you do, so he can follow." We start to walk, and Gina was right. Freckles sometimes runs ahead a little and sniffs some bushes, but then he joins us again each time. I relax, sort of.

"Gina, do you have brothers or sisters?" Maybe she can help me figure out what to do with Amarilis.

She nods. "I have two of each."

"Do they live far away?" I've never seen any family come to their house.

"Nope, they're about ten minutes away, where we all grew up."

"That's nice! You must go see them a lot."

Gina shakes her head. "They stopped talking to me when Mabel and I got together a few years ago."

"Why?!" Even when I'm super mad at Amarilis—like now—I know she'll always be a part of my life. At least I assume that. But what if I'm wrong? If other families stop talking forever, maybe that could happen in mine too. I gulp just thinking about it.

"Well . . ." Gina pulls a plastic bag out of her pocket and bends to pick up Pepper's waste. "They didn't approve of my—quote, unquote—'new lifestyle.'" She ties up the bag and keeps walking on the trail. "I was married to a man for eight years, and my family wanted to see me spend my life with a man."

"Oh," I say.

"I should have left him much sooner." She closes her eyes for a second and grimaces. "I finally walked out forever when he broke my jaw."

I gasp. "He . . . did what?"

165

"He was very abusive," Gina says, "and every time I ran away from him, my mother said it must have been my fault, that I should be a better wife to him."

"Wow, I'm so sorry."

"Thanks, but that's all behind me now. I'm really happy and doing great." Gina smiles a little too big, then speeds up to follow Freckles, who is sniffing away along the path.

Poor Gina. She wanted to leave that horrible guy, but no one would help her. "Gina?"

"Yes?"

"What if he hadn't broken your jaw? Do you think you'd still be with him?"

Gina shakes her head again. "Abusers don't stop. Even if he hadn't broken my jaw, he eventually would have done something else unbearable, and I would have decided it was enough."

When Amarilis said she and Rich were going through a rough patch and everything would be okay, I wanted to believe her, even though that didn't sound right. Now I'm sure it's not true. Unfortunately, Amarilis doesn't seem to know that.

We walk in silence for a little while. "Gina?"

"Yes?"

"Why did your mother like your husband so much?"

Gina shrugs. "I think she was scared about having a daughter like me, and she thought I would never get married, so when I brought him home, she was thrilled to pieces. Truth be told, I only married him to make her happy. I thought I could learn to love him."

Life sure can be complicated. I always feel sorry for myself because I don't have a mother, but at least I know my mother

166

would love me no matter what if she were around. Well, that's what Papi says, and I believe him. Gina's mom sounds horrible.

"My siblings were in favor of me leaving him, so they were supportive about that," Gina says. "They turned on me when I told them about Mabel."

"Wow, that's kind of messed up, huh?"

Gina chuckles sadly. "It's very messed up. And then . . ." she says tentatively, "there's the whole race thing too."

Of course. "Why does race always have to be a thing?" I say. "You and Miss Mabel are perfect for each other! It doesn't matter that you don't have the same skin color."

Gina squeezes my shoulder gently. "That's the truth."

We wait for Freckles to settle on a spot he's circling around. When he finishes pooping, I scoop it up in a bag. Gina and I keep walking as the dogs run ahead and pee on all the same bushes and fallen twigs.

"How did you and Miss Mabel meet?" I ask.

"Actually, we were good friends in college. My husband slowly convinced me to stop calling my friends, so we grew apart. Then I saw her again in the ER. She treated me the night of the broken jaw, and she gave me the phone number of a hotline for victims of domestic violence." Gina picks up Pepper, who is standing on her hind legs batting at Gina's knees. "Mabel saved my life."

"Do you spend time with Miss Mabel's family?" I ask.

"Not really. She's an only child, and her parents live in Georgia. We visit once a year, but she gets annoyed because they keep trying to set her up with single men from their church." Gina shrugs. "They didn't even come to our wedding."

"So . . . the two of you are all alone here?"

167

Gina gives me a sad smile. "We're fortunate to have a number of very dear friends. But Mabel's the only family I've got."

"Well, you have us," I say. "We can be your family next door."

Gina smiles for real this time. "That's very sweet. I think we'd like that. I think we'd like it a lot."

Chapter 29

B Y THE TIME I GET HOME, I'm more confused than ever. I don't
want Amarilis to end up like Gina, not talking to the family
and feeling like she can't trust us to help and support her. But I
have to admit I'm kind of mad at my sister. Callie and I drove all
that way to save her, and she brushed us aside. Is this how Abuela
feels when she yells at Tía Felicia? Is this what it's like to have a
sister who's a mess?

But that isn't the real Amarilis. My sister always has everything in order. She takes care of herself and everyone else too.
Jacinto and I go to her for advice and support, and she's there for
us. At least, that's how it used to be. And how it should be, right?
After all, she's our big sister.

I turn on the computer and pull up the video of my first day
of life. There's my mother looking at me and saying she loves
me, and there I am, staring at her like I'm trying to soak her in.
When a pair of arms on the screen reach in to take the bundle of
me from my mother, I'm ready to stop the video like I always do
at that point. But for some reason I don't.

"Mami! Mami!" A small Amarilis runs in and wraps her skinny arms around my mother's neck.

"Ven, mi amor." My mother helps Amarilis onto the bed. "You too, Jacinto."

My brother climbs up beside my mother and rests his head on her belly. "Where's the baby?" With his chubby cheeks and big eyes, he looks like a baby himself.

"She's over there with Papi." My mother points outside of the camera's range.

"Is she coming home with us?" Jacinto asks.

Mami laughs. "Yes, of course."

Amarilis cups Mami's face in her little hands. "You look tired, Mami. Are you okay?"

"I'm a little tired, mamita." She puts an arm around each of them, and they cling to her like ivy on a sturdy building. "I just need some sleep." She closes her eyes for a second.

"Hey!" Amarilis jumps up, her eyes twinkling with excitement. "I have a great idea! Let's go home and you take a nap. Don't worry about Miosotis. I'll take care of her."

Mami smiles. "You're a good big sister."

"And I'm a good big brother, and a good little brother too!"

"You certainly are, papito. And I'm sure Miosotis will be a wonderful little sister. I want the three of you to always be there for one another."

Amarilis and Jacinto nod. "I promise. Cross my heart." My sister makes an X across her chest.

"Me too." Jacinto copies Amarilis.

Mami squeezes them and smiles real big. "We're so lucky to have a great family." Then she takes a deep breath and her

170

arms drop away from Amarilis and Jacinto.

"Corazón, are you okay?" Papi's voice says. Then the video ends.

I stare at the blank screen for a few seconds before turning it off. I've always been jealous of Amarilis and Jacinto because they got a chance to know our mother and I didn't. But they look so tiny and helpless on that screen, with their shiny eyes and excited voices. What was it like for them to have a mother to hold on to and love every day, and then, suddenly, she's gone? I pity myself because I never knew her, but they're the ones I should feel sorry for.

And my mother was right to say the three of us should help one another. Amarilis has always been there for me. Just because she's the oldest, that doesn't mean she never needs help. We're a team, and it's about time I pull my weight.

I call Callie before going down for lunch. "You said you did some research to help Amarilis," I say. "I want to read what you found."

"Oh, kiddo," Callie says. "Those articles are too grown-up for you."

"I'm twelve! And I need to help my sister!"

"All right, all right. I'll look for them and send you the links, okay?"

"Thanks, Callie." I'm a little relieved as I hang up. I need to know what I'm doing, and this is a start.

Downstairs, Papi is using his speakerphone voice to yell into the receiver. "Amarilis? ¿Cómo estás, mija?" He walks to the door saying, "Um-hm, um-hm," then opens it and steps onto the porch.

Is Amarilis telling Papi about Rich? Probably not, because he seems pretty calm. I walk into the kitchen, where Abuela is frying some burgers. "What's going on with Amarilis?"

"Your father called to remind her about your mother's birthday party tomorrow." Abuela slips the spatula under each burger and places them on a giant plate.

I stand by the door, which Papi left ajar. "Yes, he's certainly welcome to join us," Papi says. "Should we pick you up?"

"Is she coming?" Abuela whisper-shouts, startling me.

I walk back to the kitchen. "Yes, but she's bringing Rich with her."

"¡Fantástico! After all, he'll be part of the family soon." Abuela hums as she scoops mashed potatoes out of a deep pot and into a glass bowl.

I reach in the cupboard for the plates. Should I tell her about Rich? What would she say? I set the plates on the counter and open the silverware drawer. "Um . . ."

"Did you say something?" Abuela turns her head and looks at me. Her straightened hair is in a bun and the makeup on her face is a shade lighter than her neck.

I shake my head. Abuela probably couldn't help me get Amarilis away from Rich, even if she wanted to, which maybe she wouldn't. She might make excuses for Rich, the way Gina's mom did for her husband, and I don't want to hear them. I take the dishes and utensils to the table.

"That's too many plates, mi amor!" Abuela says. She puts the napkins on the table and goes to the bottom of the stairs to call for Jacinto.

I look at the table and see I set a place for Amarilis too.

We all wear my mother's favorite color the next day. "She loved this," Papi says about his skinny yellow tie, which looks bright against his white shirt and tan suit. Abuela has on a yellow dress under her black shawl, and she ironed a yellow polo shirt for Jacinto.

I'm wearing a hand-me-down dress from Amarilis, with a pleated skirt and big yellow polka dots on a white background. The wide patent leather belt belonged to my mother and matches the polka dots perfectly. Amarilis wore this dress to her sixth-grade dance. I was thrilled when she gave it to me last year. I thought wearing the belt and dress my mother and sister once wore would make me feel closer to them. But I don't feel close to Amarilis right now. I don't understand her and I don't know how to reach her.

I also wonder if my sister will even show up. What will she say when Papi and Abuela and Jacinto ask about the stitches on her face? Will they believe Rich's ridiculous story about her having an accident? When she spoke with Papi yesterday, Amarilis told him she and Rich would be here before ten. Then we'll all go to 10:30 Mass before walking to the cemetery. It is 9:40 now and still no Amarilis. Papi is freaking out.

"Jacinto, call your sister to see if they're on their way." Papi paces back and forth in the living room.

"Calm down," Jacinto says as his thumbs glide across his phone. "I'll text her, but you know it only takes ten minutes to get to church."

I go into the kitchen where Abuela is slicing rolls. "Do you need help?"

"Gracias, mi amor," Abuela says. "Put four pieces of salami on each sandwich, please." She opens the pantry and takes out a box of plastic baggies. "Your mother loved salami sandwiches. Did I ever tell you about our trips to Brighton Beach when we lived in New York?"

I don't want to hear about how my mother looked like Amarilis in her bathing suit or loved playing in the sand like Jacinto. "Let's hurry and finish these sandwiches," I say.

Abuela cuts each sandwich in half and puts them in the baggies. "We would pack salami sandwiches and a big thermos of icy lemonade. It took us over an hour to get there on the subway, but it was worth it." Abuela slides her fingers back and forth across the seal of the last baggie. "Corazón always made sure I got a seat on the train, even if it meant elbowing someone out of the way." She laughs, then pulls the cooler out of the pantry. "She was a tough cookie, like you."

I smile. "Did Abuelo go with you?" I hand the sandwiches to Abuela.

"No, he was always at work when we went." Abuela piles the sandwiches into the cooler. "He never liked the beach, since he would get as red as a lobster." She chuckles. "Corazón liked to tease him and ask how he could have grown up on a tropical island and be allergic to the sun." Abuela snaps the cooler shut. "She was such a joker, always laughing."

"Did she swim?" I've never heard about these beach trips before.

"No, but she loved to play in the water. When I kissed her goodnight after a day at the beach, she said she felt like she was still riding on the waves, being rocked like a baby. She always

174

slept well those nights." Abuela pulls the big thermos out of the pantry and rinses it out with hot water. "Sometimes when it snows and I take you sledding on that hill at the college, I think of your mother."

"Why?"

"The way you laugh when you come down the hill, how your cheeks light up when you drink the hot cider we bring with us. It all reminds me of her at the beach." Abuela looks at me as I hand her the lemonade mix. "It's good to remember the joy she brought to my life, and being with you reminds me of that." She scoops the mix into the thermos and hums as she stirs it with water and ice.

"Let's go to Ocean City one day this summer," I say. "It's not far. We can do it in a day."

Abuela reaches over and squeezes my arm. "Why didn't I ever think of that? Yes, let's do it!"

Chapter 30

AMARILIS AND RICH ARRIVE AT 10:01, in time to stop Papi from having a heart attack. Amarilis has a square Band-Aid covering most of her cheek and sparkly blue eyeshadow around her eyes. Rich hands a giant bouquet of yellow roses to Abuela. "For the grave," he says.

"¡Ay, gracias!" Abuela hugs him tightly.

"Also, I'm very sorry for your loss," he says.

Amarilis looks at me with wide eyes. Jacinto and Abuela give Rich a confused look. Hopefully, they'll think Rich means my mother, but Amarilis and I know Rich is talking about the fake death Callie made up the other day.

"Let's go," I say. "Papi's already in the car." Which is true. He grabbed the cooler and thermos and ran to the SUV as soon as Amarilis and Rich pulled up.

Papi is tapping his fingers on the steering wheel as we all climb in. "Is everybody's seat belt fastened?" he calls out, looking in the rearview mirror. He turns around and frowns at Amarilis. "What happened there?" He points to the Band-Aid.

Amarilis brings her hand to her cheek. "I have a huge zit."

"Hmm." Papi turns back to face the road and starts the car.

From where I'm sitting right behind her, I can see Amarilis hasn't put her hand down, and she's looking at her lap. Rich reaches over and takes her other hand, then smiles at her like he's the nicest person in the world. He doesn't even feel guilty about hurting her or about being the reason why she's lying to Papi. Jacinto is next to me with his eyes closed, listening to music through his earbuds, completely unaware of Amarilis's pain. And what about Papi? Does he suspect anything? Maybe, like Abuela, he's filled with happy thoughts about my mother. Am I the only one who can help Amarilis?

We get to church fifteen minutes early and park near the entrance to the cemetery, then head across the street for Mass. As always, Abuela makes us sit near the front so she can hear when my mother's name is mentioned during the petitions. We could have heard from the back row too. It's a good thing I'm behind a super tall man so the priest doesn't see me fidgeting with the missal and glancing over at Amarilis. She's three seats away, with Papi and Jacinto in between us. Repulsive Rich is at the end with his arm around her like he's afraid she'll fly away.

After Mass, we go to the car and get everything out of the back. Papi pulls out the two folding chairs he and Abuela have sat in to watch our soccer matches and baseball games for as long as I can remember. He loops the frayed straps over his left shoulder, then reaches back into the car for the giant heart-shaped wreath he picked up from the florist last night.

"I'll help with that, Dr. Flores." Rich takes the chairs from Papi and grabs the thermos.

"Thank you, Richard." Papi hands the wreath and the sandwich cooler to Jacinto and gives me the picnic blanket. Abuela places the yellow rose bouquet in Amarilis's arms like it's a delicate baby, and Papi takes the one with amaryllis, hyacinth, and forget-me-nots in it. Then Abuela gets out a box of potted African violets for Abuelo.

"What a beautiful day," she says as we follow the brick pathway to our family's plot.

Papi lifts his face toward the sun and closes his eyes for a second. "It's perfect."

After we unfold the blanket and chairs, Abuela wipes the tombstones with a towel. She and Papi arrange the flowers, then sit to admire their work. "You know what I was thinking about today, Oscar?" Abuela says as I hand her a sandwich. "Remember how Corazón loved movies?"

"How could I forget?" Papi laughs and turns to Rich. "She was my English tutor when I first arrived as an international student at Penn. She recommended I watch movies to practice, so I took that as a hint to ask her out on a date." Papi takes a bite of his sandwich and looks at my mother's engraved name with a smile on his face.

"Was that your first date?" Rich asks.

"Um-hm." Papi swallows and gulps a swig of lemonade. "We saw *Ghostbusters*, which was her favorite movie. She had already watched it several times, and was excited to see that the student union was running it again." He points his sandwich at me. "You should see that film; it's funny and silly but also a little scary, like those movies you like."

"She liked scary movies?" I kneel on the picnic blanket and inch a little closer to Papi.

"¡Ay, sí!" Abuela says. "She would laugh and make fun of the characters and the foolish choices they made."

Papi nods. "You two would have had a blast watching those *Sharknado* movies together."

"So that's where you get your obsession with goofy movies!" Jacinto says. "I guess you weren't dropped on our doorstep after all."

I stick my tongue out at him, but I can't help but smile. Papi and Abuela tell some more stories about my mother, and I don't interrupt or change the subject. Even the ones about her being like Amarilis or Jacinto are okay. I mean, she's a part of all of us, right?

Soon we finish the sandwiches and lemonade, but we're not ready to leave yet.

"Is there a bathroom nearby?" Rich stands.

"Yeah, it's near the church entrance, on the first floor." Jacinto stands too. "I'll show you."

After Rich and Jacinto walk away, Papi and Abuela talk about Abuelo. They're great stories, and I want to hear them again, but I need to talk to Amarilis. I don't know when I'll get another chance without Rich around, so I ask her to walk with me.

Amarilis links her arm with mine as we follow the path toward the parking lot. "I hope you're not mad about what happened in my dorm the other day."

I'm not holding onto Amarilis like I usually would. Maybe I *am* mad, but I don't want to be. "I'm more sad than mad," I say slowly.

"Sad? Why?"

"I'm worried about you, Amarilis. You shouldn't be with Rich. He's no good for you."

We stop at our car and lean against it. "Rich really is sweet, once you get to know him," Amarilis says. "I know it looks bad when he gets angry, and I've thought of breaking up with him a few times because of it. But then he apologizes, and I know he means it, and I do love him."

"But why? What do you love about him?"

"Well, he's cute and smart and friendly and funny. When I first met him, you wouldn't believe how many girls at school were chasing after him. And he chose *me*!" Amarilis looks at me like she thinks I'll understand, like she thinks this all makes sense. But it doesn't.

"Does he love you?"

My sister bites her lip. "I . . . think so." She doesn't say anything for a little while. "He's under a lot of pressure. His professors are really unfair to him, and he needs me to be there for him."

"But . . . I know I'm just a kid, and I've never been in love or anything, but I don't think people are supposed to hit people they love. And you shouldn't put up with it."

My sister's eyes fill with tears. "What if this is all my fault?" she says. "What if I'm the one making him act this way? Maybe I'm not good enough for him . . . or for anyone."

My eyes are about to pop out of my face. "Are you kidding me? You're awesome! You're smart and sweet and beautiful and talented at everything you do. You're way too good for him!"

"You didn't think so the other day when you called me dumb and said you were ashamed to be my sister."

"Ay, Amarilis, I'm sorry I said that. You know I didn't mean it. I was mad because I'm scared about Rich hurting you again, and I don't understand why you're not scared too."

"I know he's a great guy," Amarilis says. "You should trust that I know what I'm doing."

I don't say anything. I have always trusted my sister, and she's usually right about things. But I'll never believe it's right for her to stay with someone who would hit her. So what can I say?

"Abuela sees how wonderful Rich is," Amarilis says.

"Abuela doesn't know everything about him." I don't actually know if it would make a difference if she did. After all, Gina's mom didn't stop liking Gina's husband when she found out he was an abuser. "Besides, it doesn't matter what Abuela thinks. What matters is that this isn't right and you need to get away from Rich. When Papi finds out, he'll make you cancel your wedding."

"Papi can never find out! Promise me you won't tell him, promise me!"

"Are you ladies running away?" Rotten Rich is walking toward us with Jacinto beside him. "What's wrong, baby? Have you been crying?"

"Thinking about my mom," Amarilis says. She reaches for me and squeezes my hand.

I want to cry too. Even though she's right here, I still feel like my sister is miles away.

Chapter 31

"**W**E NEED TO GET BACK TO school," Amarilis says as we pack up the car at the cemetery.

"What?" Abuela says. "I thought you were coming back to the house with us! I'm making bacalao for dinner."

Amarilis laughs. "I love your codfish, Abuela, but we've been eating all afternoon. I'm stuffed! Plus, finals are coming up and we have to study."

I give my sister a tight hug in front of Rich's car and watch as she gets inside. At least she'll be home in two weeks, after she's done with exams. I'll talk some sense into her then.

As soon as we get home, I head for the stairs. "I'm going to change," I say. "Gina's expecting me."

"Now?" Abuela says. "Doesn't she know you're busy today?" She looks at Papi for support.

Papi raises an eyebrow. "If Miosotis made a commitment, she should keep it."

Freckles yips and jumps when I walk into Gina's house. He scratches my knees a few times, but it's not his fault that his little nails are too long. "That's one happy boy!" Gina says with a laugh.

I get on the floor and rub his belly when he rolls onto his back. My teeth unclench and my shoulders relax for the first time all day. Being with Freckles always feels so easy. Without saying a word, he helps me feel calm and understood. Why can't it feel this good to hang out with people? Even Zoe and Olivia stress me out sometimes, like with this whole science project thing. And now Amarilis . . . But I don't want to think about any of that now.

Freckles closes his eyes and scoots a little closer to me. I can't believe this is the same dog who growled and nipped at me under the table less than two months ago. And I helped him get comfortable by being there for him and being patient. Is this what I need to do for Amarilis? Will that really work?

"Pepper found a forever home." Gina holds Pepper close and kisses the top of her head. "I'll miss you, sweetheart," she says in a high-pitched voice. Pepper licks Gina's lips and chin, and Gina giggles.

"When is she leaving?" I ask.

"The day after tomorrow." Gina settles Pepper onto her lap and looks at me. "Happy Puppy asked me if Freckles is ready to be placed in a forever home."

I hold my breath and my shoulders tighten up again.

"We have a few applications from people who might be a good fit for him," Gina says. "But I know you've become attached to him, and he certainly loves you. I handed in your application and asked them to put you at the top of his list. Is that okay?"

"Yes! But . . . you know my dad said we can't adopt until after school is over, right?"

"When's that, about a month from now?"

"More like one and a half months," I say softly.

Gina shrugs. "Truth be told, he's not ready yet, so I said he still needs a little more work. I want to spend a few weeks getting him acclimated to new environments and different people so he won't be so fearful. By the time he's ready, you'll be almost done with school. I can hold onto him for an extra week or two, if necessary."

That's a relief. But should I tell her Papi won't let me have a dog until I get those As? If I don't get the grades, will Freckles miss out on another home that might be ready for him right away? And what about Abuela? Is Freckles hypoallergenic? I still don't know.

Freckles's eyes are half closed. He's really enjoying this belly rub. He definitely needs me, and I need him too. Freckles will be my dog, no matter what.

Gina has to prepare for the two new dogs she's getting next week, so she takes Pepper to the backyard and I go on a walk with Freckles. He even lets me put a harness on him. He flinches when he sees the leash, so I hold it close to me and crouch down to speak softly to him. "It's okay," I say. I put the leash on the floor between us and pet it. "See, it's a good leash, it won't hurt my sweet Freckles." Freckles sniffs at the leash and then at me. When I pick it back up, he watches, but he doesn't pull away. I snap the leash onto the harness and keep talking to him. "See, you're fine, Freckles. We're going to have a nice walk together now." And we do.

-⋘◆⋙-

When I get back home, I follow my family's voices into the dining room. Papi and Abuela are flipping through a bunch of photo albums and talking over each other to explain the pictures to Jacinto. "What's all this?" I ask.

"Old pictures of your mother," Abuela says. "I'm glad she insisted on printing out her photos. That's much better than looking at them on a computer."

I open one book and flip through the plastic-covered loose-leaf pages. Mami in a yellow bathing suit, holding a baby. Mami in a sunhat and gardening gloves, surrounded by flowering bushes. Mami on the couch with a small white dog on her lap. I have never seen these photos before. "Where have these been?" I ask.

Papi tilts his head and squints at me. "In the hall closet, like always. We take them out every year."

Oh, I remember now. I usually go to my room and read about dogs when they do this whole picture thing.

"Who's this baby?" Jacinto asks.

"Hmm." Papi leans forward and lifts his glasses up. "I believe that's Amarilis."

"No, it's Jacinto," Abuela says.

While they argue about it, I feel like I don't belong. We all know that baby isn't me. I reach for another book. It has a cross-stitched cover with the words *My Scrapbook* surrounded by small blue flowers. The first page has my newborn hospital photo and bracelet. I turn the page. The rest of the book is blank.

"That's the scrapbook your mother made for you," Papi says. "I should have continued filling it in. And there's Jacinto's." He picks up a book with the same three hyacinths that hang on

Jacinto's bedroom wall. "It ends with his kindergarten photo. Your mother wanted to add each year's birthday and school photos, plus report cards and that sort of thing."

I run my finger over the blue flowers on my book. My mother knew my name before I was even born, and she planned to celebrate all my special moments, and Amarilis's and Jacinto's too. I don't know why she was taken away from me before I could know her, but this wasn't her fault, and she was a great mom. If she wanted to have everything in one book for me so I wouldn't forget these occasions, then I want to help with that. "We still have this stuff somewhere, right?" I say. "Let's fill in the books ourselves."

Abuela clasps her hands together. "That's a wonderful idea! Now, where did we put all those things?"

While Papi and Abuela scramble to find photos, report cards, art projects, and doctors' notes showing our heights and weights over the years, I open one of the super old photo albums. "Do you know who this is?" I ask Jacinto.

He examines the discolored photo with frayed edges. "Yeah, that's Tía Felicia holding Mami as a baby." We go through all the pictures, and I watch my mother grow up. When Jacinto goes upstairs to study, I close the book, turn it over, and start again from the beginning.

Chapter 32

Zoe and Olivia have a lot of questions at school the next day. "How's your sister?" they ask.

I shake my bottle of apple juice and think about Amarilis. She made me promise not to tell Abuela, Papi, and Jacinto, but she didn't say anything about my friends. And I need some help. So I tell them. Everything.

"Wow," Olivia says. "Your poor sister. I hate that Rich." She punches the table.

"For sure," Zoe says, "this wedding can't happen."

"I know, but I can't stop it by myself, and I promised her I wouldn't tell the family. Should I break my promise?"

"Actually . . ." Zoe taps her chin and raises an eyebrow. "You didn't promise not to tell them about Rich. You only promised not to tell them you saw her in the hospital. I mean, she asked you to promise yesterday, but you didn't get a chance to answer, right?"

"Oh, please, Zoe, you're being lawyerly about this," Olivia says. "Amarilis doesn't want her to tell, and she needs to believe she can trust Miosotis." She looks at me. "She'll never trust you if you tell."

Olivia is right. But, technically, so is Zoe. Amarilis can't say I broke a promise I never even made. And if I save her life by telling, she'll get over the trust thing. Or will she? "Zoe has a good point, but so do you." I sigh. "I guess I'll think about this. Maybe I'll wait for her to come home from college and then decide."

"That's a good idea," Zoe says.

"Don't worry, everything will work out," Olivia says. "Amarilis will ditch that creep, you'll get an A in science, and then you'll have your very own dog, and life will be perfect!"

"Ugh, I was going to study for the science test this weekend, but I forgot." Now I won't get my dog, either.

"Do you want my flash cards?" Zoe asks. "The test isn't until Thursday, but I'm done with them."

"Honest?"

Zoe nods and hands me her stack of cards.

"You're the best, Zoe!"

-≪≪◆≫≫-

Miss Mabel is sitting on the couch with a crochet project when I go next door in the afternoon. "Are you off today?" I ask.

"No, just relaxing before I leave in a few hours."

"I'm taking Pepper in for one last shot," Gina says. "We want to give her new owners a clean bill of health from the vet when they pick her up tomorrow. You'll walk Freckles for me?"

"Of course!" I sit on the floor and Freckles snuggles beside me with his bottom pressed against my thigh.

"It doesn't look like that guy wants to go anywhere right now." Miss Mabel chuckles.

Gina smiles. "Whenever he's ready—no rush." She scoops up Pepper and strokes her little face. "Tomorrow's a big day for you, sweetheart." Her voice cracks a little before she clears her throat. "I'll be back, ladies." She turns to Freckles. "And gentleman."

After Gina shuts the door behind her, I look at Miss Mabel. "What are you making?"

"A washcloth. Nothing fancy." Miss Mabel's hand dances across the little square she's forming with the thin and shiny crochet hook. My own hand trembles over Freckles's ear. He lifts his head and gives me a short lick, then rests his nose on my knee and looks at me with encouraging eyes.

"Miss Mabel?" I say. "Gina told me about her husband, and how you saved her from him."

Miss Mabel puts the washcloth down. "Gina gives me too much credit. She saved herself."

"But you helped, right?"

"I was there for her, yes, letting her know she had someone in her corner at all times." Miss Mabel gazes out the window. "I suppose I did help, and I'm glad I stood beside her, especially since she had no one else. But Gina did the real work." She picks up the yarn and hook again.

"So Gina made her own decision to leave her husband?"

"Certainly."

"What if she had wanted to stay with him?" I ask. "How would you have gotten her away from him?"

Miss Mabel stops in the middle of a stitch and looks at me. "I wouldn't have. She's an adult and she's in charge of her own life. All I could do was let her know I loved and respected her."

Miss Mabel sounds like Callie, and this doesn't make sense.

"But what if she made the wrong decision?"

"What's right and what's wrong in someone else's life isn't for me to say." Miss Mabel puts the yarn and hook in a bag beside her, then folds her fingers together. "Is there something going on with you, sweetie? Do you want to talk?"

I look at Freckles, who is struggling to keep his eyes open. Amarilis didn't say anything about telling Miss Mabel. But why would she? She would never imagine I would tell her, and she probably wouldn't like it if I did. "You know the girl I told you about from the hospital?"

"The one whose boyfriend hit her?"

I nod. "I know her."

Miss Mabel gasps. "I'm so sorry, sweetie! No wonder you were upset that day."

"I want to help her, but I don't know how."

"I see," she says. "Well, like I said, you should let her know you care about her and will help in any way she wants."

"That's it?" I was hoping for better advice. "The thing is, she doesn't want my help."

"You can't force it," Miss Mabel says. "It's like that saying: If you give a man a fish, you feed him for a day, but if you teach him to fish, you feed him for a lifetime."

I stare at Miss Mabel. What the heck is she talking about?

"Let me put it another way. You could take your friend and literally yank her away from her abuser, and what have you done for her?"

I glance at Freckles. This must be a trick question. "I've made her safe," I say.

"But for how long?"

"If I keep her away from him, then forever!"

"And how will she feel about herself if you act like she's so weak you have to take care of her?"

"But sometimes we need people to take care of us, right?"

"Yes," Miss Mabel says. "And sometimes we don't. What if your dad did all your homework for you and said you couldn't do it yourself? What would that do to your self-confidence?"

"Um . . ." I hadn't thought of it that way.

"I guarantee you her separation from him won't be permanent if it's not her own doing," Miss Mabel says.

"But I don't know how to get her to make this decision on her own." This is feeling hopeless.

"I know, sweetie, this is tough. You have to strike a delicate balance."

I nod, but I feel even more confused now.

"Don't take this the wrong way, but you really should get an adult involved. Someone whom this girl knows and trusts, who has her best interests in mind. This is too big an issue for a child."

"I can't. I promised I wouldn't tell."

Miss Mabel sighs. "I understand, but if you want to keep her safe, she probably needs to talk to a professional, and a trusted adult can guide her in the right direction."

Freckles opens his eyes and stands, then stretches into a downward dog position.

"Thanks for your advice, Miss Mabel." I get up and head toward the leashes.

"We adults can surprise you," Miss Mabel says. "More often than not, we can be very helpful."

I give her a little smile before I walk out the door with Freckles. She might be right, but what if she's not? What if I tell someone, they can't help, and Amarilis finds out and is mad at me? Plus, if there's nothing anyone can do to talk Amarilis out of loving Rich, what's the point of telling my family?

I call Callie after dinner. "Did you send me those links about domestic violence yet?" I ask. "I didn't get them."

"I'm sorry, kiddo. I've been swamped with schoolwork, but here's a book you can get from the library to help you understand what Amarilis is going through."

I write down the information. "Have you seen Amarilis lately?" I ask.

"No, but I did talk to her."

That's good news. Rich has been trying to keep Callie and Amarilis away from each other, so maybe this means my sister isn't letting him boss her around anymore.

"She's studying for finals now," Callie says. "I'm hoping to spend more time with her after her school year ends."

"Has she said anything about Rich?" I ask.

"They're still together, if that's what you mean. But don't worry. We'll have all summer to work on her."

Callie has a point, and I feel a little better after talking to her. Still, I text Amarilis every night, hoping she'll tell me she broke up with Rich. All she says is that she's studying and will see me next week.

I can't concentrate on my homework. When I show it to Jacinto, he changes everything and goes on and on explaining

192

where I went wrong. I nod and say "uh-huh" a bunch of times. On Thursday I walk into science class and realize I never even took out Zoe's flash cards to study. And, just my luck, the test is super hard.

"I failed!" I say to Zoe and Olivia at lunch.

"Oh, please," Olivia says. "You know this stuff. Even I probably got most of the answers right."

I drop my forehead onto the sticky table. "I can't concentrate."

"Don't worry," Zoe says. "There's still one more test at the end of the year. Plus, the big project."

"Ugh, I haven't done any work on that either."

"Don't worry about the science project," Zoe says. "We've got this."

"Yeah, you focus on your sister and your other classes," Olivia says. "We'll get the presentation ready for you in about two weeks, right, Zoe?"

"For sure. And then you'll have a whole week to practice."

"It's due in three weeks?" I say. I didn't realize it was that soon. "Yep!"

I am so glad Zoe and Olivia are helping me.

Chapter 33

AMARILIS CALLS THE HOUSE ONE EVENING as we're finishing dinner. Papi puts the phone on speaker and places it in the middle of the table.

"¡Hola, mi amor!" Abuela yells into the phone.

"¡Hola, Abuela!" Amarilis sounds super cheerful. "I'm taking a study break, so I thought I'd check in on all of you."

Everyone starts to talk at once. Jacinto says he broke some record in track, Abuela asks what she ate today, and Papi wants to know if her studies are going well. Amarilis laughs. "One at a time, please!" Then she answers all their questions. "Is Miosotis there?" she says.

"Yep," I say. "Are you having dinner with us on Sunday?" Sunday is Mother's Day, and Abuela wants us all together, like every Mother's Day.

"Actually, I wanted to talk about that," Amarilis says. "I still have one more exam on Monday, so I'm kind of stressed. Could we go to a restaurant near here so I can get back to studying afterward?"

"Certainly!" Papi says. He suggests a place near campus, and Jacinto gets out his phone to make reservations.

I'm trying to picture my sister right now. She truly sounds happy. Maybe she was right about Rich, and everything will be fine. I mean, if he's in a good mood while studying for finals, then maybe that other stuff wasn't the real him. "How's Rich doing?" I ask.

Amarilis pauses for a second. "Good," she says. "He's at his parents' house. He has two big finals next week, so his dad wants to oversee his studying."

"That's probably for the best," Papi says. "You two won't distract each other this weekend."

"Yeah, that's what his dad said." Amarilis sighs. "Well, I'd better get back to work."

We say good night, and I feel a little better knowing my sister will be safe this weekend.

-«‹«◆»›»-

We drive into University City on Sunday for our nice Mother's Day dinner. Amarilis meets us at the restaurant, wearing a fresh Band-Aid on her cheek.

"What's that?" Abuela asks.

"Oh, it's the zit I've been covering up." Amarilis stares at her bread as she crumbles it between her fingers.

"Still?" Abuela says.

"Acne is natural at your age," Papi says. "You shouldn't feel like you have to hide it."

Amarilis shrugs. "I just don't like it."

Abuela pats her hand. "Listen, I understand. But don't worry, pimples will be in your past soon enough."

Amarilis hands Abuela her Mother's Day gift. My grand-mother loves the cross-stitched pillow. She hugs it and even cries a little. "It matches the other pillow on my bed. The one your mother made for me."

"I know." Amarilis holds Abuela's hand and they look at each other with moist eyes.

When Abuela tells the story of how my mother ruined a bunch of fabric while learning to sew and cross-stitch, we all laugh. Everything seems normal. Amarilis holds her stomach, throws her head back, and cracks up at one of Jacinto's silly jokes. She looks happy and relaxed. If she didn't have that Band-Aid on, I'd think I had imagined what happened in the hospital just a little over two weeks ago. Maybe Amarilis is right and this was a one-time thing. Maybe everything's going to be all right with her and Rich after all. Maybe? Hopefully.

-≪≪◆≫≫-

The following Tuesday, I'm relieved when Mr. Nesbitt tells us our second—and last—test of the quarter will be multiple choice. He passes out a list of the topics that will be covered, and it's not very long. This is good news because I got a C on that first test, so I need an A on the second one. I also have to ace my presentation. Zoe gives me the perfect notes she prepared for my project, and Olivia shows me her beautiful drawings for it, which she emails to me during lunch. I'm feeling like I can do this.

After school, the three of us walk to the Free Library to pick up the book Callie told me about. "I reserved a book last week," I tell the man at the front desk. "I got an email today saying it's in." I show him my library card.

The man tilts his head and gives me a sad look as he hands me the book. "Good luck with everything," he says.

"Thanks."

"Why did he look at you like you're pathetic or something?" Zoe says while we walk away.

"He probably thinks you're the one being abused," Olivia says. "Let's tell him that's not true."

I kind of want to. But why? Would I be ashamed to have a boyfriend who hits me? Is Amarilis embarrassed about that? Do I think she should be? If I do, I won't be much help to her. "No, we don't have to tell that man anything," I say. I hold up my head and open the library door.

When I walk out of Gina's house that afternoon, Papi is pulling into the driveway with Amarilis in the passenger seat. The SUV is overflowing with all the stuff that had been in her dorm room. I wait for them to get out. "Amarilis!" I hug her. She's wearing short sleeves, and she hugs me back super tight. She has a fresh Band-Aid on her cheek but no new cuts or bruises that I can see, and a big smile on her face. "I'm glad you're home."

"Me too, mamita."

Amarilis is super chatty at dinner. "Rich and I put a hold on looking at wedding venues because we were so busy with school. But we have two appointments this week and another one next week. Then we'll be ready to make a decision and pick a date!"

Abuela giggles with her, and Papi and Jacinto ask a bunch of questions about what she wants and how much each place costs and how far they are from our house and how many people they

197

accommodate and on and on and on. Amarilis's arms fly around as she describes the spectacular views from one place, the magnificent chandeliers at another place, and the cozy wood-paneled walls somewhere else. Jacinto's voice climbs excitedly when he answers her questions about flowers, Abuela's eyes twinkle as she gives Amarilis advice on the menu, and Papi smiles and smiles. I feel like I'm watching a movie, and I can't jump through the screen to join them.

Amarilis is still hyper and smiley in our room after dinner. "You're being awfully quiet, mamita," she says. "Is everything okay?"

"Not really. I'm worried about Rich hurting you."

"Shh." Amarilis rushes to close the door. "I told you, everything's fine. Don't you trust me?"

I think about what Miss Mabel said and how I don't want my sister to feel like she can't make good decisions for herself. I definitely don't want to give her the look the library man gave me. I nod slowly. "Yes."

"Good. Now, stop worrying, and tell me about you. How's your science grade? Are you on track to get your dog?"

Amarilis looks happy. And healthy. She knows what she's doing, right? I breathe out. "My grades are pretty good so far. I got one bad grade in science, but I can still get that A as long as I ace the last test and do a great job on my science in the news project."

"Great!" Amarilis claps. "What's your project about?"

I show her Zoe's notes and Olivia's drawings. We spend the rest of the evening unpacking her things and talking about dogs and my project.

"This weekend you should do a dry run of your presentation so I can give you pointers, okay?"

That's a good idea. I feel like I have my sister back.

Chapter 34

On Friday afternoon, Gina and I gather up the dogs and take them to the nature trail. Freckles won't leave my side, so Gina is in charge of her two new dogs: a big fluffy guy named Lucky who was found dodging traffic in the middle of South Philadelphia, and a one-eyed schnauzer named Bella who was shipped here from North Carolina. All three dogs are fascinated by one spot underneath a prickly bush.

When the dogs step away from the bush with a bunch of burrs stuck to their faces, Gina and I laugh and try to pluck them off. "Ouch!" I use my T-shirt to remove the burrs from Freckles, but I can't get them all.

"Let's keep going," Gina says. "We'll snip them off with scissors when we get back." She wiggles a finger at Freckles. "Look at that messy face! That's a very cute messy face you have there, mister!" She straightens up and smiles at me. "Are you sure you want this troublesome young lad?"

"I'm very sure!" I grab Freckles and give him a kiss on a burr-free spot. "He's perfect!"

"If you say so, but you still have a chance to back out," Gina says teasingly.

"Hah, never!" Freckles jumps up and licks my ear.

When I get back home, Amarilis is on the couch next to Rich. They're holding hands and laughing.

"Hey there, little sis!" Rich stands and opens his arms out to me.

"I need to wash up." I run upstairs and into the bathroom.

I guess Rich is staying for dinner. And the two of them will go on and on about the wedding venues they've seen this week. And my family will happily talk about this marriage without knowing what he did to her. Can I sit there and smile with them? Amarilis has seemed so happy and normal the past few days that I had decided she was right about Rich. I was going to pretend that day at the hospital never happened. But now, seeing him, I can't do that.

"Are you excited about starting your accounting internship on Monday?" Papi asks Amarilis at dinner.

"Absolutely. It's a great firm, and the people seem really nice!"

"And where are you working this summer, Richard?"

"Ugh, nowhere." Rich sits back. "My dad messed up and didn't get me that internship I wanted."

Papi squints at Rich. "Your dad?"

"I need some suits for work," Amarilis says in a loud voice. "Can I go shopping with Emily tomorrow? Her summer job starts on Monday too."

Papi blinks and turns away from Rich. "Sure, take the credit card."

"I'll go with you too, babe," Rich says. "I'll help you pick something nice."

"Oh! Sure . . . great." Amarilis keeps her eyes on her plate.

Papi rubs his chin and watches the two of them for a few seconds. He looks around the table at Abuela, Jacinto, and me. Our eyes meet, and I look away.

When we're done eating, Rich pats his belly and turns to Abuela. "Thank you for yet another delicious meal!"

Abuela shoos away the compliment as she clears the table.

"Do you want to sit on the porch?" Amarilis asks Rich. "It's nice out tonight."

"Sure!" Rich stands and takes my sister's hand. "Will the rest of you join us?"

"You kids have fun," Papi says. "I have work to do; all grades must be submitted by tomorrow."

"It's my turn to help Abuela clean up the kitchen," Jacinto says.

"So, it's the three of us, huh, little sis?"

I shake my head. "I need to study for my social studies test."

"You're studying on a Friday night?!" Rich laughs.

"Yes. I am." I walk upstairs without looking back.

I reach into my backpack to get my social studies notebook, but instead I pull out the library book Callie had recommended. I open it and start to read.

It's late when Amarilis comes into our bedroom. I quickly shove the book back into my bag.

"You're still awake?"

"Yeah." I get up, open my dresser drawer, and pull out some pajamas.

"You weren't very nice to Rich tonight," Amarilis says.

I move my stuffed dogs and get my bed ready without a word.

"I've forgiven him for losing his temper, and you should too."

I look at my sister and think about what I just read in that book. Rich does a lot of things the book says are sure signs of an unhealthy relationship. If I point them out, maybe she'll realize how wrong he is for her. Then, like Miss Mabel said, Amarilis will feel good about breaking up with him forever because it will be her own decision. "Have you noticed," I say slowly, "how nothing is ever his fault?"

Amarilis's eyebrows crinkle close together. "What?"

"I mean, why does his dad have to get an internship for him? You got your own internship, right?"

"Yeah, but . . . his dad has connections and he promised to help him."

"And why should his teachers give him good grades if he doesn't earn them?"

Amarilis glares at me. "Why are you focusing on his faults? Nobody's perfect! You certainly aren't!" She storms out of our room and shuts herself in the bathroom.

-≪≪◆≫≫-

The next day, I try to forget how Amarilis didn't look at me before going to sleep; how she didn't blow me a kiss from her bed and say, "Buenas noches, mamita"; and how she turned her back to me and concentrated on her phone. Being with Freckles helps a lot. He whips his stubby tail like a windshield wiper on high as soon as I enter Gina's house.

"How are you, little Freckles boy?" I get on my knees and rub his neck.

"I'm so glad you want to adopt him," Gina says. "You two are a match made in heaven!" She snaps leashes onto Lucky and Bella, and hands me one for Freckles. "Also, remember that Happy Puppy always calls prospective adopters to go over the information on the application. In your case it's a formality, since I already know you, but remind your father they'll be calling him before your application is officially approved."

"Sure!"

I'm in a pretty good mood when I leave Gina's house. Then I see Amarilis and Rich get out of his car carrying three plastic suit bags by the hangers. Rich waves. "Hey there, little sis!"

I lift my hand a little.

When we get inside, Amarilis looks at her phone. "My grades have been posted!" She jumps up and down. "I got all As!"

Papi hugs her and says "Congratulations!"

"That calls for a celebration!" Rich says. "Let me take you out to dinner tonight."

Amarilis throws her arms around him.

"What about you, Richard?" Papi says. "Are you happy with your grades as well?"

Rich shrugs. "I didn't get them yet, but I will by the end of the day. My classes are a lot tougher than Amy's, so if I get all Bs and Cs, we'll both have good reason to celebrate."

After Rich goes home to get ready for dinner, I follow Amarilis into our room. That library book says it's important for your loved one to know she has your unconditional support. "I hope you have a nice time with Rich tonight," I say as she rummages through her clothes looking for something nice to wear.

Amarilis turns around and faces me. "Thanks, mamita." She

walks over and puts an arm around my shoulders. "I'm sorry I got mad last night. I know you're looking out for me, but please trust me. Rich is a wonderful guy and we're going to be very happy together."

I sigh. "Okay, if you say so."

"Look, if you didn't know about this one little thing"—she points at her Band-Aid—"you would think he's great, right? I mean, you liked him before, didn't you?"

I nod.

"Then think about the Rich from before. Because that's the real Rich. It's not fair to hold one mistake against him forever."

Maybe she's right. "I guess so," I say.

She smiles and gives me a hug.

-⋘◆⋙-

I'm about to go to bed when Amarilis gets home from her date with Rich. "How was dinner?" I ask. "Where'd you go? What'd you eat?"

"It was okay." Amarilis's voice is small. She sits on the edge of her bed and stares at her hands.

"Are you all right?" I sit next to her.

"Rich failed two classes, and he's really upset."

"Oh."

We sit in silence, and I feel my heart thumping. Finally, I ask, "Is he mad that you got all As?"

"No, no, no, absolutely not," Amarilis says. "We're fine. Everything's good with us."

I let out a breath. "So, what's he going to do?" I ask.

Amarilis shrugs and stands. "I guess we'll figure something

out." She pulls out a T-shirt and some pajama pants, and puts them on her bed. "I need to take off this makeup."

I stop her before she goes into the bathroom. "You know it's not your fault when Rich gets mad, right?"

Amarilis squeezes my hand. "I know. Thanks, mamita."

I try to stay awake in case my sister wants to talk when she comes back, but it's hard. I close my eyes and sink into my pillow. I guess I fall asleep right away, because I don't notice when she comes back into the room.

Chapter 35

I'M STARTLED AWAKE IN THE MIDDLE of the night. Amarilis is sitting up in bed, sobbing. She blows her nose and hiccups.

"What's wrong?" I ask.

"Huh?" She looks at me, surprised. "Nothing. Go back to sleep."

"It's not nothing. You're crying." I get out of bed and sit next to her. "What happened?"

My sister's shoulders slump. "Rich lost his temper again tonight."

"What do you mean? What did he do?"

"He just got mad, that's all." Amarilis looks away from me. "I need to . . . think this through."

The room is dim with just the night light on, but if my sister had any more cuts or bruises, I'd be able to see them. Luckily, I don't. "What about that hotline number they gave you in the hospital?" I say. "You should call them."

Amarilis opens the night table's bottom drawer and rummages through some notebooks and papers. Finally, she pulls out a business card and stares at it. "They're open twenty-four seven." She grabs her phone, jumps out of bed, and tiptoes out of the room and down the stairs.

-‹‹‹‹◆›››-

When I wake up Sunday morning, Amarilis is already dressed. "Good morning, mamita!" She hops onto my bed and holds her fist toward me. "See what was in the mailbox today!"

I stare at the gold-and-diamond bracelet sparkling around her wrist.

"And it had a note." Amarilis pulls an index card out of her pocket and unfolds it. She clears her throat. "'My dearest Amy. Congratulations on another perfect semester. With all my love, your biggest fan, Rich.'" She holds the note on her lap and smiles at me. "Isn't it beautiful?"

"So . . ." I sit up. "He's bribing you with jewelry?"

Amarilis rolls her eyes. "No, he's showing me he genuinely cares about me." She fiddles with the bracelet. "But I know what you mean. I had a long talk with the lady at the hotline last night, and she scheduled me for an appointment with a therapist on Friday. They're near work so I'll go during lunch." She gives me a hug. "Thanks for talking me into calling."

"You're welcome." I let out a breath and my shoulders relax. One or two meetings with the therapist is all my sister needs to realize Rich is bad news. She'll drop him like a prickly cactus and we'll never see him again.

-‹‹‹‹◆›››-

Our science presentations start the next day, and Zoe is up first. Of course, she's fabulous. "Did you notice how quiet the room was?" I say on our way to lunch. "The whole class was listening to you."

"I hope so!" Zoe is all fired up. "Because every little bit counts. Plastics are consuming our oceans! Hopefully, everyone took home ideas to work on this serious problem."

The thing I love about Zoe is that, even though she gets straight As, her grades aren't the most important thing to her. She gets those good grades because she cares about what she's learning. Olivia and I don't usually share her passion, but this project has Olivia excited too.

"I think I'm ready for my presentation tomorrow," she says. "But can I practice on the two of you now?"

We nod, and she sits up straight and talks about chemicals in lipstick. She doesn't even have to read her notes. I think about the notes Zoe wrote for my report on healing dog bones, and how I don't even remember what's in those notes. Should I have prepared something myself? I don't want to be like Rich, always expecting other people to do my work for me, but this is different, right?

My presentation is on Friday. I don't have time to write anything new, at least not if I want an A. I'll memorize Zoe's notes, get my A, and then Freckles will be mine.

-‹‹‹‹◆››››-

Olivia does her science presentation the next day, and it is awesome. I'm sure she's getting an A on it, which will be a first for her. Her slideshow looks like it was done by a professional artist, and it's obvious she did more than read the one article. She's learned so much about the way lipstick is made that she sounds like an expert when she explains it to the class.

I'm happy for her, but I'm a little worried about my project. I really need to study Zoe's cards when I get home. I should probably do extra research too.

⫷⫸

Amarilis hums and snaps her fingers when she walks in the door right before dinner. "That smells delicious, Abuela! I'll be right down after I change."

I follow her into our bedroom. "So, you had a good day again?"

"I did," she says. "My boss is nice, and the work is really interesting." She hangs up her suit jacket in the closet. "Plus, Rich and I saw our last wedding venue this evening."

"Oh," I say. "You're still planning the wedding?"

"Absolutely!" Amarilis unbuttons her shirt and slips her arms out of it. When she turns around to take a T-shirt from her dresser, I see two giant purple bruises on her back.

"What's that?!" I yell.

Amarilis throws on the T-shirt and runs over to me. "Shh! Papi and Abuela might hear!"

"What happened?"

"Remember when I told you Rich lost his temper after dinner the other night?" she whispers. "But don't worry, I've got it under control. Rich apologized and the therapist will help me figure out how to deal with him in the future."

"But—" My eyes start to tear. "Doesn't that hurt?"

"No, no, no, I'm absolutely fine." Amarilis wraps her arms around me. "Everything's going to be okay. I promise."

I open my mouth to say more but close it again. Amarilis

210

will change her mind about the wedding after she talks to her therapist on Friday. It's better if I let her make this decision on her own. But it's really hard.

Chapter 36

RICH IS ALL SMILEY WHEN HE comes over for dinner on Thursday. "My dad talked to the dean," he says, "and they're changing those two Fs to incompletes, which is only fair because those professors were so terrible I couldn't pass their classes."

"Did everybody fail?" Jacinto asks.

"Well, no . . ." Rich dabs the corners of his mouth with his napkin. "But, anyway, nobody graduates in just four years these days, and the professors teaching those classes next year are better, so I'll get good grades this time." He strokes Amarilis's hair. "Besides, now I'll get an extra year in school with my sweetie."

"Have you considered a tutor?" Papi asks.

"Yeah, I had a tutor last time, but he wasn't much help."

Amarilis puts her hand over Rich's. "I remember that guy. He would never answer your questions, right?"

Rich snorts. "He said I needed to figure things out myself. Then what I was paying *him* for?" He shakes his head. "The guy was useless."

Amarilis nods sympathetically.

Papi and Jacinto glance at each other with raised eyebrows. I have to admit I agree with them. Even if I didn't know how awful he is to Amarilis, I'd be thinking Rich is pretty pathetic.

-⫸⫷⟡⟩⟩⟩-

"Are you ready?" Zoe and Olivia surround me when I walk into science class on Friday.

"I think so." Zoe's cards are in my hands, and I'm ready to pull up Olivia's slides. I did a practice run at home, and Amarilis said it was great.

"Okay, settle down, class," Mr. Nesbitt says. "We have three science in the news presentations scheduled for today, starting with Mei McNamara."

As Mei drones on and on about bees and how they'll be extinct soon and why we can't live without them, I look at the script in my hands. These are Zoe's words, not mine. The pictures on my slide show are Olivia's. When Papi said he wanted me to get an A in science, is this what he meant? Did he want me to let other people do my work, or did he want me to learn? I've been studying hard and taking notes and doing all my reading for my other classes, and I'm understanding the work and getting better grades than ever before. I may not get all As, but I'm proud of the work I've done on my own, and I won't feel good if I get an A by presenting Zoe and Olivia's work.

When Mr. Nesbitt calls my name, I don't get up.

"Flores, are you ready with your presentation?"

What if I do my own project? Can I still get an A? Maybe, if I find something really interesting to me, like Olivia did.

"Flores?"

I look at him. "I'm sorry, but could I go next week? I still need a little more time."

"Well, yes," Mr. Nesbitt says. "But I'll have to deduct five points for each day your presentation is late."

That's going to make it harder to get an A. But not impossible. I can't breathe and my hands tremble as I clutch Zoe's notes. Her definitely-an-A notes. But they're also definitely not mine.

"Flores?"

I look at Mr. Nesbitt. "Can I go on Tuesday?"

Mr. Nesbitt looks at his clipboard. "Yes, that would work. I didn't schedule anyone else on Tuesday because of the Memorial Day weekend."

"So, that's just one day late, right?"

Mr. Nesbitt frowns. "Technically, yes."

"Okay, I'll be ready on Tuesday." I say it quickly before he decides to change the rules.

"All right. Next up is Robert Johnson."

-«««◆»»»-

"What happened? Did you get nervous?" Olivia runs up to me as soon as class ends.

"It's better if you get it over with," Zoe says.

I walk to my locker with the two of them on either side of me. I don't know what to say. They worked so hard, and they did it all for me. Their work shouldn't go to waste, but that's what's going to happen, unless . . .

"Look, I'm sorry." I turn the knob to my combination. "But this doesn't feel right. I mean, the two of you did all this work, and I didn't do anything. Maybe you could present it for extra credit or something."

"And what will you do?" Zoe doesn't need the extra credit. "How will you get your A now that your project will be late?"

"I'll look for another article." I place my science textbook in the locker and pull out my social studies one. "I'll work on it all weekend. I could still get an A in the class, right?"

"I don't understand," Zoe says. "Don't you like what we did?"

"I love what you did!" I close the locker and look at her. "It's just that it's not my work, it's yours. I don't want to be a cheater. I don't want to be like Rich."

"But what about your dog?" Olivia asks.

I look at her and try to blink back the tears. "I'll earn him fair and square."

Chapter 37

THAT AFTERNOON FRECKLES GOES WILD WHEN he sees me. He runs through Gina's living room, into the dining room, and back to the living room, then does the loop again two more times before ending up in my arms, licking me all over. "He's going to love living with you," Gina says. "Can you believe that's the same scared little guy we first met a couple months ago?"

I cannot. And now I can't believe I didn't present my science project today. What was I thinking? Can I really do a presentation as good as the one Zoe and Olivia prepared for me? I have to, for Freckles.

After I get back from Gina's house, I head straight to the computer to search for a good science article. I'm not sure what to look for. The last time I found articles about abused dogs, they were too upsetting. And, to be honest, Zoe's article about dogs with broken bones made me cringe. Maybe science isn't my thing, and I'll never find an interesting article.

I don't know what else to do, so I click to the video of the day I was born, and I watch the whole thing again. Like the baby me in the video, I look closely at my mother's face. Her cheeks are plump and her hair is thick and shiny. Papi and Abuela say she was a healthy person, that her death was a shock to everyone. How could something like this happen?

I click back to my browser and search *women dying in child-birth*. I find an article that says more women in the United States die from pregnancy-related problems than in any other developed country. That they're usually women of color, regardless of education or economic status. And other developed countries prevent those deaths by doing certain things. Scientific things.

I found my article.

—«««•»»»—

"May I look through the photo albums?" I ask Papi after dinner.

"Certainly. What are you looking for?" Papi opens the hall closet and gets on his tiptoes to reach the top shelf.

"Pictures of Mami." I hold out my arms while he hands me three thick books. "For my science project," I add. Then I bolt into my room and get to work.

It's pretty late when Amarilis comes upstairs. I've finished scanning all the photos I plan to use for my slide show, and I'm in my pajamas because Abuela made me get ready for bed a half hour ago. But I'm back on the computer now looking for more images to use, like pictures of hospital rooms, blood pressure monitoring cuffs, and hemorrhage carts. I only have three days to get this done, so I can't waste time on stuff like sleep.

Amarilis stands behind me and looks over my shoulder. "Is this your science project?"

"Um-hm."

"Do you need any help?"

I don't want her to do my work for me, but I do have some questions. "What exactly did Mami die of?" I ask.

My sister sighs. "I was about your age when Papi finally explained it to me." She sits and runs her fingers over the stitching on one of her pillows. "She had really high blood pressure. She told her doctor that happened with all of her pregnancies, but he said she shouldn't worry, that he knew what he was doing." Amarilis looks at me with tears in her eyes. "They didn't do anything to control her blood pressure after the birth, and she had a stroke. If they had listened to her, she'd be here with us right now."

My sister sniffles and I don't say anything at first. The day of my mother's fiftieth birthday celebration was the first time I really listened to stories about her. Before then, I would walk away or change the subject when my family would talk about her. I was always afraid they might look at me in the middle of their story and think, *This is all your fault.*

"Amarilis?"

"Yes?"

"Do you wish I had never been born?"

"What—no! Why would you ask that?"

"Because I'm the reason she died."

"No, you're not. It's her doctor's fault. Her blood pressure went up with all of us, and her first two doctors took better care of her. She could have died with me or Jacinto too, if she'd had a rotten doctor with us." Amarilis stands and grabs my shoulders. She looks me in the eye. "Nobody blames you for her death. Nobody."

I melt into my sister's arms.

Chapter 38

I WORK ON MY PRESENTATION ALL WEEKEND, only taking a break to eat and walk Freckles with Gina. My legs feel wobbly when I walk into science class Tuesday morning. What if I freeze and can't speak? What if Mr. Nesbitt thinks this is a terrible project? What if I get an awful grade? I already got a C on my first test; I can't afford to mess this up too. Ugh, maybe I should have gone ahead and used Zoe and Olivia's presentation.

"Miosotis Flores, you're up," Mr. Nesbitt says after we all settle down.

I stand and walk to the front of the room.

"My article is called 'Maternal Mortality in the United States.'" I suck in a breath and talk about the statistics in the article, the causes of maternal deaths, and the things our doctors and hospitals can do to prevent these deaths. My slides show medical equipment, cells enlarged through microscopes, and drawings of pregnant women.

When I finish talking about the scientific parts, I turn to the next slide, and I clear my throat and blink again and again.

"This is me with my mother," I say. "That's the day I was born, which is also the day she died." I show more photos of my mother: with Amarilis; with Jacinto; with her dog, Osito; with Papi; with Abuela and Abuelo. I tell my class how healthy she was, how well she took care of herself and her family, how this shouldn't have happened.

"Throughout the world, maternal mortality has been going down, but not here," I say. "The United States is the only developed nation where those numbers are rising. We know controlling high blood pressure early and measuring blood loss during delivery can save women's lives, but most hospitals in this country don't do those things. Also, all women aren't treated the same. For example, in New York City, a Black woman is twelve times more likely to die from a pregnancy-related illness than a Caucasian woman.

"Having the knowledge and the ability to prevent deaths isn't good enough," I say. "We need to actually do things, because otherwise, healthy women who are loved by their families and needed by their children just . . . disappear. Forever." I put down the clicker and say, "The end." Then I excuse myself and run to the bathroom to cry for my mother, for the first time ever.

After the bell rings, Olivia and Zoe meet me outside the bathroom. "Are you okay?" Olivia hands me my backpack and pats my shoulder.

I nod.

"That was fabulous," Zoe says. "Mr. Nesbitt will for sure give you an A, even if you were one day late."

I sigh. I'm satisfied with my project, whether or not I get that A. I learned a lot, about science and medicine, about our society, and about my mother and my family. I also learned that Miss Mabel was right: It feels good to take control and do my own schoolwork. It was nice of my friends to help me, but it's nicer that they—and I—know that I can prepare a good presentation by myself. I'll remember that the next time I have a challenging project to do.

—«««◆»»»—

That afternoon Gina has company. "This is Kristin, the director of Happy Puppy."

"It's nice to finally meet you, Miosotis. And to see Freckles again."

I say hello and squat to pet Freckles. "Is everything okay with him?"

"Yes, he's coming along very nicely."

Gina nods. "Did I tell you we took him to a barbecue this weekend?"

"Oh," Kristin says. "How did he do?"

"He was great! A little shy but very calm."

Kristin smiles at me. "This is great news for you. We always make sure a dog doesn't have aggressive tendencies if we're putting him in a house with children."

Freckles climbs onto my lap and rests his little face on my arm. "He's super gentle," I say. He did nip at me one time, but that was long ago so it doesn't count.

"He certainly seems comfortable with you." Kristin shuffles through a stack of papers in a folder. "So, I see you'll be ready to take him in about . . . three weeks?"

I nod.

"Well, then, I'd better call your parents soon." She leans forward and puts a hand on my shoulder. "Don't worry, your application has pretty much already been approved, but we need to follow all our procedures."

"My dad's right next door if you want to ask him anything."

"Thanks, but I'm running late to another appointment." Kristin stands. "I'll call him next week to go over your information and to answer any questions he may have. You can be there too, if you'd like."

"Okay," I say. "I'll tell him you'll call. Do you know what day?"

Kristin pulls a calendar out of her shoulder bag. "Will next Tuesday at four o'clock work for you?"

"I think so."

"Great! I'll write you in. If that's not good for your dad, let Gina know and we'll reschedule."

Gina closes the door behind Kristin and gives me a smile.

Chapter 39

It turns out Papi isn't available next Tuesday. He has office hours for the summer class he's teaching. "Ask her if Wednesday will work." He scrolls through his calendar. "If not, then maybe one day the following week."

"Okay, I'll tell Gina tomorrow."

Papi stops me on my way upstairs. "Don't let this distract you from doing your best in school," he says. "Even if the application is approved, you still need the grades we agreed on."

"I know, I know." I shuffle upstairs to get ready for bed.

"How was your therapy appointment?" I ask Amarilis when she comes in. I was so busy with the presentation, I forgot she was supposed to see a therapist on Friday.

"Oh . . . that." Amarilis putters around gathering her pajamas and hair stuff. "Listen, I'm not going to be able to see a therapist after all."

"Why not?"

"It's very busy at my internship—I can't leave in the middle of the day. And I can't go in the evenings because then what would

I tell Papi? He expects me home at a certain time." She tilts her head and shrugs.

"Papi doesn't mind if you stay out late sometimes," I say. "You know that."

"True, but . . ." Amarilis takes my hands and looks me in the eye. "I've decided I don't need therapy. I talked to Rich about my discussion with the counselor from the hotline, and he was so apologetic and understanding that I'm sure he'll never lose his temper with me again. So everything's fine now."

I snatch my hands away. "But you said that before, remember? And now you have giant black-and-blue marks on your back!"

"Shh! You don't want Papi to hear!"

"No," I say, "*you* don't want Papi to hear. *I* think you should tell him."

Amarilis purses her lips and frowns. "Well, I'm not going to tell him, and neither are you!" she hisses.

"You can't tell me what to do," I say. "If I decide that telling Papi is the right thing to do, then I will." If Amarilis can make her own decisions, then I can make mine.

My sister chuckles and strolls over to the dresser. She picks up her hairbrush and looks at me. "Rich says you're not going to tell because it'll be your word against mine, and who's Papi going to believe anyway?" She has a mean smirk that I've never seen before.

My chest heaves up and down and my face feels warm. "Oh, really? *Rich* says that? He doesn't know anything!" I throw open the door and stomp down two steps at a time. Papi is sitting on the couch in the living room. I stand in front of him and yell, "I have something to tell you!"

Amarilis is suddenly right behind me, rubbing my shoulders like a boxing coach. "No, she doesn't." She fake-laughs and sounds like she's got something stuck in her throat. "Come on, mamita, it's time to go to bed. You have school in the morning."

Papi has put down his newspaper and he's squinting at the two of us. He slides his glasses down from the top of his head and onto his nose. "What's going on here?"

"Rich hits Amarilis."

"¿Qué?" Abuela appears beside us and clutches Amarilis's arm. "Is this true?"

Amarilis pulls her arm away and looks at the floor. "It was—it was an accident."

Papi stands up. "What happened? What did he do to you?"

"Nothing!" Amarilis is crying now. "We argue occasionally, but every couple does."

"Listen, it's normal to have a few pleitos, mi amor," Abuela says, "but why did Miosotis say he hit you?"

"Because he did!" I turn to Papi to make sure he isn't buying Amarilis's phony story. "More than once. That Band-Aid on her face isn't covering up a pimple. She went to the hospital and got stitches because he cut her! And the other night when he took her out to dinner, he hit her again and now she has a bunch of morados all over her back."

Abuela stares at Amarilis with her mouth hanging open.

"Is this true, Amarilis?" Papi asks.

My sister stamps her foot like a toddler. "It's not that bad. Miosotis is making this sound like a big deal."

"If he's violent toward you, it's a huge deal," Papi says.

"I love him and we're going to work this out!"

225

"Work this out? There's nothing to work out." Papi says. "That's it—you're not marrying a criminal."

"What are you talking about? He's not a criminal." Amarilis chuckles like Papi just made a silly joke.

"He assaulted you." Papi's expression is super serious. "He could have been arrested, and he should have been."

Amarilis folds her arms across her chest. "It was an accident. Everything's fine between us now."

"No, it isn't," Papi says. "This time you got away with injuries you can recover from. The next time you might not be so lucky."

"There isn't going to be a next time." Amarilis rolls her eyes like Papi is being ridiculous.

"You're right, there isn't." Papi gives her a steady look. "Because you're staying away from him."

My sister's mouth drops open. "Are you kidding? You can't do this." She turns to Abuela. "Tell him he can't do this."

"Ay, Amarilis, no seas terca," Abuela says. "This boy doesn't deserve you, and you shouldn't put up with that."

"I'm not being stubborn. I love him, and if you care about me, you'll support me!"

Papi and Abuela shake their heads. "The wedding is off," Papi says.

"You can't tell me what to do!" Amarilis heads for the steps. "And you"—she points at me—"I trusted you, but I won't make that mistake again." She runs upstairs and slams the bedroom door.

Papi sits and leans his forehead against his palms. "She won't be angry forever," he says. "In the long run, she'll appreciate our concern and help."

226

I'm not sure I believe him. He barely sounds like he believes himself.

"You were right to tell us." Abuela pats my hand.

I throw my arms around her. I'm so relieved she isn't sticking up for Rich, and I feel a little silly for thinking she would. When I pull away from her, she has tears in her eyes. She cups my face in her hands.

"Go get some sleep, mi amor," she says. "Your father and I will figure out how to protect your sister. Don't worry."

I walk upstairs slowly and slip into our room. Amarilis is sobbing on her bed. I'm partly relieved I told Papi and Abuela. Maybe they can help her since I haven't been able to. But what if they don't know what to do either? This probably isn't how Miss Mabel handled it when she helped Gina. Maybe I made a big mistake.

"Amarilis?" I stand beside my sister's bed and reach for her shoulder, then pull back my hand without touching her. "Amarilis?"

"What do you want?!" She bolts up and glares at me with wet red eyes.

"I-I'm sorry. I was trying to help and—"

"Well, you didn't help. You ruined my life." She grabs a wad of tissues and blows her nose.

I sit on the edge of my bed. "It's just that he keeps hurting you, and I thought Papi could do something to make him stop."

Amarilis frowns. "That's not true. You were angry and trying to get me in trouble."

I open my mouth to argue, but the words don't come out. I really do care about Amarilis and I really want Rich to stop

227

hurting her and I really thought Papi might be able to help. Honest. But what my sister is saying might also be right. I was mad and I wanted to show her she can't push me aside and let Rich control me too. Maybe I was tattling to Papi. But doesn't my sister know she's already in trouble and Papi has nothing to do with that? "I'm sorry," I say again.

"Apology not accepted." She lies down with her back to me.

I bite my lower lip, pull back the covers, and crawl into bed.

Chapter 40

AMARILIS DOESN'T TALK TO ME ALL week. We get dressed in silence every morning, and she doesn't make eye contact through the mirror while she flat irons her hair. At dinner on Thursday, she serves herself rice and looks at the beans, which are next to me. "Jacinto," she says. "Could you pass me the beans, please?"

Jacinto grimaces. Papi told him what happened, and he thinks Amarilis is being ridiculous, but he doesn't want to get involved. "Could you hand me the beans, please, squirt?"

I roll my eyes, pick up the beans, and place them next to Amarilis.

"How was work today?" Papi asks her.

"Fine." She chews and swallows quickly, finishing her meal in ten minutes flat. "May I be excused? I'm tired."

Papi nods, and Amarilis stands, puts her plate in the sink, then bolts upstairs.

"What are we going to do?" Abuela asks.

Papi rubs his chin and stares at the water pitcher. "Give her time. She'll be fine."

"Shouldn't we encourage her to go to counseling or some-thing?" I say.

Papi shrugs. "I'll support her if she wants to go, but the important thing is to keep her away from that boy, and I've taken care of that."

"How?"

"I called his parents." Papi puts an elbow on the table and points at each of us. "Can you believe those people? They said their son would never do such a thing! They said they no longer support this wedding because they can't believe we would accuse him like that."

"They called Amarilis a liar?" Jacinto's eyes are wide.

"They certainly did." Papi slaps the table and stands. "It's a good thing we nipped this in the bud now. Imagine if we found this out after they were married!" He takes his plate and starts to unload the dishwasher.

"But . . . they haven't broken up," I say. "She called him this morning."

"Ay, ay, ay," Abuela says. "I'd better talk to her."

"Why don't you wait a few days?" Papi says. "She's still angry."

"You're right. I can usually get through to Felicia after she's had time to cool off."

"Won't she get angrier if you try to boss her?" I ask.

Abuela shakes her head. "Listen, I know what I'm doing."

Maybe she does. I sure hope so. Abuela hasn't read any books or websites about helping people in Amarilis's situation, but that doesn't matter, right? Tía Felicia always appreciates her advice, so maybe Abuela just naturally knows what to say. I pick up the bowl of leftover carrots and hand it to her. I take the empty rice platter to Papi at the sink. "Oh! Papi, I almost forgot," I say. "Gina said Kristin can talk to you next Wednesday like you said, so she's calling at four."

Papi takes off his glasses and rubs his eyes. "Ay, Miosotis, I don't know about this."

"She can call another day, if Wednesday isn't good anymore."

"No, that's not what I mean." He puts a hand on my shoulder. "This is not a good time, with everything going on with Amarilis. We have to put off this dog thing."

"Put it off? What do you mean? I'm getting good grades!"

"I promise you'll get a dog eventually if you get those grades like we agreed. Just not now."

I can't believe this. "But where's Freckles going to live? He isn't a new backpack or a pair of sneakers we can buy later. He's a living, breathing being who needs a home now!"

"I know, mija, and I'm certain another loving family will take him in, but resolving Amarilis's situation should be our number-one priority right now. A new dog would be a huge distraction."

"Listen to your father," Abuela says. "This is a big problem, and we need to focus on it above all else."

Even Jacinto nods. Am I a horrible selfish person for wanting Freckles now? I don't think so. I mean, he matters too. And so do I.

—⟨⟨⟨◆⟩⟩⟩—

"That's so unfair!" Olivia waves her brush and splatters paint on her shirt. "You had a deal with your dad!"

"It's not like any of this is your fault." Zoe paces in Olivia's basement.

231

It's the next day, and I'm trying to sit still so Olivia can capture my "essence" for her art club portrait project. "I care about Amarilis too, but how will me not getting Freckles help her? And how will me getting him hurt her? None of this makes sense."

"What if you stick with your end of the deal?" Zoe says. "Get your two As and then go back to your dad and appeal to his sense of fairness."

"He already said I can get a dog if I get the two As, just not now." I gulp and try to hold back the tears. "Not Freckles."

"What if your sister breaks up with Rich before school ends?" Olivia says. "You can have Freckles then, right?"

I shrug. "Maybe, but what do I tell Gina? The rescue group wants to talk to my dad."

"What if . . ." Olivia strokes her chin and stares at her canvas. "What if the rescue group talks to someone else, and thinks they're talking to your dad?"

"Who else would they talk to?"

"That's the question." Olivia swirls her paintbrush around and around on the palette.

"I got it!" Zoe claps her hands. "I'll do it!"

"*You'll* pretend to be my dad?" Zoe is usually brilliant, but this is a terrible idea.

"No, no, no, I'll pretend to be your grandma. They know she lives with you, right?"

I nod.

"And they don't know she doesn't speak a lot of English, right?"

I nod again.

232

"I do a great grandma voice. See? *How are you doing there, sweetie?*" Zoe's old lady voice is pretty funny. Olivia and I laugh.

"I don't know," I say. "What if we get caught?"

"We won't get caught," Zoe says. "I'll come to your house next Wednesday and you make sure to answer the phone when it rings at four."

"I'll come too for moral support," Olivia says.

I'm not sure about this, but I don't want to miss out on getting Freckles. Plus, Papi is being unreasonable. After Freckles is cleared to come live with us, Papi will see that this is best. And, like Olivia said, Amarilis might have broken up with Rich by then. I can tell my dad they didn't need to talk to him because Gina told them how great we are, which she did, so this is totally believable.

So that's the plan, and it's a pretty good one.

Chapter 41

THE NEXT DAY, MY HANDS ARE all sweaty when I go to Gina's house for my usual Saturday visit with the dogs.

"Is everything okay?" Gina says. "You seem quiet today."

Freckles looks me in the eye as I pet him. "Well . . . there's a big problem in my family now."

"What is it? Do you need anything from us?"

"Thanks, but we'll be okay. At least, I hope so." I tell her about Amarilis and Rich, but I don't mention what Papi said about Freckles. "I don't get it," I say. "I mean, Amarilis has all these people who love her and are telling her Rich is bad news. Why won't she listen to us?"

Gina rubs Lucky's neck and adjusts Bella on her lap. "You've met Rich, right? Didn't you think he was sweet and charming?" I nod. "Well, that's probably who he is most of the time." She takes the leash I hand to her. "Your sister fell in love with the charming Rich, and she wants to believe the violent Rich is a fluke who won't appear anymore. Unfortunately, that guy always comes back."

"What am I supposed to do?"

"Let her know you're there for her. Always."

Why does everyone keep saying that? Don't they know that isn't working? "But she won't even talk to me."

Gina squeezes my shoulder. "I'm sure this is hard for you. Truth be told, it's much harder for your sister, so don't give up on her. She might not show it right now, but she really needs you."

When I get home, I tiptoe up the steps. If I can slip into our room without Amarilis noticing, I can avoid her evil glare, at least for a little while. Before I reach the door, I hear Callie's voice. I stand in the hallway and snoop on their conversation.

"If you say your relationship needs work," Callie says, "then why don't you go to the therapist and see if she can help?"

"I want to but, to be honest, I'm kind of afraid."

"Of what?"

"I don't know." Amarilis doesn't say anything for a little bit. "I guess . . . that she'll tell me something I don't want to hear."

"Look, I've been to therapy, and all they do is guide you as you figure things out for yourself. It's really helpful. And now that your family knows about this, you don't have to worry about sneaking around to get help."

"Yeah, I guess you're right."

"I know you're mad at your sister," Callie says. "But if you think about it, she actually did you a big favor by telling. Isn't it better to have this all out in the open?"

"Yeah." Amarilis sighs. "Plus, she's just a kid. I shouldn't have asked her to keep such a big secret. She was only trying to help."

I bite back a smile and sneak downstairs to get a snack.

235

"Hey, kiddo!" Callie says when I burst into the room a few minutes later.

"Hi, Callie." I glance at Amarilis while I grab some clean clothes. She gives me a tiny smile. "See you later." I head for the shower.

When I come back in the room, Amarilis and Callie are gone. Still, I know Amarilis has forgiven me and she'll talk to me the next time I see her. I hum as I gather up my schoolwork. I finish writing a paper for English and I study for my math and science final exams. I have to do all I can to get Freckles, no matter what Papi says.

Amarilis is a little nicer during dinner. She chuckles when Jacinto tells a corny joke, and she looks right at me and asks me to pass her the concón. Then she says something that brings a little smile to all our faces.

"I'll be home a little late on Tuesday. I made an appointment with a therapist."

Papi nods. "I can pick you up when you're done."

"No, that's okay. I'll take the train."

Abuela squeezes my sister's hand. "It's good you're moving past this Ricardo phase. Talking to someone will really help."

"It's not a phase, Abuela! I'm not ending things with Rich," Amarilis says. "The therapist will help us work through our problems."

Abuela clucks and shakes her head.

"I know all of you hate Rich now, but he's still the same wonderful guy you got to know and love," Amarilis says.

"We don't *hate* him," Abuela says. "We just think he's no good for you."

"But he is! And we're in love."

"You might believe that now," Abuela says. "But you're kind and pretty and smart. Before you know it, you'll find a young man who's good to you, and you'll see what love truly is. And if he's not so handsome, that's okay, because what's important is that he treats you like the princess you are."

Did Abuela just encourage Amarilis to date someone who looks like us? I mean, we all know that's what she means when she says "not so handsome." Jacinto opens his eyes wide at me and puts his hands to his chest in shock. I giggle, then cover it with a fake cough.

"But Rich *is* good to me," Amarilis says. "This has been a stressful year for him."

"Life is full of stressful situations, mija," Papi says. "Hurting your loved ones is not an appropriate reaction."

Amarilis sighs. "I know, and Rich knows too. He promised to get help. He's willing to do anything to stay with me."

I'm not convinced, and I can see from the looks on their faces that no one in my family is either. But we don't say anything more. Hopefully, the therapist will help Amarilis see she's better off without Rich.

That night, as I change into my pajamas, I think about how my sister must feel. For some reason, she really loves Rich and wants their relationship to work out. I don't understand why, but still, I made her a promise and I broke it. Our relationship is important too, and I shouldn't have hurt her feelings like that. "I'm sorry I told about Rich," I say. "I just—I didn't know what else to do."

Amarilis puts down her phone and looks at me. "I know. It must have been scary for you to see my bruises."

I nod.

"I know this has to stop," she says. "And it will, I promise." Amarilis stands and comes over to me, her arms outstretched. "I'm sorry I asked you to keep that a secret, and I forgive you for telling. Do you forgive me?"

I nod and hug her back. I had told myself I didn't care if Amarilis never spoke to me again, that I wasn't going to let her ruin my life, but I have no control over how I feel. I want her to be happy and I don't want her to be mad at me. I breathe a sigh of relief when I get into bed, and I fall into a deep and restful sleep.

Chapter 42

WHEN THE PHONE RINGS ON WEDNESDAY at 4 p.m., Zoe, Olivia, and I are sitting in a circle on my bedroom floor huddled around the cordless handset I grabbed from the kitchen. The caller ID says *Happy Puppy Rescue*, and my heart practically beats out of my chest. Zoe hits the speaker button. "Hello?" she says in her old-lady voice.

"May I speak with Oscar Flores?" says the voice on the other end.

"My son-in-law isn't here right now. May I help you?"

"Yes, this is Kristin from Happy Puppy Rescue Association."

"Ah, yes, he told me you would call! He had to deal with a work emergency, but I can answer your questions, young lady."

Olivia gives Zoe a thumbs-up. I have to admit she sounds old lady legit, even though she doesn't sound anything like Abuela.

"Is this . . . Marta Camilo?" Kristin asks.

I nod to Zoe.

"Yes, dear, what can I help you with?"

"I assume you're aware of your family's application to adopt a dog from our organization?"

"Yes, we're all very excited to have Freckles come live with us," Zoe says. "My granddaughter is here with me right now, and she really loves him."

"Hi, Kristin," I say into the phone.

"Hello there! It's good to talk to you again. As you know, Gina has told us great things about you. So, I'll make this quick, okay?" We hear Kristin flip some papers on her end. "First, how much time will the dog spend alone each day?"

I shake my head at Zoe. She looks confused.

"None!" I say. "My grandmother is home all day."

"Yes, yes, I'm retired so I'll be with Freckles *aaaall* day long," Zoe says.

"Good, good," Kristin says. "Are there any allergies in your family?"

I could explain that Abuela might *maybe* have a little allergy to dogs, but that's not necessary, right? I shake my head again.

"No, dear," Zoe says.

"Excellent. One last question: Will you take the dog to the vet regularly?"

"Yes, dearie," Zoe says.

"We've already picked out a vet," I add.

"Beautiful." Kristin rustles some more papers. "That's all I have. Gina has assured us that a home visit is not necessary, so this is the end of your application process. Since you're friends with her, we'll let Gina know our decision and all the details about picking up your dog, okay?"

"Okay, thanks!" I can't believe that's it. This was way too easy. We hang up the phone and cheer.

"You are so approved for this dog!" Olivia says.

"I know!" I say. "Thanks, Zoe, you were great. I hope no one finds out."

"For sure," Zoe says. "But your dad's not keeping his end of the deal, so it's okay if you bend the rules a little, right?"

She has a point. Now all I need is that A in science. We haven't gotten our grades for our presentations yet, but our last test is this week, and I need to ace it. "Let's study for the science test now," I say. I don't think I've ever said those words before. But I'd do anything to get Freckles, even if it means spending my weekend cramming a bunch of boring science facts into my brain.

Zoe and Olivia join us for dinner. "What have you young ladies been up to this afternoon?" Papi asks.

It's hard not to talk about Freckles, but fortunately, we still have science on our minds. And we've done so much work since the phone call that we can give him an honest answer without sounding suspicious. "We finished preparing flash cards for our science test on Friday," Zoe says.

"We made three sets," I say. "One for each of us."

"Now all we have to do is review, review, review," Olivia adds with a dramatic hair flip.

"Excellent," Papi says. "It sounds like you have this all under control." He looks at Amarilis. "And . . . how's the internship?"

"Pretty good." Amarilis picks up her knife and carves her steak slowly. We all watch her, but she doesn't look up and she doesn't say anything more.

Jacinto clears his throat. "I got my SAT score."

"Oh!" Papi raises his eyebrows. "And?"

"Well"—my brother shrugs—"my score improved, but it's still not perfect. It should be good enough to get into Penn, though."

I roll my eyes. His score was good enough for Penn the first time. "What do you need, one more point to be perfect?" I say.

"No, smarty pants," Jacinto says. "*Twenty* points."

"That's a great score, mijo." Papi reaches over and pats my brother's back. "I'm proud of you."

"Thanks."

When Zoe asks Jacinto for SAT study tips, my brother goes on and on. I expect Amarilis to join in, but she doesn't. Abuela watches her with worried eyes and raises an eyebrow when she catches me looking at her.

"Are you okay?" I ask my sister after my friends have left and the two of us are alone in our room.

"Um-hm," she says. "I went to therapy yesterday."

She said she was going on Tuesday this week, but I haven't wanted to ask her in case she didn't want to talk about it. "How did it go?"

Amarilis brushes her hair. "It was actually really good. I like her a lot, and she's helping me understand things."

"That's great!"

She puts the brush down and fiddles with her engagement ring. It reflects the light from the floor lamp beside her.

"So . . . is Rich talking to anybody about all of this?" I ask.

"Not yet, but he'll go when he has time." Amarilis opens her little box of hairpins. "We'll probably go to couples counseling soon."

"Oh."

She parts her hair down the middle and brushes it around her head into a doobie, clipping it with the hairpins. Her face looks calm. She isn't wearing the Band-Aid anymore, and the scar on her cheek is fading. It's going to be a while before that half-inch-long darkened line is entirely gone, though, if it ever goes away.

"Do you still want to marry Rich?"

Amarilis nods. The past few days she only talks about Rich when somebody asks, but I know she texts him all the time. "We won't have a big fancy wedding, since Papi is being stupid about this and Rich's parents are mad that he called them. But we're absolutely getting married." She puts the last pin in her hair and turns to look at me. "Things are getting a lot better between us. With some couples counseling, we'll absolutely make this work."

I'm not sure what to say. I want to shake her and yell at her to dump that loser already, but Miss Mabel's voice pops into my head and I remind myself that this isn't my decision to make. At least they won't get married until after Amarilis graduates. Hopefully, her therapist will help her see Rich is no good for her before then. If not, then forget Miss Mabel, Callie, and all the experts and their books and articles. I'll stop that wedding no matter what.

"Okay, well, I'd better go to sleep," I say. "I don't want to doze off in class tomorrow."

"Goodnight, mamita." Amarilis pulls out her phone and holds it close to her face as she texts, like she does every night. I shake my head and go brush my teeth.

Chapter 43

THE NEXT DAY, GINA HUGS ME when I walk into her house.
"Congratulations! You're officially a dog owner now!"

"Huh?"

"Kristin called last night and said you can have Freckles whenever you're ready. All you need to do is pay the adoption fee."

I gasp and hug Gina back. When Freckles jumps up and paws at my knees, I drop to the floor and let him lick me all over. "He knows too," Gina says.

I think she's right. Unlike me, though, Freckles is just plain happy. I'm super nervous because school ends next week, and I'm running out of time to convince Papi to let me keep him. I still can't believe he thinks Freckles can just go live with someone else, as if he were a stuffed animal or something. It's not easy for a dog to trust and get attached. Papi doesn't understand dogs, and he doesn't care about them. But Freckles is definitely coming to live with me, even if I have to sneak him in and keep him hidden in my room.

"That's . . . not really a good idea," Zoe says before science on Friday when I tell her and Olivia about my idea of hiding Freckles.

I sigh. "I know, but I have to do something. And I've been studying for this test all week, so I'll definitely ace it."

Olivia agrees. "Once he sees your grades, your dad will change his mind, I just know it."

Mr. Nesbitt claps his hands. "Settle down, people! Take your seats." He hands out the exams as soon as we all sit.

I don't think about Freckles or Papi or even Amarilis for the next hour. I'm focused on air masses and the water cycle and natural hazards. I concentrate on every question and make sure I pick the right answers. Before I know it, I've gotten to the end of the test. When I look up, there are ten minutes to spare, so I look everything over one more time, and I make one change. Then Freckles comes back into my mind, and I squeeze my elbows to keep from squealing. I am getting my dog after this!

That afternoon Gina gives me more great news. "Mabel and I are leaving in an hour for a wedding in the city, and we're staying overnight. Kristin is coming over to stay with the dogs, but since Freckles is technically already yours, you can take him home for the weekend to meet your family if you'd like."

"Really? Tonight? Don't we have to pay the fee?"

"No, you've met all the criteria, so you would basically be fostering him for the weekend," Gina says. "We'll need the fee before you take him home permanently next week."

That's not a problem. I have two years' worth of birthday and Christmas money saved up, which is more than enough to pay the fee. "Wow, that would be great, but I have to ask first."

"Of course."

Freckles doesn't squirm when I carry him into my house. Amarilis is on her way out with Callie and Emily. "How cute!" they say.

"Why is this dog here?" Papi gives me a suspicious look.

"Gina asked me to babysit him for the weekend. I said I had to check with all of you first." I turn so he can look right into Freckles's adorable eyes. "Can I do it, please?"

Papi looks at Abuela. "If it's okay with your abuela, then it's okay with me."

"Claro que sí," Abuela says.

"Thank you!" I run back to Gina's to pick up some dog food and a crate. This is perfect. My family will fall in love with Freckles, I just know it. Then Papi will realize it doesn't make sense to put off getting a dog, and when I give him my grades next week, he'll tell me to go ahead and bring the little guy home forever. I won't have to hide Freckles in my room after all.

"Where are you putting that crate?" Papi asks.

"Over there?" I point to the corner by the TV. "I won't need it upstairs, since he'll sleep in my bed with me."

Abuela sneezes into her elbow. "Ay, no, mi amor. His new owner might not want him on the bed, so it's better if he doesn't get into that habit."

I guess I can't tell Abuela and Papi that we're the new owners. I grab the crate, scooping Freckles up in my other arm, and head upstairs. I text Zoe and Olivia to let them know I have Freckles for the weekend. *Can we come over tomorrow to meet him?* I say yes, of course, then I plop myself on the floor to play with my dog. He walks all over the place with his nose to the ground, figuring out all these brand-new smells.

"So, what do you think?" I say. "Do you like it here?"

Freckles looks at me and tilts his head to the side. He comes over and licks my hand, then rolls onto his back for a belly rub.

"You're a little belly-rub addict, aren't you?" I laugh as I rub away. "Let's get to know the rest of the family," I say after a while.

Freckles follows me into Jacinto's room and jumps into his lap.

"Whoa!" Jacinto rolls back in his desk chair. "Who's this little guy?" He smiles and scratches Freckles's neck.

"Freckles." I close the door and lower my voice. "I really want to keep him, and Gina says I can if I want to. Could you help me convince Papi? Please?"

Freckles is getting comfortable and enjoying the neck scratch. It looks like Jacinto kind of likes it too. "I don't know," he says. "Papi's really worried about Amarilis."

"Me too! But Freckles could actually help her. I mean, don't you feel great sitting here with him right now?"

Jacinto chuckles. "Yeah, I guess."

"So, will you talk to him?"

"I'll try, but I might not be able to convince him."

"I know, but thanks." I open the door, and Freckles pops up and leaps down. He follows me down the steps and heads right to Papi.

"May I help you?" Papi smiles at Freckles, who is sniffing his ankles intently.

Freckles gives him a friendly bark. He sits and watches Papi, panting with his little pink tongue dangling to the side.

"Are you thirsty?" I say. "Let's get you some water." I rummage through the pantry until I find a plastic bowl.

"Cuidado, mi amor, or you'll step on him," Abuela says.

Freckles is right behind me. "When did you get here?" I pat his head and fill the bowl with water. "Do you need any help?" I ask Abuela as Freckles slurps up his water.

She shakes her head and blinks again and again. "Go tire him out before we sit down to eat." She turns her head and sneezes into a napkin.

I already walked Freckles when I got to Gina's, but Abuela's probably afraid of stepping on him, so I take him to the little park down the street. A few other people are there throwing Frisbees and balls with their dogs. I take off Freckles's leash and let him run around with his new friends. When he comes back to me and puts his head on my lap, I know this was a good idea.

"Amarilis seems to be doing really well," Jacinto says during dinner.

"Yes," Abuela says. "It's good she's with her friends tonight, instead of talking to that good-for-nothing Ricardo."

"That's a really cute dog, Miosotis." My brother points at Freckles, who is snoozing under my chair. "Amarilis would probably love hanging with him."

"Yeah, dogs are great at helping people feel better." I look at Papi. "Did I tell you about the therapy dogs I saw at the hospital?"

Papi's eyes dart between Jacinto and me, looking suspicious. "No . . ."

I tell my family about Taco at the hospital. "His special job is to calm people down when they're anxious. Isn't that cool?"

"Hmm." Papi rubs his chin.

I glance at Jacinto, and he gives me a little smile. Then he changes the subject, which is a good idea. We don't want to overdo it here. I can tell Papi is going to think about it. This will

248

be a good night. Freckles and I will take a nice walk under the moonlight after dinner, then he'll cuddle in bed with me, and in the morning we'll go for a long hike. Then, while he's curled up on my lap looking adorable and content, I'll ask Papi—again—if I can keep him forever, and this time Papi will say yes.

Abuela sneezes.

"Are you all right?" Papi says. "It sounds like you're coming down with something."

"Maybe." Abuela pulls a tissue out of her pocket and blows her nose.

"You should go rest," he says. "The kids and I will clean up the kitchen."

Abuela sneezes again. Her eyes are red and watery. "Yes, that's a good idea."

She must really feel sick. Even when we help in the kitchen, she has to be around to supervise. I glance under my chair. Wait—could this be because of Freckles? Suddenly, my eyes feel watery too.

Chapter 44

Freckles and I have just gotten back from a long after-lunch walk on Saturday when I get a text from Olivia. *My dad and I are on our way to pick up Zoe, then he's dropping us off at your house.* Ten minutes later, the doorbell rings, and I leave Freckles in my room while I run downstairs. "Hola, niñas," Abuela says to Zoe and Olivia. She's still sneezing today, but it doesn't seem any worse than yesterday.

"Come on, Freckles is in my room!" I sprint upstairs with Zoe and Olivia right behind me. We walk into my room and look around.

"Where is he?" Olivia asks.

A crunching sound is coming from beneath Amarilis's bed. I get on the floor and peer under there. "What are you doing, Freckles?"

He's eating something—a candy bar! Everyone knows chocolate is poisonous to dogs!

I grab Freckles by the leg and drag him out from under the bed. He growls and clamps down his teeth when I pull on

250

the chocolate in his mouth. I get a piece of it, but he gobbles up the rest and swallows quickly. "Where's the wrapper?" I ask.

"I'll check under the beds." Zoe crawls around, then sits back up and shakes her head.

I gasp. "He probably ate it." I scoop up Freckles and run downstairs. Papi is reading on the couch. "He ate a chocolate bar, wrapper and all," I say.

Papi puts his book down. "Is Gina back home? Should we take him to a vet?"

"I'll see if Gina's there." Even if she's not, Kristin will know what to do. Zoe, Olivia, and I run next door, but, for a second, I pause in front of Gina's door. What if Kristin decides I'm too irresponsible to keep Freckles?

I shake my head and knock. Saving Freckles is all that matters now.

Gina opens the door and looks from Freckles to me to Zoe to Olivia with her mouth open. "What's the matter?"

"He ate some chocolate! I'm sorry!" What was I thinking? I can't take care of a dog, not now, not ever! Tears run down my face.

"Did this happen just now?"

I nod and hiccup.

"What kind of chocolate? Dark? Milk? And how much?" Gina takes Freckles and cradles him like a baby.

"Um, milk chocolate," I say. "One big bar, I think."

"Oh, good, milk chocolate isn't as bad. I'll give him hydrogen peroxide to induce vomiting. If that doesn't work, we'll call the vet."

Gina pours the stuff down Freckles's throat with a dropper, then we all go to the backyard and sit in the chairs to wait.

"He doesn't seem distressed," Gina says. "And it takes about two hours to digest. If he throws up all the chocolate now, he won't suffer any effects from it."

I wipe my face and sniffle. "What about the wrapper?"

"He ate the wrapper too?"

"I think so."

"Hopefully, he'll throw that up as well."

The four of us watch Freckles sniff all over the yard. Gina's other dogs join us. They run around and chase some toys Zoe and Olivia toss to them. Freckles just watches. I don't take my eyes off of him. I can't believe I almost killed the poor little guy after having him for less than a day. Papi's right: reading about dogs and even helping Gina out a little each day isn't the same as taking care of a dog full-time. Maybe I'm not ready for this.

Freckles sits on the ground and looks straight ahead. The other dogs run in circles, chasing one another, but Freckles stares past them. Then he lifts his hind legs into a squat. He jerks his neck forward, then back again, over and over, like a bobblehead doll. Finally, he gags and a bunch of brown stuff spills out of his mouth. The wrapper too.

"Grab him before he eats it again," Gina says.

I jump up and scoop Freckles off the ground. "Thank you, Gina. I'm going to get rid of all the chocolate in my house right now!"

"That's not necessary." Gina chuckles. "Just keep it out of his reach, okay?"

I nod.

Gina stands and pats my shoulder. "Come on, you two should go home now and spend quality time together."

I don't move. "Actually . . . he should stay here." I put Freckles into Gina's arms.

"Oh, Miosotis, don't get discouraged! Before you know it, the two of you will be in sync and you won't even remember life before he was your dog."

"The thing is . . . he's not really my dog, and I don't deserve him."

"Come again?"

I have to tell Gina the truth right away, so I blurt it out without taking a breath. "My father said we have to hold off on getting a dog until after my sister's problems are resolved, so he wouldn't talk to Kristin, so . . ." I glance at Zoe. I don't want to rat her out, but I don't want to lie anymore. Plus, Gina doesn't even know Zoe, so she can't get mad at her. "I—I asked my friend to pretend to be my grandmother, and she did the interview. My family doesn't even know the application was approved."

I peek up at Gina. For the first time ever, she looks angry.

"How could you do this to me, Miosotis? My credibility is at stake here! I told them they didn't need to check your references or your home or anything! I trusted you!" She holds Freckles close and heads to the door. "You should go home now."

"I'm so sorry, Miosotis!" Zoe says when we're outside. She and Olivia follow me to my house.

"We should have told her it was all our idea," Olivia adds.

"It doesn't matter whose idea it was," I say. "I'm the one she trusted." I sit on the front steps and put my head on my knees. Zoe and Olivia sit on either side of me, and we don't say anything for a while. "The thing is, I never thought about how this would affect Gina. I only thought about myself. And Freckles. I guess I'm not a very good friend."

"Oh please, that's not true!" Olivia says. "You're a great friend! You help me out all the time, no matter what."

"Yeah, me too," Zoe says. "But when you have a grown-up as a friend, you forget they need stuff too."

Olivia nods. "That's because adults can do whatever they want."

"But they can't," I say. "They have to follow rules too, and they pay the price when things go wrong." I stand. "I should apologize to Gina—eventually."

"Why not now?" Zoe says.

"She's too mad right now."

We run up to my room and hope Papi and Abuela don't notice. But they do.

"How's the dog?" Papi opens my door while knocking.

"He's fine. Gina got him to throw up the chocolate, but she's going to keep him now."

Papi stands in the doorway and looks at the three of us sitting side by side, staring at our fingernails. "Are you okay?"

I nod.

"I'm certain Gina understands this wasn't your fault," he says. "Accidents happen."

I nod again.

"Okay, well, dinner's almost ready. Zoe and Olivia, you're welcome to join us. Wash up and come downstairs."

I get up and close the door behind Papi. "Should I tell him what happened?"

"I don't know," Olivia says. "He might get really mad, like Gina."

"But what if Gina tells him herself?" Zoe says. "Won't that make things worse?"

I plop back onto the bed and bury my face into a squishy stuffed bulldog. "It doesn't matter. He'll never let me get a dog anyway. Amarilis and her problems are more important, plus I might not get that A." I sit up and look at my friends. "I should have left everything alone. Now I can't even hang out with the dogs at Gina's house." I get up. "Could one of you take this crate back to Gina?"

"Sure, we'll do it on our way out," Olivia says. We drag ourselves downstairs and put the crate by the door, then go to the dining room.

"Are you feeling better?" Papi asks Abuela during dinner.

"I'm fine, why?"

"I thought you were coming down with a bad cold," he says. "You've been sneezing a lot since last night."

"Oh, that! It was because of the dog."

"I'm sorry, Abuela," I say. "I didn't mean to make you sick."

"Don't worry about it, mi amor. You asked, and I said it would be okay. But, listen, I'm glad Gina took him back, because my eyes were itching terribly. They probably would have been swollen shut by tomorrow if he had stayed all weekend."

Abuela says all that in Spanish, and Zoe and Olivia don't understand. They look puzzled, so Jacinto translates for them.

"I didn't know your grandmother was allergic to dogs." Zoe gives me this look, and I know what she's thinking: I lied to her and Olivia too.

I look away from my friends. After dinner I walk out with them and carry the dog crate to Gina's door. "I'm sorry," I say.

255

"I should have told you about my grandmother's allergies, but I didn't want to get you mixed up in another one of my lies. Plus, I was hoping she wasn't really allergic."

Olivia nods. "I get it."

"Me too," Zoe says. "But you know you can tell us anything, right?"

"I know. I'm sorry." I hug them goodbye and go home before they knock on Gina's door.

After Zoe and Olivia have left, Amarilis comes back from her sleepover with Callie and Emily. "Did you have a good time, mija?" Papi asks.

Amarilis nods, puts her bag over her shoulder, and goes upstairs. I follow her up and burrow into the sea of stuffed dogs on my bed.

"Why are you so sad, mamita?"

"I lost Freckles."

"You lost another dog?! Where?"

"No, no, not like that." I sit on the edge of my bed and face her. "I mean I can't adopt him now."

"Why not?"

"Abuela's allergic to him." Not that Papi would have let me keep him anyway.

"I'm sorry." Amarilis puts an arm around me. "I know how special Freckles is to you."

My sister looks as sad as I feel. She doesn't even like dogs that much. But she knows this is important to me, so now it's important to her too. "Thanks." I rest my head on her shoulder.

Chapter 45

I'M CONFUSED WHEN ABUELA WAKES ME up Sunday morning. "What's wrong, Abuela?"

"You're late, mi amor. Gina's waiting for you."

"Oh." I lie back down. "She doesn't need me today."

"Then why did she call?"

"She called?!" I jump up, get dressed, and run to brush my teeth. Maybe Gina's not mad anymore. Or she realized I'm such a great helper she can't live without me. Or maybe there's something wrong with Freckles after he ate the chocolate. Oh no, that's it. Freckles is sick!

I race out of the house without even drinking a glass of orange juice (the minimum breakfast required by Abuela), and I practically crash into Miss Mabel as she unlocks her door.

"Hello there, sweetie! You're in a hurry today." She steps inside and holds the door open for me. "Gina, are you here?" she calls out.

"We're coming!" Gina's voice is immediately followed by four dogs tumbling down the steps, with Freckles in the lead. He heads straight to me and jumps and jumps, licking my face over and over again.

"I'm so glad you're fine." I get on one knee and rub him all over the way Abuela does to me when I'm sick, like I'm feeling for broken bones.

When Gina gets to the bottom step, she and Miss Mabel look at each other and then at me. "I assume you two have some things to discuss," Miss Mabel says. "And I need to sleep." She gives Gina a quick kiss on the cheek and heads upstairs.

I stay on the floor and rub Freckles's belly. "Hi, Gina."

"Hi." Gina's voice is soft and a little sad. "Come sit with me." She goes to the couch and pats the seat beside her.

"I'm really sorry," I say as I sit. "You're my friend and you trusted me. I lied to you and I'm so, so sorry."

Gina opens her arms and gives me a hug. "We all make mistakes. The important thing is that you own them, right?"

I sit back and look at her. "I hope I didn't make things bad between you and Happy Puppy. If you want me to talk to Kristin, I'll call and tell her it was all my fault and you had no idea I was lying and—"

"Not necessary." Gina holds up her hand. "I told them there was an allergy in the family no one knew about beforehand. These things happen all the time. People back out and we find new homes for the dogs. No problem."

I'm glad Gina doesn't seem mad anymore. But I need to be sure we're okay, so I have to tell her everything. "That's actually the truth."

"What is?"

"My grandmother was sneezing nonstop when Freckles was

around. My dad told me we needed a hypoallergenic dog, but I wanted Freckles so bad I didn't listen to him."

"I guess it's a good thing your paperwork now says there are allergies in your family and you need a low-shedding dog."

"My paperwork? You mean, I can still adopt a dog?"

Gina nods.

"You're not too mad at me?"

"No, but I am disappointed. Miosotis, you could have talked to me about what was going on. I would have tried to help you. Instead, you chose to scheme and go behind everyone's back. Why?"

I think about Gina's question. "I guess I thought no one could help me," I say. "I figured if I wanted Freckles, I had to do it myself."

"Well, you're wrong. There are a lot of people who love you and will do anything they can to help you. And having someone in your corner, helping you along, always makes any task easier." Gina's gray eyes are warm and sincere. "Don't shut out your family and friends. We need you and you need us."

That's what Mami would have said. It was what she told Amarilis and Jacinto when I was born. I'm lucky to have Gina and my other friends. And I'm definitely lucky to have my family. We may not always agree on everything, but we do our best to take care of each other. Papi and Abuela don't have all the right answers about how to help Amarilis, but talking to them turned out to be a good thing for her. If I had been honest with them about Freckles, maybe that would have helped too.

I look around at the dogs in the living room. Bella the schnauzer is curled up with a tiny Chihuahua in the crate in the corner, their little bellies going up and down in unison. Lucky is looking extra fuzzy under the coffee table, and Freckles has squeezed himself in between Gina and me, his bottom pressed against my thigh and his head on her lap.

"Where do you think Freckles will end up?" I ask. I hope someone loves him as much as I do, that he's happy in whatever new home he finds, but the thought of never seeing him again makes my heart hurt. I breathe hard, and then the tears come.

Gina reaches over and pats my shoulder. "My friend Peggy put in an application to adopt him after you did. She and her family met him two weeks ago and they all fell in love with him. They're fabulous and I know he'll be happy with them."

"That's good." But I don't stop crying.

Freckles looks at me and clambers onto my lap, sniffing me all over. I can't help but laugh. "I'm going to miss you, Freckles," I say. "You're perfect, and I love you." Then I hug him and cry some more.

"I know how you feel," Gina says. "It's hard for me when the dogs come and go, but I'm helping all of them, which is the most important thing." She hands me a tissue.

"You're a great person, Gina." I wipe my eyes and blow my nose. "I'm sorry I let you down. I hope we can still be friends."

"Of course we can."

"Can I keep helping you with the dogs? Please? Well, if my dad lets me after he hears what I did."

"Why does your dad need to know about this?" Gina says.

I look at her. She isn't going to tell him?

Gina sighs. "I was twelve once too, and I did some dumb stuff. You're a good kid, Miosotis, but you need to look deep into

260

your heart and make the choices you know are right, even if you don't really want to, okay?"

I nod.

"Now, do I have my helper back?"

"Yes, yes, yes!"

Chapter 46

WE'RE CLEARING OFF OUR DINNER PLATES when there is a light knock on the door. "I'll get it!" I put the dishes down and run through the living room.

Callie and Emily are fidgeting on the porch. "Hey," Callie says. "Is Amarilis around?"

"Sure, come in."

Papi chuckles when he sees them. "Welcome, ladies, but aren't the three of you sick of one another yet?"

Amarilis rushes over to her friends. She grabs their hands and heads for the steps. "We'll be right back."

I wait until I hear our bedroom door close, then I tiptoe up the stairs. Even with my ear pressed to the door, I can't hear everything they're saying. But Emily's whisper voice is pretty loud. "You lied to us!" she says.

"I didn't want to get you in trouble," Amarilis says. Then she mumbles something else.

"What if your dad had called my house?" Callie doesn't bother to lower her voice now.

"Then you would have told him I was at Emily's, which is what you thought, right?"

"And if he had called my house?" Emily is practically shouting now.

"Look . . ." Amarilis mumbles something, and then her voice gets loud. "If you were real friends, you'd cover for me!"

"What?!" Callie screams. "We're not real friends now?"

"Huh!" Emily says. "And who is your real friend? The guy that beats the crap out of you?"

I can tell from the deafening silence that this conversation is over. I leap into the bathroom in the nick of time as Callie and Emily march down the stairs.

"What did Callie and Emily want?" I ask later as we get ready for bed.

"Um . . . just to talk about something." Amarilis puts the last clip in her hair and jumps into bed.

I reach for my phone. Callie will tell me what's going on. Except I pretty much already know. Amarilis's sleepover wasn't with her friends, and she lied to the two of them too so she could see Rich. Now she's angry at them and they're angry at her. And if she finds out I'm sneaking behind her back talking about her with Callie, she'll be mad at me too. I put the phone down and turn to my sister. "Amarilis?"

"Yeah?"

"How's it going with the therapist?"

"Really good," Amarilis says. "Rich went with me on Thursday. The therapist recommended someone for him to see separately, so he's going to do that." She gets up and sits on the edge of my bed. "Buenas noches, mamita." She hugs me and goes back to bed.

I turn out the lights. I hope my sister has everything under control, but if she's sneaking around and lying to Papi and her friends, something isn't right.

-«««◆»»»-

Mr. Nesbitt hands back our tests on Monday, and I get a 100 percent. "I haven't finished grading your projects yet," he says. "I'll get those grades to you in a couple of days."

I stare at my test, not sure how to feel. On the one hand, I'm happy and proud that I did this, and all by myself at that. On the other hand, it doesn't seem to matter anymore. I mean, I can't have Freckles anyway, so what's the point?

That afternoon I meet Gina's friend Peggy and her two daughters. They're all nice and the girls are very gentle with Freckles. The little one giggles when he licks some sticky stuff off her face and the bigger girl kisses his ear and says she loves him. Freckles runs around the yard with them, then plops on the grass with his head on my lap. I scratch his favorite spot behind his left ear and he licks my nose. "I'm going to miss you," I whisper.

"You're welcome to visit him whenever you want," Peggy tells me as she loads Freckles into her car. "We live right across the street from the middle school."

"Really?"

"Yep. We'd love to have you." Peggy gives me a hug. "Thank you for taking such good care of Freckles. He's so sweet and well-adjusted, and you had a lot to do with that. You should be very proud of yourself!"

I wipe my tears. I really am happy Freckles found a great

home. But I'm happier now that I know I can still see him sometimes.

-⟪⟪◆⟫⟫-

The whole class is jittery on Wednesday morning. The last day of school is two days away. All our classes are having parties or watching movies, and there isn't anything more we can do about our grades. What's done is done. Mr. Nesbitt places the write-ups we emailed to him for our presentations facedown on our desks. "There are two grades on your papers," he says. "The top one is the grade you received for your final project, and the bottom one is your grade for the quarter."

I stare at my paper for a few seconds without turning it over. I still don't look at it when I slide it into my backpack. Mr. Nesbitt starts a lesson about some topics that came up during the presentations. We won't be tested on any of this, but it's interesting anyway. I take out my notebook.

"Did you get your A?" Zoe asks as soon as we enter the cafeteria.

"I did!" Olivia screams. She waves her paper in the air and does a little dance.

Zoe and I hold onto Olivia and jump up and down with her. "What about you? What about you?" they say to me.

"I haven't checked yet."

"What?!"

I shrug. "It doesn't matter now anyway."

"Oh, please!" Olivia says. "You'll find another dog you love, a hypoallergenic one, and then you'll be happy you got this A."

"*If* I got this A." I sit and put my face in my hands. "I guess

I'm scared I didn't, but not knowing won't change anything." I reach into my bag. "Let's get this over with." I close my eyes, pull the paper out quickly, and shove it toward them. "Well?" I open one eye.

Zoe and Olivia look at each other and smile a little. "This is good, right?" Olivia says softly.

I take the paper and look at the red letters on the top corner. A– over A–.

"That means you actually got an A on your project, since he dropped it down for being late," Zoe says.

"Will your dad let you get a dog with an A minus?" Olivia asks.

"I think so," I say. "Maybe? I don't know." I had convinced myself there was no way I was getting an A, that I would have to be happy helping Gina for the rest of my life. But now, maybe I can get my dog, even if I have to wait a few months. Even if he's not as perfect as Freckles. Still, all dogs are basically wonderful, so . . .

I grin big. "Oh, my goodness, I might get a dog!"

We squeal together.

At home I don't say anything about my science grade. I'm still a little scared Papi will say an A– isn't an A, so I want to show him my whole report card. I'm sure I got an extra A in there somewhere, and then he might say I can still get my dog, after Amarilis is doing okay, and after I find another perfect pup. There's no telling when that will be, and even though I will do my best to learn interesting stuff at school, I don't want to worry about my grades again. At least not for a dog.

Still, I can't sleep that night, and I won't be able to until I fix something. I know Papi is awake, so I put on my slippers and go downstairs. He's sitting on the couch, reading the newspaper, and I sit next to him. He folds down a corner of the paper and looks at me. "Why aren't you in bed?"

"Can we talk?"

Papi puts the paper aside and laces his fingers together. "What's the matter?"

"Well . . ." I think about how Gina said Papi didn't need to know about my dog lies, but I also remember she said I should look into my heart and do what is right. "I lied about Freckles." I concentrate on my palms because I do not want to see what Papi is doing with his face right now. "I told the rescue people the whole family was on board with getting him and no one had allergies. That weekend was supposed to be for us to get to know him before keeping him for good."

I wait, biting my lip and picking at a blister on my hand. Papi is quiet. Finally, I look up. "Why did you do that?" he says.

"Because . . ." Why *did* I do that? "Because it didn't seem fair. I mean, we made a deal. We shook on it and everything! And then, because of Amarilis's problems, you say it can't happen, that Freckles doesn't matter. That I don't matter." I whisper the last sentence because I don't want to seem pathetic. But it's how I feel. "I mean, I love Amarilis and I want all of us to do whatever we can to help her and protect her from Rich. But why does that mean I don't get a dog?" I look at Papi because I really, really want an answer.

Papi opens his mouth, then closes it again. He stands and walks around the coffee table, his hands in his pockets. "I'm sorry I went back on our deal. That was wrong of me. I feel overwhelmed with the Amarilis situation, and I didn't want to think about anything else. But you do matter. You always have and you always will." Papi stops pacing and looks into my eyes. "*However*, lying is *never* the answer. And you haven't gotten your final grades yet, so why would you believe you could get the dog now? Plus, we agreed the dog would be hypoallergenic."

I stare at a loose thread on the rug and nod. "I . . . didn't know if Abuela would be allergic to Freckles because he's a mix of different breeds, so . . . I guess I wanted so much to keep him that I hoped it would work out."

Papi sits beside me again. He doesn't say anything.

"I'm really, really sorry," I say. "Gina said it was okay if I never mentioned this to you because she found someone else to adopt Freckles, so everything is fine with him now. But I wanted to tell you because I don't want to live with this lie for the rest of my life!" My lips tremble, and I try to hold back the tears. "I'm sorry," I say again.

Papi shakes his head slowly. "Thank you for telling me." He reaches over and strokes my hair. "I hope this never happens again."

"It won't, honest."

"I'm very disappointed in you for lying," Papi says. "And there have to be consequences, so you're grounded for the first two weeks of your summer vacation."

I nod. That seems fair.

"However, I'm proud of you for coming clean. So, if you keep your end of the deal, I'll keep mine, okay?"

"I—I can still get a dog?"

"If you keep your end of the deal," Papi says.

"Thanks!" I jump up and hug him. Then I sit back down.

He looks at me with his eyebrows raised. "Is there anything else?"

"Yeah, um, why do you want me to get As?"

Papi jerks his head back, and his eyes open wide in surprise. "Why *wouldn't* you want to get As?"

"It's not that I don't want good grades. It's just that, well, what's the point of them? And what do they have to do with being a good dog owner?"

"Hmm." Papi taps his chin. "What I want is for you to do your best, and I don't believe you do that. Your notebooks are always empty—do you even pay attention in school? And if a particular class isn't your favorite, you should still try to understand the material and see if you can get something out of it. A good education can open a lot of doors. It certainly did for me. I want you to have the best possible life. Do you understand?"

"Yes, but whenever I work hard and get a B, you're disappointed," I say. "And when Amarilis and Jacinto do my homework and I get an A, you're happy. Do you want me to cheat?"

"Certainly not!" Papi says. "I'm sorry if I gave you that impression. But I know you can do well if you try. I want to encourage and motivate you. Perhaps insisting on As isn't the best way, but that's what always worked with your sister and brother, so I thought it would work with you too."

"I probably shouldn't admit this, but it did work a little," I say. "I mean, this quarter I really paid attention in class, and I've been taking notes and doing my reading, and my grades are pretty good. But not all As."

"See! This old man isn't wrong about everything, huh?"

"I guess not," I say. "We had this big project for science. Zoe and Olivia helped me at first, and they prepared an A-plus project for me. But it didn't seem right, so I scrapped that and did my own project. I learned a lot and I'm proud of the job I did. And I got an A minus. That's good, right?"

"That's excellent! I'm happy you took pride and ownership in your work," Papi says. "That's what I wanted all along. It's not only about getting As."

For once, Papi and I are on the same page. He's not so hard to talk to after all, and I can sleep now.

Chapter 47

A MARILIS GETS HOME RIGHT BEFORE DINNER on Thursday, like she's been doing every Tuesday and Thursday since she started therapy. "I'll be right down, just need to make a quick phone call." She runs upstairs.

I know snooping isn't nice, but I can't help myself, so I follow her upstairs.

"Hey, Callie, can we talk? Let's conference Emily in too, okay?"

When Amarilis starts to apologize to her friends, I sneak back downstairs to give her privacy.

-《《◆》》-

The last day of school is a half day, and Papi and Abuela take Jacinto and me out to lunch. The diner is packed with kids from school, and Papi tells Jacinto to go ahead and sit with his track friends. He deserves it because of his straight As, Papi says. Then he catches me looking at him and says, "Not because of the As, but because you worked hard and did your very best."

I take out my report card and shove it across the table toward Papi without saying a word. I'm hoping the A– I got in English and the B+ in math will help even though I don't have a solid A in science. Plus, Papi knows I did my best, right? He lifts his glasses to the top of his head and nods as he examines the paper. "Not bad," he says.

"So, can I get a dog?"

He puts his glasses back on and looks at me. "You will continue to do your best in school next year?"

I nod again and again.

"You won't shirk your academic responsibilities to spend all your time playing with your dog?"

I shake my head.

"And you'll take care of this dog by yourself, walking it and feeding it and keeping track of vet appointments?"

"Yes, yes, yes!"

"All right, then."

I jump up and throw my arms around his neck. "Thank you, thank you, thank you!"

--- ‹‹‹•›››‹ ---

When I get to Gina's house, there's a new dog in her big crate. "Who's this?" I peer in. "Puppies!"

Gina stands beside me. "Poor Lola was thrown out by this awful puppy mill owner. He said she was defective because she wouldn't get pregnant. As soon as Happy Puppy took her in, they noticed she was about to give birth."

"I guess it was lucky for her that guy was too stupid to notice."

"That's the truth!"

Lola is licking her puppies, and they're squirming around and squishing close to her. "How many are there?" I ask.

"Four," Gina says.

"Is she a miniature poodle?"

"Yes, these little guys would have been sold for a lot of money at a pet store," Gina says. "We'll find good homes for them, and for her too. She's a sweet and beautiful girl."

The puppies are too young to go outside, so Gina stays home to keep an eye on them while I take Lucky out. He's still waiting for a forever home, and Gina expects him to be with her for a while since he's a little older and kind of wild. She's definitely letting herself get attached. "This big boy needs to run around," she says in her baby voice as she rubs his neck with both hands. "It's boring here with all these old ladies and babies, isn't it, Lucky?"

As I jog through the nature trail with Lucky loping along beside me, I wonder what Freckles is doing right now. Does he remember me? Does he miss me?

What's important is that he's happy in his new home. At least that's what Gina would say.

—◄◄◄◆►►►—

Amarilis, Callie, and Emily are whispering in our room when I get back from Gina's. "Oh, hi kiddo!" Callie jumps up and stuffs her hands in her pockets.

"How's school?" Emily says with a super big smile on her face.

"Fine." I squint at them. "We're done for the year now."

"Oh, good, good," they say together.

Amarilis waves her hand. "It's okay, she already knows everything anyway."

"What's going on?" I ask.

"I was telling them about my therapy, and how I had a heart-to-heart with Rich and set some limits with him." She smiles. "He's very committed to making this work, and I feel confident we're going to be okay."

Callie gives Amarilis a sad look. "I'm glad you're making progress."

"Me too," Emily says. "But—and I'm saying this because I love you—there are lots of fish in the sea, so if you ever feel like it isn't working out, it's okay to end it. You do know that, right?"

Amarilis stares at her hands as she picks at a cuticle. "I guess. But what if I never meet anyone as great as Rich?"

As great as Rich?! Is she kidding? I glance at Callie and Emily, who look at each other with raised eyebrows. "Remember what Abuela said," I say. "Mejor sola que mal acompañada."

"What does that mean?" Emily asks.

"It means it's better to be alone than with someone who's no good for you," Amarilis says. "I agree with that, but . . . I don't know." She stands. "I'm hungry, and Abuela made a banquet for us tonight. Let's go."

Nobody talks about Rich or therapy over dinner. Papi and Abuela seem to have decided that if we pretend Rich is out of the picture, then he really is. Even though that giant ring is still on Amarilis's finger.

That weekend, Rich calls Amarilis every night before bedtime. I only hear her side of the conversation, but it sounds like he's begging her not to leave him. "I love you, Rich," she says.

"And I plan to marry you, but you have to keep your end of this deal too. You have to go to counseling and get your anger under control." She stops and listens for a little bit, and I take my time getting my bed ready. "Well, if it hurts your feelings when I tell you what I want out of our relationship, then maybe you're the one who doesn't love me." Amarilis sounds like her old self when she talks to him—the confident and self-assured sister I've always known—and every night I just know this is the night she's going to break up with him. But every night she ends the conversation by saying she loves him and will talk to him tomorrow.

Chapter 48

THE SUN IS RISING WHEN I wake up Monday morning. I'm annoyed when I look at the clock and remember I don't have to get up for school today. A sliver of light is seeping through the blinds and right into my eyes. I can't get back to sleep now. Maybe Amarilis is awake too. I sit up and look at my sister's bed. I blink a few times to make sure I'm seeing right, and I am. Amarilis's bed is neatly made, with all her pillows in their right places. But there's no Amarilis. I get up and pick up the folded piece of paper on top of the pillows. *TO MIOSOTIS AND JACINTO*, it says.

"Jacinto?" I knock on my brother's door as I open it.

"Huh?" He puts a pillow over his face.

"Amarilis is gone."

"What?!" Jacinto springs up like a jack-in-the-box. "Where?"

"Shh, I don't want Papi and Abuela to hear." I show him the paper from Amarilis's bed. "She left us this note."

Hey you two. Rich and I are getting married this morning in
City Hall. I always wanted my whole family at my wedding,

*but I know Papi and Abuela will freak out if they know. After
the wedding, they'll have to accept Rich no matter what.
Anyway, I didn't want you to be surprised and upset. I'm still
your big sister and I will always be there for you. The next time
you see me, I'll be a married woman!*

Love,
Amarilis

"This is bonkers!" Jacinto says. "She can't do this!"

"We have to go to city hall now," I say. "She must want us there or else she wouldn't have told us."

Jacinto jumps out of bed. "Let's get Papi."

"No! He'll freak out and make things worse."

"You want to go into the city without telling Papi?"

I nod. "You can drive."

"No way. Papi will have a heart attack if he wakes up and his car is gone."

My brother has a point. "Callie and Emily might go with us." I text Callie.

We'll be right there! she says.

Abuela comes out of her room as we're heading to the steps. "Did I oversleep? Did you make your own breakfast?"

"Go back to bed, Abuela," I say. "There's a special, um, summer reunion thing at the school today and we have to be there early." I grab Jacinto's arm and drag him downstairs before he can give us away with his guilty look.

"I can't believe she didn't tell me about this." Callie swerves through traffic like a race-car driver.

"Me too," Emily says. "Although we probably should have guessed, the way she kept talking about all the progress Rich has been making."

"We should have taken the train." Callie clutches the steering wheel and bites her lower lip. "Parking around city hall is impossible."

Emily looks at her phone. "There's a train into the city stopping at Overbrook Station in seven minutes. Let's park there and take the train the rest of the way."

-~«‹‹◆›››~-

"So . . . what will we do when we get there?" Jacinto takes a seat on the train and looks at us.

Callie and Emily blink. They seem lost and desperate, which is how we all feel.

"We tell her we love her and we've come to be with her on her special day," I say. "And we let Rich know we're not going anywhere, that he can't push her away from us, ever."

Callie smiles. "That sounds perfect."

-~«‹‹◆›››~-

Rich and Amarilis are sitting in a waiting area when we arrive. "What are you guys doing here?" my sister asks.

"We got your note and we wanted to be here for your wedding," I say.

Amarilis gives Rich a sideways glance, then sits up straight and smiles like she's posing for a school picture. "Well, thanks!"

Rich frowns at Amarilis. "What note?" he says. "We agreed not to tell anyone until after we finished here."

"I know," Amarilis says softly. "But I wanted my brother and sister to know—"

"For what?! So they could tell your dad and he could come ruin this again?" Rich stands and paces back and forth, red-faced and out of breath.

"We didn't tell our dad," I say, inching closer to Amarilis.

She stands and rushes over to Rich. "See? They're here to support us, not to ruin anything." She wraps her arms around him.

Rich pushes her away. "What about them?" He turns to Callie and Emily, and wags a finger in Callie's face. "That one has always been out to get me."

"That's not true," Amarilis says. "Callie loves me. She wants what's best for us." She strokes his arm gently.

Rich yanks his arm away and shoves her away from him. She topples backwards and Jacinto catches her before she hits the ground. Amarilis blinks back tears as my brother helps her stand.

Jacinto holds Amarilis and glares at Rich. Callie rubs my sister's shoulder, and Emily and I take her hands. She holds on tight and looks at me with now-dry eyes.

A woman opens the door in front of us and pokes her head out. "Richard and Amarilis, we're ready for you."

"Come on, babe." Rich walks toward the door.

Amarilis doesn't move, and neither do we.

"Babe, come on, we're getting married." Rich stretches his hand out to my sister.

She doesn't take it.

"Look, I'm sorry." Rich slaps his thigh impatiently. "I was

upset because you lied to me. But it's okay now. I forgive you and we love each other. Now, come on."

Amarilis doesn't look at him. She twirls the diamond ring around on her finger, then pulls it off. Tears run down her cheeks as she drops the ring into Rich's hand. "I can't do this," she whispers. "I love you, Rich, I always will, but I can't do this anymore."

Rich blinks and blinks. "But . . . we're getting married. Today."

Amarilis shakes her head and keeps looking at her hands.

Rich starts to speak, then looks at all of us standing beside Amarilis. He closes his mouth and sighs. "I'll always love you too," he says softly.

I step in front of Amarilis and put my arms around her neck. The four of us circle her as she cries on my shoulder. We don't let go until Rich's footsteps are far away.

Chapter 49

"**I** HAVE TO GET TO WORK," AMARILIS says after a while. "I'm supposed to be there by ten."

"Me too!" Emily hands out tissues and we all wipe our faces and blow our noses.

"I'm sorry I made all of you come down here," Amarilis says.

"You didn't make us do anything." Callie presses her hand over my sister's. "We're here because we love you and you can't get rid of us, no matter what."

"Yeah, especially us." Jacinto points at me. "We're stuck to you like gum in your hair."

We walk outside laughing.

"Amarilis did *what*?!" Papi says when Jacinto explains where we were.

"But she backed out of it," I say. "It was her decision, and she's going to stick to it." I grab his arm and look him in the eye. "We should be happy for her."

"I suppose you're right."

Nobody mentions the almost-wedding when Amarilis gets home from work, and she seems relieved about it. She even talks about therapy and Rich during dinner. "I realized that one reason I stayed with Rich was because I was afraid of what he would do if I broke up with him," she says. "My therapist says that's normal, and very smart. Abusive partners sometimes kill their exes, especially in the first year after the breakup."

Papi looks shocked. "Did he threaten you?"

"No, but he might later," she says. "I want to live at home next year and commute. I'll feel safer that way."

"Certainly," Papi says.

"That's a wonderful idea." Abuela looks relieved.

Jacinto nods.

"What about you, mamita? Are you okay with having a roommate again?"

I laugh and throw my arms around her. "You can stay forever!" I'm so glad Amarilis is protecting herself from Rich—that she knows she has to. But keeping a person safe is more complicated than rescuing a dog. Rich might still come after her. All we can do is huddle close to her like we did in city hall, and hope he stays away.

—⦓⦔◆⦕⦖—

On Father's Day we decide to take Papi to his favorite Japanese restaurant, where he can chat with the strangers sitting next to him and catch shrimp in his mouth. Before we leave the house, Abuela bursts into my room with an armful of hair stuff. "¡Ay, Dios mío, mira ese pajón!" She plops three different kinds of hair gel and some heavy-duty brushes and combs on the dresser. "Hurry, we don't have much time to fix your hair!" She plugs in Amarilis's blow-dryer and flat iron.

"I'm not straightening my hair today," I say.

Abuela's eyes practically pop out of her face. "You want to go out looking like that?!"

"She looks fabulous, Abuela!" Amarilis says. She and I worked this out yesterday. We're both wearing our hair curly today. Hers hangs down her back in ringlets. My curls are tighter and stop at my shoulders. Not to be conceited or anything, but I look really cute. And Amarilis is gorgeous, as always. Of course, Abuela does not agree.

"Ay, niñas, por favor," she says. "What will people think?"

"They'll think we have adorable curly hair, which we inherited from our beautiful ancestors." Amarilis puts an arm around my shoulders and stands tall. So do I.

Abuela rolls her eyes and mumbles something about esta juventud loca, then leaves the room.

I let out a loud breath.

"Don't worry," my sister says. "Abuela will get over it."

I know she's right, but I feel sorry for my grandmother. Why doesn't she see that her thick hair and smooth brown skin are beautiful, like Abuelo used to tell her practically every day? It's sad that every time she looks in the mirror, she doesn't like what she sees. Like Papi says, though, we all have flaws. Abuela will always love and defend us, and I will always do the same for her. I have to accept her for who she is, because I can't change her. But that doesn't mean I have to be like her. When I look in the mirror, I do like what I see, and I'm glad I resemble her. She might never understand that, but she can't change me either.

"Let's finish getting ready," Amarilis says.

I look at the cross-stitch above my bed while she zips up my dress. The blue flowers over the neat *FORGET-ME-NOT* are kind of sloppy, but I'm proud of the job I did after my first lesson from Amarilis. My next project will be better, I am sure.

Chapter 50

THE DRY AUGUST LEAVES CRUNCH UNDER my sandals as I walk down our front steps. "Have fun in New York!" I hug Abuela before she opens the car door. "Say hi to Tía Felicia for me."

Papi hoists Abuela's bags into the trunk. "I'll be back in an hour or so," he says, "after she's safely on the train. You kids behave, okay?"

I run up the steps to Gina and Miss Mabel's house.

"Here's the new doggie mama!" Gina greets me at the door with the smallest of Lola's puppies in her arms. She looks like a reddish-brown version of my mother's dog, like an actual little teddy bear.

"Hi, Osita!" I lift the puppy and hold her close. "Are you ready to come home, sweet baby?" I say in that Gina baby voice.

Osita stares at me with moist black eyes. I read an article once that said dogs make people fall in love with them by looking deep into our eyes. It's science, and it's definitely true. The first time she opened her eyes, I knew Osita was the dog for me. Her brothers and sister were already climbing on Lola with their eyes wide open, and they barely noticed when I reached in to change their blankets. But Osita looked right at me, and I fell in love that very minute. Now she's finally old enough to be separated from her mom, and she's coming home with me.

Lola is snoozing on the couch, her head nestled under a pillow.

"Will they miss each other?" I ask. "I can bring Osita over every day for a visit."

"No, Lola's going to her forever home tomorrow. Truth be told, she seemed relieved each time one of her puppies left. Osita is the last one, so now Lola can rest."

"Oh," I say. Do mothers get sick of their kids?

"Dogs grow up faster than humans." Gina seems to read my mind. "And they easily attach to people, so Osita and Lola will both be very happy."

I hold Osita closer.

"Do you need anything?" Gina asks.

"Nope. I have a crate, a bed, food, bowls, leashes, and poop bags." I look around Gina's living room. "Oh, and toys too! Should I get anything else?"

"It sounds like you're all set!"

"Okay, we'll come back after she's had all her shots and can hang out with your new dogs!"

Amarilis and Jacinto jump up from the couch when I walk in the door.

"OMG, she is sooo precious!" Amarilis kisses Osita on the head and snuggles her while Jacinto takes a million pictures. I pull out my phone to snap a few also. When Amarilis first broke up with Rich, she cried a lot, especially when she listened to the dozens of voicemail messages he left for her every day. Deep down, though, she knew he wasn't right for her, so she didn't call him back. She still goes to therapy and hangs out with Callie and Emily. And we have lots of fun together. Sometimes she seems a little sad, though. It's great to see her smile so big with Osita in her arms. These photos are definitely keepers.

I take my puppy and put her down on the floor. She sniffs the rug, the sofa leg, and the TV stand. "Osita, do you want a treat?" I place two biscuits on the cushion in her crate. She steps inside, sniffs them, and putters around in a tight circle before curling up and closing her eyes.

Amarilis, Jacinto, and I kneel in front of the crate and watch her little back rise up and down with her breaths.

"I'll go with you when she needs a long walk," my brother says. "We can run through the nature trail and tire her out."

"And I'll help you bathe her," my sister says. "I saw this all-natural dog shampoo online. We should get some."

I shake my head, ready to tell Jacinto and Amarilis that this is *my* dog and I'll take care of her *my* way. But then I remember my mother saying the three of us are a team, and Gina reminding me that the people who love me can help me, and Zoe and Olivia pointing out that we all need each other. I think of how Miss Mabel was sort of right about getting Papi and Abuela to help with my sister. And how Callie insisted we stick by Amarilis no matter what. I couldn't have helped my sister by myself, and I would never have gotten Osita on my own.

"She's too little to run the whole trail," I say. "But we can start her off walking half of it."

"You got it, squirt."

I turn to my sister. "Let me see that website so we can pick a shampoo."

"Absolutely, mamita."

I reach for their hands and we stay in front of the crate watching Osita as if she were a movie. When I glance at Amarilis, I remember Abuela's saying about how it's better to be alone than in bad company. Amarilis is definitely better off now that she doesn't have a boyfriend, but she's not alone, and she never will be. Neither will I, and that's something I'll never forget.

Author's Note

THE DAY I BECAME A LICENSED attorney, I went to the hospital to meet my first client: a woman with several fractured ribs and a punctured lung. She had suffered these injuries at the hand of her husband, who was arrested after this incident. Wincing in pain and struggling to breathe, she gave me the information I needed to prepare her request for a Protection From Abuse order. Once granted by the judge, that order would require her husband to stay away from her.

A few days later, she called to tell me she no longer wanted the order. She was gathering up her savings to bail her husband out of jail, and everything would be fine because they were in love. I was shocked. What was she thinking? Didn't she know she wasn't safe with him? I tried to talk her out of this decision, but she would not listen. When I hung up the phone, I felt like I had failed at my job because I could not convince her to do the "right" thing.

I never saw that client again, but I subsequently represented more victims of relationship violence, including a few teenagers.

Some were ready to leave their abusers forever and some were not. I was often frustrated, confused, and even angered by my clients' choices, just as Miosotis was when she found out about her sister.

Then I volunteered with an organization that helps victims of domestic violence, and I learned to listen to my clients and let them know about the resources available to them when they were ready to break free from their abusers. I didn't push them because I knew they had to make their own choices. I have to admit, though, that I was able to accept my clients' decisions because I knew that, as their lawyer, my role in their lives was limited. It would not be appropriate for me to meddle in their personal lives. But I wondered, what if a victim was a close friend or relative? What if this happened to one of my sisters? It was from these thoughts that this book was born.

While Miosotis and Amarilis are fictional characters, their story is not uncommon. According to the National Domestic Violence Hotline, one in three adolescents in the United States is a victim of physical, sexual, emotional, or verbal abuse from a dating partner. That is a *lot* of young people in unhealthy relationships. How does it happen? Usually, it's very gradual. Many times, college students find themselves away from home for the first time ever, making decisions and figuring out new relationships on their own. These relationships can be confusing. The abuse could start with social media stalking, asking for passwords, and demanding immediate responses to messages. If the victim says they feel uncomfortable with some of the abuser's demands, the abuser will make the victim feel like they're "crazy" or unreasonable. Little by little, an abuser will exercise control over their victim until the victim feels powerless and trapped.

But there are ways to end these feelings, regain control, and have safe and healthy relationships. The National Domestic Violence Hotline at 1-800-799-7233 or thehotline.org provides free and confidential help for domestic abuse victims and their loved ones. Through the hotline, you can speak with a counselor by phone or live chat, get information about legal help, and find a domestic violence advocate in your area.

If you're a witness to domestic abuse, it can be difficult to know what to do. You may stumble and not always make the right choices, as Miosotis did at first when she lashed out at her sister in anger. But Miosotis definitely did some things right: she trusted the instincts that told her Amarilis and Rich were not in a healthy relationship, she did research to understand how best to assist Amarilis, and she did not give up on her sister. Helping a loved one—or yourself—get out of an abusive relationship is not a quick and easy task, but it can be done with steady patience, love, and the support of trained professionals. As Miosotis and Amarilis learned, abuse is never the victim's fault, and everyone deserves to feel safe in their relationships. So, whether you are a victim or a witness, be kind and patient with yourself and your loved one, and don't give up. You and your loved ones are worth it.

Acknowledgments

I CANNOT FORGET ALL THE SUPPORT AND assistance I have received and continue to receive in my writing journey. I am very thankful to:

The Lee & Low team, especially Cheryl Klein, who believed in this story when it was just starting to sprout, and expertly guided me to nurture and shape it to completion;

My writing critique group—Susan North, Laura Parnum, Amy Sisson, Nicole Valentine, and Nicole Wolverton—for reading and reading and reading, and giving me great feedback, encouragement, and friendship;

My husband and my son, Wayne and Ruben Wynn, who gave me a fresh reader's perspective when I asked them to read my "final" drafts—which is very important when you've reread your own words hundreds (or thousands?) of times;

Las Musas writing collective, for the camaraderie, support, and education—I have learned so much from all of you;

Everyone who generously answered my seemingly random questions about dogs, classrooms and school curricula, track teams, proms, Spanish grammar, and other things, including veterinarian Dr. Lauren Connolly, teachers Margarita Carruthers and Valerie Lamb, my kids Claudia and Ruben Wynn, and fellow Musa Yamile Saied Méndez;

Lissy Marlin and Neil Swaab, for yet another beautiful book cover;

My mother, Hilda Maria Burgos, who always believed I could accomplish anything; although she is now gone, she'll never be forgotten; and

My family, friends, co-workers, and neighbors, for your kindness and support. The year 2020 was a difficult one, beginning with the loss of my mother in January. To my father, José Burgos; my sisters, Rosemary Burgos-Mira, Josephine Burgos Starr, and Margarita Carruthers; and the rest of our family: I'm grateful that we have each other to lean on during challenging times, and that, like the Flores family, we'll always stick together like chicle, no matter what.